YOU MAKE ME weak

USA Today bestselling author
Juliana Stone

You Make Me Weak
Cover by Sara Eirew
Copyright © 2016 by Juliana Stone
All rights reserved.

No part of this book may be reproduced in any form or by any electronic or mechanical means, including information storage and retrieval systems, without written permission from the author, except for the use of brief quotations in a book review.
ISBN: 978-1988474038

CHAPTER ONE

Crystal Lake held a lot of bad memories for Hudson Blackwell and he remembered every single one of them on the long drive back from Washington, DC. By the time he crossed the bridge that separated the north side of town from the south, his mood was black and a scowl transformed his handsome features into something dark.

He pulled up at the main stoplight downtown, fingers drumming along the steering wheel, eyes scouring the quaint buildings that lined each side of the street. The place had gotten a face-lift since the last time he'd been home, and he noted a few new shops. Mrs. Avery's flower depot was about the only one he recognized, and his scowl deepened as he thought of the last time he'd been inside.

God, he hated coming back here.

The light turned green, but instead of heading out to the family home on the lake, he made an abrupt U-turn and a few minutes later pulled into the parking lot of the Coach House. Hudson killed the engine of his black F-150, gaze on the building.

Now this place hadn't changed a bit, and for the first time since he'd begun this trip home, a slow smile curved his lips. The parking lot was shit, potholes galore, the tin roof looked rusted as hell, and the front entrance and door needed a new coat of paint. The overhead sign hung crooked, held in place by one hinge, and it looked like a good gust of wind could knock the damn thing clear off. He didn't remember it being this bad, but hell, it was something he could live with.

As he walked inside the darkened interior, he was assaulted by the smell of stale beer and that certain mustiness only a place like this could hold. Hudson had never been one for change, so he'd take the sticky floors and crap smell over new any day.

It was an early Monday afternoon, late September, and the place held few customers. Hudson didn't make eye contact, though he took note where each of them sat, and headed for the bar, taking the last stool at the far end. Neon beer signs twinkled down at him, casting shadows along the wall of bottles lined up in a row. He pushed aside a damp used coaster and, out of habit, reached for his cellphone. He paused and then let his arms rest on the bar.

Work was a long way away and, at the moment, the least of his worries.

"What'll ya have?"

A huge, hulking man stood in front of him, a faded black wife-beater stretched thin across wide shoulders and bulging biceps. His head was shaved clean and glistened with sweat, while his handlebar mustache and full beard did nothing to hide the colorful tattoos that lined his neck. Hudson had never seen him before and frowned, glancing to the end of the bar.

"Where's Sal at?"

The bartender's eyes narrowed, and he tossed a rag over his shoulder. "You from around here?"

Hudson nodded, leaning back on his stool as each man took measure of the other.

"Sal's been taking some time off."

Huh. As long as Hudson could remember, the owner of the Coach House could always be found behind his bar, serving up drinks (which was the reason you'd be there) and advice (whether you wanted it or not).

"He okay?"

The bartender took his time answering, wiping up the edge of the bar though his eyes never left Hudson. "As good as you'd expect. Now, what'll you have?"

Hudson considered digging deeper, but something told him he probably wouldn't like what he'd find. "Cold beer would be good."

"Draft or bottle?"

"Draft."

Less than a minute later, Hudson cradled a cold mug of Guinness and settled in to watch the game. With the MLB pennant race on, it was as good a way as any to pass the afternoon, and the fact that he'd rather watch it here than at the house said something. What that something was he didn't want to dwell on. No sense in going there just yet.

He was well into his second Guinness when someone took the stool a few places down from him. A quick glance in the mirror behind the bar told him it was a male, early to mid-thirties, an A's ball cap pulled low over clipped dark hair. The length of his arms told Hudson he was tall, and the tattoos told him ex-military. His clothes were on the dirty side, as if he'd been working outdoors, but the watch on his wrist was a Rolex.

The fact they were close in age told Hudson there was a good chance he knew the guy, but he paid him no mind. Quite frankly, he didn't care. He was content to sip his beer and watch the Red Sox get their asses kicked. He wasn't ready to head down memory lane just yet. Hudson lifted his mug and took a good long drink, eyes on the pitcher as he squared up at the mound.

"How's Sal doing?" The man spoke, and Hudson's hand froze midair.

"Not good, Jake." Hulking bartender guy leaned forward, shaking his head.

Hudson's eyes widened. He knew the voice right away. Jake Edwards was a few years older than Hudson, and while they hadn't exactly been friends—Jake had been pretty tight with his own crew back then—they'd hung out a time or two. It sure as hell explained the Rolex. The Edwards family came from old money, not as old as the Blackwells, but still, their privileged asses were part of Crystal Lake's elite.

Hudson looked down at his beer, his face dark as he thought of family and the reason he'd come back here. For a moment, his vision blurred, and he slammed his eyes shut, because just like that, it felt as if he'd never left.

"You leave here now, Hudson, don't expect a welcome back if you change your mind. You're on your own and good luck with that."

His eyes flew open, and for a second, he was disoriented. Like a ghost from the past, his father's voice sliced through his head, tugging something ugly and dark from deep inside him. Hudson clutched his hands together, fisting them so tight, his fingers cramped. A slim tan line cut across his left ring finger, and he wondered how long that reminder would stare him in the face.

A reminder of what he'd lost and most likely never deserved.

With a sigh, he pushed back the unfinished beer, not really feeling the Guinness anymore, and stood to leave. He tossed a couple of bills onto the bar, nodded at the bartender, and had every intention of leaving without saying a word to Jake Edwards, but the man in question saw things differently.

"Holy shit. Hudson Blackwell." Jake slid from his barstool, pushing back the brim of his cap and offering up his hand. His smile was genuine, his handshake firm. "I can't remember the last time we were together."

Hudson shook Jake's hand and took a step back, feeling sheepish as he remembered the tragedy the Edwards family had faced a few years back. "Sorry to hear about your brother."

Jake's smile faltered a bit. "Thanks." He glanced around the Coach House. "It's weird. Being back here without him. I stop in for a beer, meet up with the guys, and expect Jesse to walk in and join us." Jake lifted his chin. "You back visiting the old man? I hear he's not doing too good."

Tight-lipped, Hudson nodded. "He's in Grandview." And just like that, he wasn't in the mood to talk. "I haven't been out to the house yet. I should get going."

Something flickered in Jake's eyes at about the same time Hudson's internal radar erupted, hitting him square in the chest and pumping boatloads of adrenaline into his system. Jake was talking, but he ignored the man, taking a step back as he scanned the Coach House. In his capacity as an FBI agent, this feeling, this sixth sense, had saved his ass more times than he cared to count. He didn't sense danger or anything like that, but something was coming for him.

The door to the bar opened, and the late-afternoon sun filtered in, haloing dust and dirt into beams of hazy light. It camouflaged the person standing in the doorway chatting to one of the customers who was on his way out, but he could tell it was a woman.

"She's been back for a while now. Working here for a couple of months."

Eyes still on the door, Hudson frowned. "What was that?"

"Rebecca."

Hudson swung his gaze back to Jake, the entirety of his world narrowing down to this one man.

"Rebecca." It was a name he hadn't uttered in years.

Jake was silent for a bit and then nodded toward the door. "Yeah. Rebecca Draper is back in Crystal Lake. Didn't you guys date back in the day?"

Date? The word didn't come close to what he'd shared with Becca. She'd been in his blood like a wildfire, one that could never be doused.

"Huds, I'm scared."

Her blonde hair fell around golden shoulders, rippling waves that glistened in the moonlight. The big blue eyes staring up at him were the kind you could get lost in. The kind that made a guy think of things. Like getting lost inside Rebecca Draper.

"I've never done this before." Her voice faltered, those big eyes falling away from him, and his chest filled with something he didn't quite understand. In that moment, he knew she was important. She meant something more. Something he needed. Something he wanted.

Hudson gathered her in his arms, his young body taut and hard and aching with desire. "It's okay," he managed to say. "We don't have to."

"But I want to." She breathed into him. "I want my first time to be with you."

He was hot. And cold. And excited beyond anything he'd felt before. But there was something warm and tender unfolding inside him. He wasn't sure what it was, but he knew it was wrapped up in the girl he held.

Rebecca Draper.

His Becca.

The memory disappeared as quick as it'd come, and, shaking his head, Hudson ran his hand through his hair. Christ, she was back here? What the hell were the odds of that? This town was small. Insular. He'd run into her for sure. He wasn't exactly sure how he felt about that. The thought of seeing her with her husband and probably a pack of kids wasn't something he relished.

That had been his dream once. Until he'd screwed it up.

"I didn't know," he muttered. "How is she?"

"You guys will catch up."

"Not sure she'd want that." The words were out before he thought better, and Jake's eyes narrowed a bit before glancing over Hudson's shoulder.

"I guess you're gonna find out."

Hudson followed Jake's gaze, settling on the woman who'd walked into the Coach House a few minutes earlier. She was at the far end, behind the bar, her back turned to him. Blonde hair was pulled back into a high ponytail, exposing the delicate lines of a neck he was way too familiar with. She turned slightly, smiling up at hulking bartender guy, and Hudson couldn't tear his gaze from the curve of her cheek, the small upturned nose, and a mouth that had driven him to the edge more times than he deserved.

She put her hand on the bartender's forearm, and damn if that didn't pull at some kind of Tarzan thing inside him. Hudson didn't like it—not one bit—and that was plain stupid. He had no claim on this woman and hadn't for a very long time. Not since the night he left town, the night he'd left her at the end of her driveway, sobbing her damn heart out.

"Take me with you."

She'd pleaded with him and the plea had turned into a scream as he'd gotten in his truck, letting the shadows cover him and the tears burning the backs of his eyes. It was a scream he heard long after that night.

He watched Rebecca for a good five seconds or so. Watched as she grabbed up several beer mugs from under the counter and set them on the bar. As she turned to the till and had a peek inside. As she scooped up a rag and moved down the bar. As she smiled at the lone customer who raised his glass in hello.

As her eyes met his and her smile slowly faded.

They were still as blue as the ocean and, damn, but Becca was more beautiful than he remembered. She was beautiful and fragile and delicate and...

He took a step forward, his body acting before his mind could tell him to calm the hell down. Her eyes widened, those lips of hers parted as if she was finding it hard to breathe. He got that. He felt like he was drowning.

Her hand went to her throat and then fell back to the rag in her other hand. She slowly turned away from him, grabbed one of the empty mugs, and began to fill it. She placed it in front of her customer, said something to hulking bartender guy, and disappeared into the back room.

Just like that, he'd been dismissed.

"I take it things didn't end well between you two," Jake said quietly.

"That would be an understatement."

Hudson stared after her for a long time before heading outside. His mood blacker than ever, he slid into his truck, jaw clenched tight, hands fisted on the wheel. He never should have come back here.

What the hell had he been thinking?

CHAPTER TWO

Becca splashed cold water on her face and exhaled slowly as she looked at herself in the mirror. She blinked and frowned because, just for a second, it wasn't her face she saw. It was his.

Hudson Blackwell. All six foot four inches of him. Gone was the young twenty-year-old she remembered. He'd been replaced by a dark, dangerously handsome man—the man she'd known he would become.

And he'd done it without her.

Her stomach dipped, and she leaned on the sink. She hadn't seen him in years. Not since that last night when he'd ripped out her heart, stomped all over it, and left her behind in Crystal Lake. The memory of the late-summer rain mingling with the salty tears on her face as she watched his taillights disappear stirred something ugly inside Becca. Her fingers gripped the edge of the sink, thank God, because it was the only thing holding her up.

When she got her shit together, she splashed water across her face once more and reached for a towel. She quickly dried off and secured her ponytail before one last look in the mirror. Her pale cheeks were now flushed, heated with an anger that wasn't leaving anytime soon. And her eyes spit fire.

Hudson Blackwell was back in Crystal Lake? So what. Rebecca didn't give a good goddamn. He meant less than nothing to her, and no way was she hiding how she felt. In fact, she had a good mind to tell Hudson Blackwell exactly what she thought of him and where to go. That particular opinion had been festering for twelve years. Maybe it was about time to let that piece of her past go as well.

Fired up and determined, Rebecca marched her butt back out to the bar, only to find him gone and the place nearly full with an early crowd eager for half-price chicken wings. More than a little deflated, she spied Tiny.

"You okay?" Tiny shouted from the other end of the bar. The man was born Julian, but somewhere along the line, Tiny had stuck.

Okay was a relative term and not at all what she was feeling, but Rebecca nodded anyway.

"Can you take the big table at the back?"

"Got it." Rebecca grabbed her tray. Mondays were busy at the Coach House, and that was one of the reasons she'd taken the part-time gig on top of her regular job at the veterinary clinic. When she'd moved back to Crystal Lake, the only house she could afford was a fixer-upper near the old mill. She loved her place—an older home, it boasted tons of character—but there was always a project on the go, and she needed the cash. Straightening her shoulders, Becca marched toward the table. She didn't have time to waste thinking about Hudson Blackwell. In the grand scheme of things, he didn't much figure in her day-to-day life. Besides, if she was lucky, he was only in town for a visit and she wouldn't see him again.

But the thing about luck is that some folks have it in spades. And unlike those particular folks, Rebecca Draper wouldn't be able to find a golden horseshoe if it hit her on the head. So it wasn't surprising any luck she did manage to find ran out exactly two days later.

Wednesday started out pretty much like any other day, if one ignored the inch of water on the kitchen floor. Once she turned off the water supply to the house, called a plumber, and dealt with the mess, she got her son, Liam, to school and was only fifteen minutes late for work. It was a lovely morning, and the sun reflecting off the lake was bright. The dew was heavy and the air crisp. As she got out of her car, the unmistakable scent of fall was in the air, and her mood improved at the thought. It was her favorite time of year, and her steps were light as she headed inside.

Crystal Lake Veterinary Clinic was located in the new development on the other side of the water and looked more like a private doctor's clinic. She supposed it was in keeping with the moneyed folk who'd moved to the luxury homes surrounding the new golf course, but she wasn't complaining. More newcomers meant more dollars poured into the town, and that meant more jobs. She liked her coworkers, and her boss, Aiden Burke, was the sweetest little old man. He was close to retiring, and the buzz in the office was that his son, Ethan, would move back to Crystal Lake and take over the clinic.

"He's back." Kimberly Higgins, one of the associate vets, stood a few feet from Rebecca, a huge smile on her face, eyes twinkling.

Rebecca slipped behind the reception counter and slid her purse into her cubby underneath. "Who?" She was almost afraid to ask as her thoughts returned to Hudson Blackwell.

"Ethan! I heard Aiden speaking to his wife on the phone."

Relieved, Becca hung up her jacket. So the rumors were true. Ethan Burke was a few years older than Rebecca and had never returned home after college. A tall, good-looking kid, he'd had a knack for finding trouble both on the football field and in the backseat of many a car. He'd been part of Hudson's crowd.

Hudson. With a scowl, she slid onto her chair just as the door opened. Mrs. Ryan walked in with her overweight pug and just behind her, a new client with a box full of mewing kittens. Thank God for distractions. Rebecca pushed all thoughts of Hudson Blackwell aside and got to work.

The day passed quickly, and at five thirty, she pulled into the parking lot of the grocery store and gave Liam his list. He was in a grumpy mood—after hockey practice, he'd wanted to hang with his buddy Michael. But groceries were their thing, and it was a thing they did together.

"I'm going to Michael's for dinner," Liam mumbled as he slid from the car. "So I don't know why I couldn't just go there after hockey." He slammed the door shut—just a little too aggressively—and Rebecca shot him a look as she got out.

"I'm not doing this with you, Liam." She frowned and watched him stomp into the store. Her son was a good kid, but lately, he'd been moody, and his mouth was starting to aggravate her. With a sigh, she followed him inside, telling herself his attitude was understandable. He'd been through a lot in the last year and a half.

Rebecca glanced down at her list and grabbed a cart. The two of them were usually able to get in and out in thirty minutes or less, and after the day she had, she wanted nothing more than to get home, put her feet up, and watch some mindless reality show while she munched on whatever was handy. It was only Wednesday, but takeout pizza might be a good idea.

She was almost to the produce section when she ran into Mr. Hines, one of the clinic's clients.

As she picked out the freshest apples she could find, she half listened to the older gentleman go on about his cat, Oliver, who'd recently suffered through a bout of crystals. She nodded and smiled where appropriate, moving on to the grapes and oranges. Of course Mr. Hines followed, and she eventually had to smile and excuse herself by pointing to her watch.

"Of course, dear. I'll see you next week when I bring Ollie in for his needles."

A headache was crawling up the side of her skull, and she undid her ponytail, groaning softly as the hair fell loosely down her back. She headed to dairy and hoped that Liam was close to conquering the cereal aisle. They usually met in the meat section, and after tossing in eggs, butter, cheese, and two cartons of milk, Becca swung past the deli and ordered up sliced ham and turkey for sandwiches before heading to the back of the store.

She was almost to the meat section when her world tilted a little off-center and she came to a halt. Liam stood near the display case and appeared to be deep in conversation with none other than the one man she did not want to see. Hudson Blackwell.

Seriously.

"Shit," she muttered under her breath, casting a quick glance around to see if anyone was paying attention. Could she grab her kid and go without causing a scene?

Her hands gripped the grocery cart, and she bit her lips as she considered her options. Was she really going to hide from him like a weak little schoolgirl? Really? She inhaled and straightened her shoulders. No. Rebecca Draper was done hiding. She'd been done for a while.

Pushing forward, she made a beeline to the pair and was proud of herself when she didn't break eye contact with Hudson when he turned to her. Dressed in faded jeans, boots, and blue-and-red flannel over a white T-shirt, he looked way better than she would have liked, but Rebecca ignored his dark good looks and paused in front of him. The words she'd wanted to say the other night bubbled beneath the surface, wanting out, but she didn't think taking a strip off Hudson

Blackwell in the middle of the grocery store and in front of her son was a smart idea.

Choices, her brother Mackenzie always said. Smart choices.

His thick, dark hair was kind of messy, as if the wind had pulled at it, or some woman's fingers had run across his scalp. And that rugged mouth of his was slightly open as his eyes widened. There were smudges beneath them—as if he hadn't slept all that much, but she chose to ignore them. What did she care?

He looked at Liam and then back to Rebecca. For a moment, there were no words, and then he spoke, his voice low and with a hint of rasp. Just the way she remembered.

"I should have known this was your kid. He looks a lot like Mac."

She nodded and managed to answer without sounding as if she was bothered by his presence. Which she was. Big-time. "He does."

"You know my mom?" Liam asked brightly, unaware of the tension between the adults.

Hudson dragged his gaze from Rebecca and smiled at her son. "I do."

Liam tossed a package of ground beef into his basket. "Like from school and stuff?"

"Yes," Rebecca answered curtly. "From school." She paused, her eyes never leaving Hudson even as his gaze swung back to her. "And stuff." She tried like hell to keep the bitterness from her voice but knew she'd failed miserably when Liam cranked his head around in surprise.

"You okay, Mom?"

"Yes, Liam. I'm perfectly fine." In fact, the slow-burning anger that bubbled beneath the surface since she had spied Hudson two days earlier was slow burning no more. It swept over her like a wave crashing against the shore, and before she knew it, she was diving under.

She was not perfectly fine. Not by a long shot. And that was what pissed her off even more. The fact that Hudson Blackwell could still make her feel this way made her angry. And after all this time. She'd worked too long and too hard to get to a place where things were good. No way was she letting him take that away from her.

He was just a ghost from the past. A ghost who'd nearly broken her, mind you, but a ghost nonetheless. He didn't matter anymore. Of course, if Rebecca had been thinking clearly, she would have realized that all the feelings coursing through her told the exact opposite story. He might be a ghost from the past, but he was also a thread that had been left dangling. One that had never been tied off. Hudson mattered. The story behind him and her *mattered*. She just didn't want to acknowledge it. At least, not right now.

Exhaling slowly, she ran a hand over her cheek and tucked back a thick swath of hair. "How long are you staying in town?" She knew she sounded rude, but didn't care, noting the full grocery cart in front of him.

If Hudson was surprised by her tone or question, he didn't show it. In fact, he seemed as relaxed as ever as he ran his hand through that mess of hair atop his head. The tattoos on his forearm were visible, and for one second, her vision blurred and she was back in a place she never thought she'd be.

"Huds, my dad will kill me if he ever sees this tattoo."

"Then don't let him see it." His kisses made her ache, and she bloomed beneath the touch of his hands. It was early morning, and the sun was just coming up, lighting their tent afire and sweeping the shadows away. Outside, the birds were already awake, singing to each other and celebrating a new day.

His mouth trailed a line of fire down her stomach until he reached the small tattoo on her right hip. He'd gotten the match on the inside of his wrist. "This is only for me."

His fingers sank inside her, and she nodded as her body began to hum. "Only for you," she whispered.

As she blinked rapidly, Rebecca's heart beat so fast she heard it in her ears and shook her head as the memory faded. Hudson and Liam were looking at her strangely.

"What was that?" she asked.

"My dad's not well," Hudson replied slowly. "I'm not sure how long I'll be around."

Right. Of course. Lips pursed, she didn't say anything.

"None of my brothers could be here, so…" He shrugged, his face now devoid of any kind of emotion, save for the hardness around his mouth. She knew there was no love lost between the Blackwell boys and their father. That was common knowledge. She just didn't know the why of it. It was, among many things, something Hudson had never shared with her.

"Right. Well, we should go." She nodded to Liam.

"You look amazing, Becs."

Rebecca's head shot up so fast, she saw stars, and for a second, she had nothing to say. Not that it mattered. Hudson gave her a small nod.

"I just thought you should know." And headed toward the dairy aisle.

The anger inside her deflated—just a little bit—and that wasn't something she'd seen coming.

"Mom. You look funny. You okay?"

She smiled wanly and motioned for Liam to head to the checkout. "I'm good," she murmured, following her son. She scooped up a bottle of wine along the way because she was so not okay. Her heart was still beating a mile a minute. She felt weak and dizzy. And on top of that, something inside her ached. It ached so much, she felt tears prick the corners of her eyes. And that was silly. Damn silly. She hadn't shed a tear since the day she walked out on David, and she wasn't about to do it now on account of some stupid trip down memory lane.

She especially wasn't going to cry over Hudson Blackwell. That well had run dry years ago.

She gave herself a mental shake and stood in line for all of ten minutes, muscles straining from tension at the thought of Hudson appearing. He didn't, and she wasn't exactly sure if it was relief she felt or something else entirely.

Deciding she wouldn't dwell on it, she grabbed her bags and headed out to the parking lot, the bottle of wine tucked under her arm. She had everything she needed. A new home and a new life. She'd escaped a miserable marriage, a bastard of a husband, and made something out of nothing. She shouldn't feel like this.

Except she did. Because down there, buried deep inside her, was an empty space that needed filling up. And she was afraid it would remain empty the rest of her life.

CHAPTER THREE

Hudson hated hospitals. The smell. The crazy order to things. The nurses and doctors. The cold tiled floors and bland walls filled with cheap prints of beaches and sailboats. His mood hadn't improved since he'd returned home, and now that he'd finally made it to Grandview, he wasn't so sure things would get better.

His phone buzzed just then, and with an apologetic glance to the nurse behind the reception desk—Ms. Daniels, according to her nametag—he pulled the device from his pocket and moved to the stairwell. It was his brother Wyatt.

"Yeah," he said roughly, leaning his long frame against the cement wall.

"You see him yet?" That was Wyatt, straight to the point.

"I'm at Grandview now."

A pause.

"Okay. Sorry I couldn't be there."

"No, you're not."

"Got me there. The last time I saw the old man, he told me I was gonna die young and not to bother calling him when it happened. I told him that would be kind of hard to do considering, you know, the whole being-dead thing. He just made that noise he always does and took a business call. Just like that, I was dismissed. Hell, I bet he didn't realize I left Crystal Lake until days later."

Hudson sighed. "Not to be on his side or anything, but that last crash was a son of a bitch." His brother had a fondness for cars. Fast cars. Unfortunately for the family, he raced them and was currently the darling of the NASCAR circuit.

"Everyone crashes and I came out of it with nothing more than a mild concussion and a few bruises."

"You were lucky."

"Look, I didn't call for a lecture. I called to see how the old man was doing."

Hudson glanced at the door. "I'm about to find out."

"You get hold of Travis yet?"

"I talked to him before I left DC. He's got his first preseason game on Friday in Toronto."

"Baby bro in the big leagues. Who would have thought?" The youngest Blackwell had lived and breathed hockey since he was three. It was their mother who'd taken them to the rink. Their mother who'd encouraged the boys when it came to sports, especially hockey. And when she died, Hudson lost his love of the game. Not Travis. To him, it became a lifeline, an escape from a home shrouded in sadness. Hell, he'd hitchhike to the arena if he had to, and that wasn't too far from the truth considering their father had pretty much disappeared from their lives after their mother passed. He provided a roof over their head, put clothes on their backs, and made sure they didn't go without. But that was about it.

It hadn't always been that way.

Hudson cleared his throat, shaking off a memory he didn't want to think about. "I'll let you know how he's doing."

"All right. I'm headed to New England for a race."

"You watch your ass out there."

Wyatt laughed. "Always, brother."

Hudson pocketed his phone and headed back into the main reception area of the fifth floor. He nodded at Nurse Daniels and strode down the hall, not stopping until he reached the private wing at the end where his father was. He didn't hesitate. He pushed open the door and entered the room.

The lighting was dim, and it took a few seconds for his eyesight to adjust. His father was asleep, and Hudson stared at him in silence, noting every detail with a clinical eye. John Blackwell still sported a full head of silver-white hair, but there was significant weight loss. It showed in the drawn features, threw shadows across skin stretched too tight over bone. His breathing sounded like shit, even with the oxygen mask in place.

Hudson shoved his hands into the front pockets of his jeans and took a few steps forward, chest tight as if held in a vise. John Blackwell had always been a big, tough, strong man with a no-nonsense attitude and a gruff disposition. He'd ruled his sons with an iron fist that left no room for softness or coddling. To see him so *less* than what he'd been was more than a little unsettling for Hudson.

There were flowers on the table beside the bed, cards propped up alongside them and… Hudson blinked and walked over, bending slightly so he could get a better look. A family photograph stared up at him, and that vise in his chest tightened. It tightened hard. Christ, he remembered the day like it just happened. They'd gone out for a day of fishing, just John and the boys. For a bunch of kids starving for the affection of their father, it had been a day to cherish.

The three of them stood side by side in the boat, each of them holding up their catch, while behind them, their father grinned, a relatively elusive thing back then. In the picture, Hudson wasn't looking at the camera but up at his father.

A knot formed in his throat, and he took a step back. Hudson could still feel the yearning, the need for a connection lost.

He gave himself a mental shake and pulled up a chair. He sat beside the bed, stretching out his long legs and resting his eyes as he settled in to wait. He didn't have to wait long.

"Hudson?"

The voice was weak, a little rough and hesitant. Hudson's eyes flew open, and he got to his feet so that he stood beside the bed. His father yanked off the oxygen mask, and pale blue eyes stared up at him.

"Hey, Dad."

John Blackwell let out a shaky breath and with lips pursed, struggled to get to a sitting position. Hudson would have helped, but his father wouldn't have it. So he took a step back and watched the man until he finally managed to get the pillows just so.

"I see you're still as stubborn as hell." Hudson shook his head and frowned. As the oldest of the Blackwell boys, his relationship with his father was a little more complicated. Mostly because he'd been nearly ten when his mother died, and he remembered a father much different from the one he'd become.

John coughed a bit and then fell back against the pillows, his chest heaving in an effort to get air into his lungs. End-stage heart disease and emphysema would do that to a man. He took another hit from his oxygen mask.

"Who called you?" his father managed to say between coughing spells.

"Darlene."

"Bah." John wasn't pleased. That much was obvious. "She shouldn't have bothered you. I know you're busy making sure those bastards don't get us again."

"Don't worry about my job. I had some time coming." As a special agent with the FBI, Hudson worked in homeland security. He loved his job. Loved the guys he worked with and, truth be told, if Darlene hadn't called to tell him his father was on his deathbed, no way would he be back in Crystal Lake.

In fact, Darlene had made a point of telling him it had been exactly twelve years since he'd stepped foot in this town and that it was damn time he rectified that. Technically she was wrong but then no one knew about his return trip, or the fact that he'd pretty much turned tail and ran as quick as he'd come back.

Darlene Smith might just be the best thing that had ever happened to the Blackwell family, but shit, there were times when she should mind her own business. Not that Hudson would ever tell her that. She just might show him the back of her hand.

He smiled at the thought.

"What about the other boys?" John's voice was a bit stronger now, and Hudson offered him the glass of water sitting on the tray beside the bed.

"They're tied up right now." It was the truth…a sad truth nonetheless.

His father was silent for a few moments, his chest heaving and rattling as he moved to get more comfortable. "You here for long?"

Hudson considered his answer for a few seconds. "As long as need be."

For the first time, a small smile touched his father's lips. "You mean until I'm gone."

"Yeah. That's pretty much it." They'd always had a no-bullshit relationship, so there didn't seem to be a point in sugarcoating things now.

"You staying at the house?"

"I am."

"Good." John Blackwell's eyes narrowed. "You been by the office yet?"

The office. The family business that had caused so much discord between himself, his brothers, and his father.

Tight-lipped, he shook his head. "Not yet, but I'll swing by tomorrow and make sure everything is running the way it's supposed to."

"You better." Voice noticeably weaker, John stifled a cough. "Sam Waters is in charge right now because there's no one else. He's adequate, but hell, I wouldn't trust him as far as I could throw him. And the man weighs damn near three hundred pounds."

Sam Waters had been his father's right-hand man for as long as Hudson could remember, and the man was more than adequate. The Blackwell holdings were diverse, the pockets deep, and there were many safeguards in place to protect the family fortune. He highly doubted the man would be the kind to steal from the hand that fed him.

"I wouldn't worry about Sam, but to ease your mind, I'll make sure everything's on the up and up."

His father nodded, seemingly exhausted, though his eyes burned with a feverish glint. Outside the room, phones rang and muted voices could be heard. But in here, cocooned in a space of illness and unspoken words, there was only silence.

"I'm glad you're here, son."

Hudson's throat tightened, and he took a step closer to the bed, but whatever words he would have said died when the door flew open and a nurse walked into the room. She was middle-aged, with a kind, round face, complemented by an equally round figure, an ample chest, and small feet. Her hair, shot through with slivers of gray, was scraped back into a ponytail, and she smiled when she spied Hudson.

"My word, John. This must be one of your handsome boys." Her accent was Southern, and he knew she wasn't from the area. She hustled over to the bed and unwrapped the stethoscope from around her neck. She glanced back at Hudson. "I just have to have a listen, and while I'm doing that, the doctor is outside. I know she'd like to speak to you."

With a curt nod, Hudson exited the room and found a tall, slender brunette chatting with a bunch of nurses at reception. She turned and smiled when she saw him.

"Hudson."

Okay. Killer body. Great legs. Nice smile. Green eyes that looked familiar. But who the hell was she?

Her smile widened as she walked toward him. "You don't know who I am, do you?"

"You got me there."

She stood a few inches from him now, a slow smile curving her generous mouth. "I'm Adam Thorne's sister. Regan."

Damn right she was. Those eyes, the same ones that Adam had. If he remembered correctly, she was a couple of years younger than him. Although…

"You look a lot different than I remember."

She laughed. "I sure hope so. The last time I saw you, I had braces, acne, and was on the chubby side. Puberty wasn't exactly my friend."

An image of an overweight, shy girl came to mind. "You decided to stay in Crystal Lake."

Her smile widened. "I like it here." She shrugged. "I had no reason to leave." Her smile faltered a bit. "We should talk." She motioned to the lounge, and he followed her over. Once there, she shoved her hands into the pockets of her white jacket and got down to business.

"So, your father isn't doing well."

There it was. The cold, hard truth. "I can see that."

"He's got fluid on his lungs and heart, his oxygen levels aren't great, and we're pretty sure he's got another blockage in his arteries."

"Can't you unblock it like last time?"

Regan sighed. "I'm not sure your father will survive another surgery. His heart is weak, and he's been sick. If we can get him stronger, more stable, then it could be an option but…" Her large eyes were expressive, and he knew the deal.

"You don't think it will matter."

"I'm sorry, Hudson. I don't think he'll live long enough to find out. There's always a chance. Always hope. But I like my patients and their families to know the reality of the situation, and right now, it's not good."

Hudson exhaled and glanced back at the door leading to his father's private room. "He's a tough son of a bitch."

"I know. But he's been fighting for a long time now. I'm just not sure how much fight he's got left." Regan glanced at her watch. "I have to make rounds." She paused and cleared her throat. "Is…is Wyatt coming back?"

Hudson shook his head. "I'm not sure when he can make it."

Her mouth tightened and her eyes flashed—which Hudson might have wondered about if he'd been paying attention, which he wasn't. And then she was all professional again.

"Okay. Well. If you have any questions about your dad, don't hesitate to ask." She smiled. "It's good that you're here. He needs you."

"Yeah," he murmured.

She took a step back and paused. "You planning on going to the barn dance at the fairgrounds?"

Surprised, his eyebrows shot up. "They still have that thing?"

"Damn right they do. We're all about tradition here. Saturday night of fair weekend." She glanced at her watch once more and began to back away. "You should come. A lot of the old crowd will be there. Adam and his wife will probably go, and I hear Ethan Burke is back in town too." She chuckled. "Everyone who leaves seems to come back at some point."

He thought of Rebecca and her little boy. He thought of the man they belonged to and gave himself a hard mental shake. He needed to shut that shit down.

"You should go. Give Adam a call. It might be fun."

Hudson smiled but said nothing as he turned and headed back to his father's room. Adam and the guys, Rebecca—they belonged to a past he'd lost touch with a long time ago, and there was no point in dredging it up now. He pushed open the door, eyes falling to the slight form on the bed. The nurse held his father's hand, her words so soft and low Hudson couldn't make them out. His father smiled at whatever she said, and for a second, Hudson caught a glimmer of the man he'd been.

But the sickly sweet smell that permeated the air couldn't be ignored. This was his reality now.

CHAPTER FOUR

Saturday night rolled around much too quickly. Rebecca spent the day helping her mother can tomatoes and rushed home to get Liam fed, so she could drop him off at his friend Michael's house for a sleepover. She made it back in record time, had a quick shower and change. She pulled on jeans, boots, and a clingy black top that was probably too low-cut for the barn dance, but she didn't care. She'd just applied her lipstick when the doorbell sounded, followed by footsteps on the worn wooden floors and then the stairs. She grabbed her purse from the bed and reached for her jean jacket just as her girlfriend Violet waltzed into the bedroom like she owned it.

"Holy. Cowz." Violet Thorne whistled and leaned against the doorframe as she looked Rebecca up and down. Her vibrant red hair spiked in all directions and her warm brown eyes glittered. A generous mouth painted the deepest red imaginable slowly curved into a smile. "Becca, you look hot as hell. Like, if I swung that way, I'd totally date you."

"I think Adam would have a problem with that."

"Would he, though?" Violet giggled. "Pretty sure that's every guy's dream."

Becca glanced at herself in the mirror. Had she overdone it?

Large blue eyes, enhanced with smoky shadow, subtle liner, and delicately shaped brows, popped and stared back at her. Lips glistened, and she hadn't meant to make her cheekbones look so…so…defined, or her skin so flawless. Wasn't her fault she found the contour kit she'd been given last Christmas and decided to give it a whirl. It was just sitting there. In the drawer.

Rebecca leaned forward. Crap. She totally should have scrapped the contour kit. Seriously. She was taking a bartending shift at the barn dance, not going clubbing in the city. She reached for some tissue.

"Don't you dare!" Violet walked over and hip-checked her away from the mirror with a wink. "Now let's go. We're going to be late, and you know how bitchy Nadine gets."

"True."

Rebecca followed her girlfriend downstairs and out into the cool night air. Their pal Nadine was a board member for the local fall fair, and she'd roped both Violet and Rebecca into volunteering for a few hours at the dance.

"Where's Adam?" Rebecca asked, sliding into Violet's Jeep. "He staying home with the kids?"

"God, no. The twins are at his parents'. He was meeting up with some of the guys, and they'll probably end up at the dance later. That's if he wants some of this tonight."

Violet giggled and slapped her butt. Married eight years, Violet and Adam were still happy and in love, and they made it work. If she didn't love Violet so much, she'd be jealous as hell, because there'd been a time she wanted all that. But for some mere mortals like Rebecca, the end game never quite happened the way she'd envisioned it.

Now a little pensive, she leaned forward as they drove across the bridge and then headed along the river toward the fairgrounds. Adam used to hang with Hudson back in the day, and, mouth suddenly dry, she shot a sideways look at Violet.

"What?" Violet asked, eyebrow raised in question.

"Nothing."

"Don't tell me nothing." Violet pulled into a parking spot and cut the engine. "I can feel you looking at me, and you're wearing Hot Spice."

"What?"

"Your lips. Isn't that Hot Spice?"

Her fingers touched her bottom lip. Shoot. Violet saw everything. "Hudson's back in town." The words fell out of her, and then silence filled the vehicle. It wasn't often her girlfriend was speechless. But right now, her mouth hung open and no words came out. The redhead shook her head, hands still gripping the steering wheel.

"What? When?"

"Since Monday."

Violet looked as if her eyes were going to pop right out of her head. "He's been home for nearly a week and this is the first time you've said anything to me?"

"I'm sorry. I…"

"It's like a thing now? Him being home?"

"No." Rebecca fell back against her seat. "It's not a thing. We're not a thing. I just…" Chest tight, she clamped down her mouth. She didn't know what she felt, and that was the problem. There was anger there—even after all these years. But seeing him again stirred up a lot more than just anger. And it was the other stuff that confused and scared the hell out of her.

"You weren't expecting to see him." Violet's voice was gentle. She'd been there, back in the day when things had gone bad. She'd seen what he'd left behind. The mess Rebecca had been.

"No. He's the last person I thought I'd ever see back here." Her voice dropped. "That last night… He said he was never coming back."

Outside, the sounds of music drifted on the air, mingled with the happy shouts and merriment from the crowd inside. Rebecca glanced over at the barn, the windows ablaze with light, the people milling about outside, and suddenly, her heart felt so heavy, it hurt.

"Do you think he'll be here?" Violet prodded gently.

Rebecca glanced at her friend. The Hudson she'd seen wasn't small town anymore. "I doubt it. If Adam didn't say anything to you, he's not reached out to any of his old friends, and really, a dorky barn dance doesn't seem his style."

"Do you want me to text Adam and ask if he's heard from him?"

Yes.

"No. God. No. I don't care either way."

Violet made a face, and Rebecca knew her friend didn't believe a word she was saying. Probably because of the whole Hot Spice thing. Why oh *why* hadn't she chosen a more subtle hue? Pink Punch would have been fine.

"I told Nadine I'd help out, and that's what I'm going to do."

"Okay." Violet reached for the door handle. "Let's do our duty. But more importantly, let's have fun."

The barn was pretty much at capacity by the time ten o'clock rolled around. The beer flowed, the band was a local favorite and kept the dance floor hopping. Of course the rumors that Crystal Lake's own bona fide rock star, Cain Black, would appear most likely helped. By the time Rebecca's shift was over, her nerves had long since settled and she was enjoying herself.

Everywhere she looked, there were people she knew. People she cared about. People who mattered to her. People who'd made coming back here and leaving an abusive husband behind so much easier than it could have been.

She was right where she wanted to be and yet…

"And yet, nothing," she muttered, tossing her apron to the next shift recruit. She grabbed herself a cold beer and decided it was time to have some fun. Violet nodded toward the dance floor just as the band swung into a rousing version of an old Eagles classic. It had been ages since she'd let her hair down and had fun, and as the music took over, Rebecca let go. She danced until sweat made her hair stick to the back of her neck. Until her cheeks were sore from laughing. Until Adam appeared and claimed his wife. Until the band slowed down and played a slow song that burned right through her.

Adam kissed his wife, uncaring of the crowd, and his hands moved down Violet's body until he cupped her butt and drew her as close as two people could be. He whispered something in her ear, and Violet laughed, wrapping her arms around the man she loved. It was a beautiful thing to see, that kind of love between a man and a woman, but Rebecca didn't want to see it anymore.

Smile slowly fading, she moved away from the crowd until the shadows that clung to the corner of the room covered her. It felt safe here, and she leaned against the wall and closed her eyes, letting the music and melody wash over her. God, she loved this song. And she hated it.

It was a dark song about desire and hot summer nights. About things forbidden and dangers unseen. About pleasure and regret and consequence.

The crowd erupted in cheers as a crisp, clear voice sailed over all of them. She knew Cain Black was in the house, and as he nailed every note of the classic, Rebecca slipped farther into the shadows and sang along, her voice soft and sad.

When the guitar solo sliced through the night, she smiled at the simple artistry that Cain possessed. He made his guitar cry, and it touched her soul, so much so she felt the hot spring of tears sting the corners of her eyes. That thing inside her, the empty space she tried not to think about, it ached. It expanded and grew and stretched so damn tight, it was hard for her to breathe.

Suddenly in need of fresh air, or maybe some quiet to temper the sadness that had sprung up inside her, Rebecca headed for the doors. Someone called her name—Violet maybe? But she ignored her and pushed her way through the dance floor, bumping into more than a few couples and stepping on more than a few toes.

Her eyes on the wide doors just beyond the ticket table, she damn near ran over Mrs. Avery, the flower shop lady, and barely managed an apology on her way out. By the time she reached the parking lot, she was wheezing and her chest hurt. She swore because her purse and inhaler were inside, but no way was she ready to go back in there. Not yet. Leaning against the nearest truck, she glanced up at the big night sky, and eventually, her breathing slowed.

What the hell was wrong with her?

But she knew. Didn't she?

"You okay?" The voice slid over her like warm whiskey. Just the sound of it sent shivers rippling across her skin, and dammit, there went her heart again. Beating like a freaking drum and making her feel weak.

Shoot. Me. Now.

Slowly, Rebecca's eyes opened. Hudson stood a few feet away, bathed in moonlight or starlight…or whatever the hell beam of light was reserved for the insanely hot and dangerous. It emphasized every single thing about him. The wide shoulders. The long legs. The chiseled, handsome features. The utter masculinity of the man.

It wasn't fair. And it pissed her off.

She pushed away from the truck, letting that anger roll over her. "Are you stalking me now?"

Was that a small smile touching his lips?

"No." He nodded behind her. "That's my truck, and I forgot my wallet." The way he looked at her made all sorts of alarm bells go off inside her. The air was thick and heavy. She needed to move but couldn't.

She stared across the space between them and nearly took a step forward before she caught hold of her senses and stopped herself. What the hell was wrong with her? This was Hudson Blackwell, for God's sake. She needed to dismiss him and get on with her night.

I need to get laid.

The thought sliced through her brain at about the same time he tilted his head to the side, in that way that was achingly familiar. His dark eyes regarded her, an intense glint within them, and she felt the subtlest vibration travel across her body as they locked gazes. It was like small invisible fingers of lightning lit the air, and this need inside her…this desire to be touched was the conduit.

It had been ages. Well over a year since she'd felt the touch of a man's hand. As the band quieted down and the stillness of the evening washed over her, she heard a ragged edge to his breathing. Saw the muscle work its way along his jaw. It was then she knew.

There was still something there between them.

That ache inside her exploded until it spread through her body like a train barreling down the track. Her heart rushed to keep up, and she stumbled a bit, dizzy and hot and suddenly more scared than she wanted to be.

She needed to be away from him.

Needed to assuage the ache inside her.

Needed to think straight.

Rebecca never said a word. She took off toward the dance and left Hudson by his truck. She didn't look back, though she felt the heat of his gaze on her. She didn't stop walking until she reached the bar and handed over a ticket to the bartender. She decided she needed the hard stuff to get her through.

She turned to face the dance floor and took a sip of the vodka and soda. Almost instantly, she caught a smile from Nate Smith. Usually, she ignored that sort of thing. But tonight? Right now? She smiled back. There were several men in the room she knew were interested in her. Several men to choose from. Maybe it was about time she took care of a few things. Maybe then she wouldn't turn into an idiot when she saw Hudson Blackwell. She had an empty house tonight, and she needed a man. It shouldn't be hard.

"You look like you're on a mission." Violet slid up beside her. "I am."

"Should I ask?"

"I need to get laid." Violet nodded. "Girl, I've been telling you that for six months." She paused and glanced around the room. "What about Derek Silver?"

"No. He used to date Nadine, remember?"

"Right. That would be weird." Violet's forehead crinkled. "Jonathan Lambert?"

"No. He's too pretty."

Violet made a face. "Braedon Sanders?"

It was Rebecca's turn to make a face. "Seriously? He's been with half the girls in town."

"I know." Violet giggled. "And he's supposed to be hung like a horse." Violet's smile faded. "This might sound crazy, but there's Hudson—"

"Are you kidding me?" Rebecca snapped.

"He's looking this way and—"

"Not gonna happen."

"Adam says he's single, divorced or something. He said Hudson was asking after you, and it's obvious you guys have unfinished business. Maybe the two of you—"

"Are you not hearing me?" Irritated, she glared at her girlfriend.

"O-kaaay," Violet replied, eyes moving over the crowded room once more. "Who's it going to be?"

Fueled by vodka and the need to do something about the pathetic state of her personal life, Rebecca scanned the room, eyes on a tall, dark man who'd just walked into the dance. He strode through the crowd until he reached Violet's husband. Of course Hudson was there, and by the looks of it, the guy was someone they all knew.

"Is that…?"

Violet followed Rebecca's gaze and frowned. "Ethan Burke. It has to be. God, he got hotter with age." Violet paused. "Isn't he going to be your boss?"

"Maybe." Was it the alcohol talking? "It's not a done deal from what I've heard."

"You don't seem to care."

Rebecca shook her head slowly. "I don't."

"Okay, then." Violet tugged on her arm. "Let's go."

CHAPTER FIVE

At his job, Hudson was the go-to guy. He was even-keeled, worked well under pressure, and had an uncanny ability to analyze a situation—no matter how dire—and make the right call. He'd dealt with cold-blooded killers, terrorists, the dregs of society, and never lost his cool. His peers called him Ice Man, and though he commanded the respect of his team, there was also a healthy dose of intimidation. No one wanted to cross him. No one wanted to see him lose control, because there was a general feeling that once unleashed, he wasn't the guy to tangle with.

In fact, some of his crew wondered if he was human.

And yet in the space of a few hours, Rebecca had managed to press just about every goddamn button he owned, and Hudson was on the fast track to losing it. Big-time. He scowled in the general direction of the dance floor, his eyes on one couple only. Christ, how many slow songs were the band going to perform? And how many times was Ethan Burke going to put his hands all over Rebecca?

"You okay, Blackwell?" His buddy, Adam Thorne, watched him closely.

Hudson swore under his breath. Not even close. His jaw was sore from gritting his teeth, and a damn headache was thudding inside his skull. What the hell was he doing here? "I should head home."

Adam followed his gaze and was silent for a few moments. "You still got a thing for Rebecca." It wasn't a question, and Hudson didn't bother denying it.

"I don't have a right to feel anything where she's concerned. Gave that up a long time ago."

"What happened between you two? You guys were the one couple everyone thought would make it."

He turned to Adam. Saw the genuine confusion there, but he didn't want to get into it. The past wasn't his friend, and he sure as hell didn't feel like revisiting it tonight.

His scowl deepened, and he considered heading back to the bar, but the thought of waiting for a cab or walking out to the lake stopped him in his tracks. A glance at his watch told him it was nearly midnight, and he'd just decided to head out when a woman stepped into his path. Athletic. Blonde. Dress that didn't cover much. Killer legs and a smile that promised the kinds of things most men wouldn't be able to say no to.

Shelli Gouthro. She'd been a good time girl from what he remembered and from the looks of things, not much had changed.

"Hey, Adam." Her voice literally purred, and his pal nodded before making a lame excuse to go find his wife, leaving Hudson alone with a woman who was sending him all sorts of invites. It was in the way she stood with her chest pushed out. The open stance of her legs. The swipe of her tongue across her mouth. And definitely the hungry look in her eyes.

"Hudson Blackwell." She managed to add at least three more syllables to his name. "Someone told me you were back in town. Glad to see the local gossip was right for once." She smiled and got right up in his personal space, glancing at his hand with a calculating look in her eye. "You single these days, Hudson?"

All that restless energy in him rushed to the surface, and, hot, he rubbed the back of his neck while considering his options. Maybe a quick screw was what he needed to get his head back in the game and Rebecca off his mind.

"You want to buy me a drink?" she asked coyly, swiping that pink tongue of hers along the edge of her mouth once more. She was a fine-looking woman, he'd give her that, and though he'd never sampled her offerings back in the day, he was pretty sure she'd show him a good time tonight. The thought of hot, dirty sex with an attractive woman had never failed to get his motor going. But when she put her hand on his forearm and leaned closer, he had to force himself not to push her away.

What the hell?

He didn't want her. Plain and simple. Well, *shit*. Cock-blocked by a memory. He looked over Shelli's head, and everything in him stilled as his gaze locked with Rebecca's. Ethan was motioning with his hands as he spoke, and sure she nodded as if listening to him, but her eyes were glued to Hudson and neither one of them was looking away. In that moment, there was just the two of them, and in a weird way, time stood still.

The spell was broken when Ethan moved and she disappeared from his line of vision.

His heart rate quickened, and he clenched his hands into fists, because the urge to stomp over there and plant one of them in Ethan Burke's nose was strong. And that was insane. Ethan was a good guy, and Hudson had no claim on Rebecca.

"Hey." Shelli sounded annoyed and tugged on his arm. "Drink?" she said again, pulling him toward the bar.

Hudson was so rattled that it took a few seconds for him to get his shit together, and when he did, he pulled his arm from her grasp.

"Maybe another time."

Hudson didn't wait around for her reaction. He spun on his heels and headed for the doors. His mood was black. His body tense. His gut churned. He never should have come here.

Hudson made it outside without having to speak to anyone else, and that was a chore in itself. He strode through a crowd of people he'd known his whole life, all of them wanting to say hello or ask after his father or one of his brothers. He kept his head down and didn't look up until he got to his truck. He made no effort to climb inside but stood there, inhaling that crisp, cold Michigan air he missed more than he cared to admit.

How long he stood alone in the dark he couldn't say, but he was cold from the damp when his brain finally told him to get his ass moving. He shoved his hand into his pocket, intent on finding his key, when something made him look up. Sixth sense? Or just the absolute awareness he'd always had for *her*.

Rebecca.

She walked toward him, a little unsteady on her feet, and when she stopped a few feet away, he realized she'd had more than she should to drink. Her cheeks were pink, all that golden hair of hers wild and crazy around her shoulders, and her eyes glittered like glass. Her mouth, that delectable pillow-soft mouth, was parted and her chest rose and fell as if she was having a hard time breathing. Worn denim clung to hips that were rounder than he remembered, and a butt that was made for a man to grab hold of. No longer was she a precocious teenager, a woman-child who'd bloomed beneath his touch. This right here was a full-on, grown-ass lady and she was…

The hottest thing he'd ever seen.

"Where're you going?" She hiccupped beneath a hand and stumbled a bit more. He didn't mind, because she stumbled toward him. Now she was only a few inches away.

The slight breeze picked up her scent, and that familiar warm vanilla smell made his gut clench.

"I was thinking of heading home." Thinking? Hell, that sounded like indecision, and the only right thing to do was get his ass home and leave her alone.

"I saw you talking to Shelli." Her words were slightly slurred and carried a hint of accusation.

Hudson wasn't exactly sure where this was headed, but he was more than willing to go along with it. Maybe it was the Michigan air, or the smell of vanilla that permeated it. Or the woman who swayed in front of him, looking up at him with a strange expression.

"She said hello."

"You taking her home?"

"No."

Rebecca cranked her neck to the side and peered behind him. "Why not?"

Hudson considered his answer and decided to be honest. Hell, what did he have to lose? "I didn't want to."

She muttered something under her breath.

"What was that?"

"I said you're probably the first guy in Crystal Lake who's ever turned her down. That has to be some kind of record." Rebecca looked defiant, and he was pretty sure she was spoiling for a fight. He knew the signs—remembered them well.

"You should get back inside. It's cold out here."

She didn't respond. Just shook her head and looked at him in silence. It was the strangest few minutes he'd had in a long while, but he'd take them. Just to be here with her. To see her again and hear her voice. To pretend that maybe she still belonged to him. It was easy to do under the cover of darkness.

"I want to go home," she said suddenly. Her voice was low, and there was a tremble in her words.

"I'll get Violet." He knew she'd come with Adam's wife.

"No." She exhaled shakily and moved past him, so close he could have touched her. She reached for the door handle on his truck. "You take me." She slammed the door shut after she climbed in.

Huh. Hudson wasn't so sure this was a good idea, and he glanced back toward the barn dance. He should get Violet. That was the right thing to do. But after a few seconds of hesitation, he sent a quick text to Adam, deciding to avoid Violet altogether. He climbed into his truck, fired up the engine, and looked at Rebecca.

She'd obviously had too much to drink, and he was doing what any good person would do. He'd take her home and make sure she got in safely and then leave. She was fiddling with the seat belt, and he had to lean over to get it locked in place. Her hands grazed the top of his, and it was like a lightning bolt shot through him. Energy, blazing-hot energy, rolled through him, and he moved an inch or so, trying like hell to concentrate, only to find that damn mouth so close to him, it was enough to drive any man crazy.

Slowly, he looked up, and the dark desire he saw on her face made his blood boil hotter than the goddamn sun.

Hudson had to clear his throat in order to speak properly, and even then he barely managed to get the words out. "Where am I taking you?"

Her gaze dropped to his mouth, and the edge of her pink tongue swept across her bottom lip. Her breath came in short, hard spurts, and something hot tempered the air around them.

"You remember the old house near the mill?"

"The one with the porch? The blue shutters?" How in hell he could remember anything was beyond him. Especially when all he could see was that mouth. And that pink tongue.

She nodded, seemingly deflated, and fell back against the seat just as he managed to lock the seat belt. Rebecca didn't say another word, and as several couples spilled out into the night, their voices echoing in the dark, he drove away and headed back across the bridge.

The trip was a short one, maybe three minutes in total, and they drove in silence. Hudson found her place, just past the mill, and pulled into the driveway. He put the truck in Park and glanced over to

Rebecca. She was looking at him, and this time, he had no idea what she was thinking.

"Do you need help to get inside?"

She scrunched her nose and shook her head. "I'm not drunk."

He raised an eyebrow at that, and she giggled. It was a sound straight out of his past, and if he could replay it over and over, he would.

"I'm not. I know what I'm doing."

He'd done his part. It was time for him to leave. Get his head screwed on right.

"It was good to see you again, Becs."

She was silent for a bit and then, after releasing the seat belt all on her own, opened the door. The night air seeped inside his truck as she slipped outside, and small puffs of frosted breath fell from her lips. For a good long while, she looked in at him, standing there with the door open, an odd expression on her face.

The air between them changed. It became heavy and hot and full of dark and dangerous things. Crazy things. Unexpected things. And, man, that motor of his was purring.

She exhaled, her forehead furrowed slightly as if she was thinking real hard about something. And then, with a soft shudder, she took a step back.

"Are you coming in or what?" She didn't wait for his answer. Rebecca turned and headed for her house. She climbed the stairs and opened the front door before turning around to look down at him.

The right thing to do was to wave good-bye and leave. Anything else was just plain wrong. Hudson Blackwell lived his life by following the rules. Doing things right. It was his code. It was what made him who he was. Hell, it was why he'd come back to Crystal Lake.

So why the hell did he step out of his truck? Why the hell did he climb those stairs and follow her into the house?

They were valid questions, and maybe later he'd think about them. But at the moment, Hudson wasn't going there.

CHAPTER SIX

Rebecca tried real hard to remember the last time she felt like this. And then she tried real hard to think about what it was exactly she was feeling. But her head was fuzzy, and she gave up. Walking into her dark, silent home, she kicked off her boots and headed straight for the kitchen, giving a wide berth to the sheets of drywall and painting supplies near the front door.

The light above the stove glowed softly. She reached for the fridge and paused when she heard a curse from the front of the house. Guess Hudson hadn't seen the drywall.

Hudson. What the hell was she doing inviting him back here?

She yanked open the fridge door and immediately went for the chocolate ice cream. It was loaded with chunks of peanut butter, and she had a spoon in her hand before Hudson found his way to the kitchen.

Her heart jumped at the sight of him. It had always been like that. One look and her body reacted. It was chemical and organic, and she couldn't seem to control it. She shoved ice cream into her mouth before she said something she'd regret. And regret was definitely on the table. But she didn't want to think about that right now. Instead, she leaned against the counter, melting that little bit of heaven in her mouth, and watched him.

It came to her then. The things unsaid. *I still want him. Even after everything.* The things she felt. Unsure. Excited. Scared. *Aroused.*

Hudson had always been a big guy, tall with broad shoulders, and the room seemed to shrink with him in it. His black leather jacket and boots lent an air of danger to the man, but they had nothing on the dark glint in his eyes, or the sensual lift to his mouth.

Rebecca tried to remember the bad things…the painful things that had ripped them apart. She thought back to that last night—saw a picture in her mind of how she'd cried her heart out. But right now, with him standing a few feet from her, she couldn't remember how it felt.

Couldn't remember because she'd obviously lost her freaking mind.

She dropped her gaze. God, she must be crazy to be considering the things in her head. She shoved another spoonful of ice cream into her mouth.

"Let me guess." His deep voice startled her, echoing in the silent kitchen, and she jerked her head up. "Chocolate ice cream with chunks of peanut butter."

She nodded slowly, swallowing the melted treat. "I'm surprised you remember that."

"I remember everything."

Her heart suddenly in her throat, Rebecca put the carton of ice cream on the counter and tried to collect her thoughts. A million things swirled through her head, and she gripped the edge of the counter with her fingers, turning the knuckles white.

"Violet said you're divorced." Okay. That came from out of nowhere, but since it was out in the open, she found herself curious about the life he'd made without her.

Hudson was silent for a few moments and then moved toward her. *Shit.* Surely he could hear her heart or see the mad flutter of the pulse at the base of her neck? Mouth dry, she wanted to run, but found she couldn't take her eyes from him.

What was he doing? Was he going to touch her? Kiss her? Was she going to let him?

He stood an inch or so away and then reached for her. Her eyes squeezed shut because she didn't want him to see the raw, uncensored need inside her. Seriously. She'd given in before he'd even started.

Several seconds ticked by and then…

"This is good."

What? Her eyes slowly opened, and she watched him lick ice cream from the spoon she'd abandoned and then go in for more. When he offered her a taste, she shook her head and waited. For what, she didn't know…but the rules had been thrown out the window, and she had no idea what they were doing or where they were headed.

The bedroom. The thought slid through her mind like a secret.

Hudson leaned back against the counter, right beside her, his long legs crossed at the ankles. He dug in for more ice cream and, and waited a few seconds before he spoke.

"I was married for just over a year. Candace and I…"

Candace. The name conjured up a tall, cool, collected woman. A supermodel maybe. Or a brain surgeon.

He shrugged. "She worked at the White House."

Of course she did.

"We hardly saw each other. Probably shouldn't have gotten married in the first place."

"Then why did you?" She glanced up at him.

Hudson frowned, and he kicked at some invisible piece of dirt on the floor. After a while, he shrugged. "I don't know. We dated for a couple of years. She was easy to be with, and she wanted a ring. It seemed right at the time."

Rebecca's heart twisted. He'd given her a ring once. He'd taken her out in the boat over to the little island in the middle of the lake. He'd packed a picnic and stolen some of his dad's beer. Not the cheap stuff kept in the boathouse, but the premium imported bottles from inside the house. They'd spent the afternoon drinking, eating, and making love on the beach. When it was time to pack up and leave, he'd given her a ring. A delicate, simple gold band with encrusted diamonds. Hudson had called it a promise ring and told her he loved her. Said they'd never be apart. A year later, he was gone.

She still had the ring.

"What about you?"

Rebecca pushed away from the counter and wrapped her arms around her body. She was cold and sad and confused and a whole bunch of things. Her chest hurt, or maybe it was her heart. She didn't want to talk about her marriage. Or her life with David, because it had sucked. The only good thing to come out of it was Liam.

"Becca?"

She shook her head because she didn't want to talk about anything.

"Becs?"

He was closer now. She felt the heat of him at her back.

"You're shaking."

Was that his warm breath against her skin?

The silence in her house was oppressive. It filled the nooks and crannies, yet slid over her body and left her feeling empty. She was so damn sick of feeling empty. She needed a connection, even if that connection was all wrong for her.

Slowly, her fingers crept downward until she gripped the edge of her shirt. Heart pounding, lungs on fire with the need to breathe, she pulled the black silky material up and over her head and tossed it to the floor.

Hudson made a noise—an animalistic sound that came from deep inside him. It touched a part of her that used to belong to him. A part of her that used to sing beneath his touch. A part of her that was no longer silent.

Was it the planets aligned properly to make her feel this way? Was Pluto orbiting some other moon or something crazy like that? Was it the fact it had been forever since she'd felt any kind of desire? Any kind of need that hurt so badly it felt better than good?

That was when it hit her. Her forever was Hudson Blackwell. He'd been the only man to make her feel this way, and God, how she missed it.

A sob escaped her. Her breasts ached. Her skin was on fire. Her sex was swollen and wet. She felt as if she were coming apart. As if she was pulled too tight and everything was too thin.

"Becca." His voice was rough, his breathing ragged. "What are we doing here?"

Her hands fell to the opening of her jeans, and before she could change her mind, she unzipped and stepped out of them. His sharp intake of breath told her the black cheeky undies were to his liking—he'd always been an ass man—and for the first time tonight, she felt as if she were in control.

Which was crazy, really, because she so wasn't.

"Rebecca." His voice was sharper now.

"I'm going to bed." She took a few steps and paused near the door. "It's up to you whether or not you want to join me."

Rebecca walked up the stairs, her footsteps slow and precise, and she didn't stop until she reached the end of the hallway. Once inside her bedroom, she took a moment to lean against the wall and tried to catch her breath. But it was hard because her heart was beating so fast, she felt light-headed. And she *was* shaking like a damn leaf.

For a long time, all she could hear was that drumbeat in her ears and the air in her lungs as she struggled to breathe. When it became too much. When her shoulders tensed so badly, the muscles corded painfully, and her stomach tumbled damn near to the floor…

Hudson appeared in her doorway.

She glanced up and watched as he took two steps into the room and stood directly in front of her. Light fell in from the window, creating shadows across his face, illuminating the hard planes, the strong cheekbones and slightly flared nostrils. His eyes were so dark, they looked obsidian, and he looked her over, lingering on her half-exposed breasts and skimpy panties.

In the half-light, he looked dangerous while she felt exposed. She bit her lip and clenched her hands, wondering what he thought as he gazed down at her. She wasn't nineteen anymore. Her body had changed. She'd had a child.

She held her breath when he reached for her, but couldn't hold back the small whimper that spilled from her lips when he touched the tattoo on her lower hip. His fingers burned her skin even as, at first, his touch was tentative. Just a forefinger tracing the outline of the ink so slowly and gently, she wanted to cry.

But then his fingers splayed wide open, and he cupped her hip possessively, running his palm up and down, his touch rougher. She was mesmerized by the sight. By the large masculine hand on her pale skin.

"Look at me, Becca." His voice had an edge to it, and she obeyed. "Are you sure this is what you want? Because I'm about as close to losing control as I've ever been, and if you want me to leave, say the word now. I'll go. We can blame this on whatever you want. The booze. The music. The full moon."

"There is no full moon," she whispered.

A half smile touched his face, and her gut clenched. "No," he said roughly. "There's not." His hand fell away from her hip, and the seconds stretched long and thin.

Hudson was giving her an out, and if she was smart, she'd take it. Rebecca tried to think. She tried to rationalize her behaviour. But how could a person rationalize something they didn't understand? She knew she should stay as far away from Hudson Blackwell as she could, because if she let him in again, it wouldn't end well for her. She *knew* this.

Oh God, but she knew this.

A heartbeat passed. The moment came and went. That perfect moment of clarity when she saw herself pushing him away and asking him to leave. She saw it in her mind, so clear it seemed real. Her hands rose in the air...her fingers reached out. They trembled slightly. They touched leather.

Then, with a groan, she tugged on his jacket, a savage pull. And then his shirt. She helped him with his jeans and belt. It was a hot, feverish manipulation of clothes and skin that left them both breathless.

There was no turning back. Clarity vanished, and raw need took over.

CHAPTER SEVEN

Hudson's willpower left the second her fingers touched his body. Gone was the urge to do the right thing. To think things through, and maybe take a step back. There'd been a fire simmering inside him since he'd laid eyes on Rebecca nearly a week ago, and it was out of control.

Thing was? He didn't care.

Him. Hudson Blackwell. The ultimate control freak who ran his life the way he ran his team. With icy precision and a wide lens that let him see everything. Action. Consequence.

Yet right now, the only thing he cared about was the heat inside these four walls and the half-naked woman in front of him. Rebecca.

My Rebecca.

With a groan, he sank his hands into the silky blonde hair on either side of her head and bent low so that he could finally taste her again. There was no hesitation. No soft nibbles and gentle sweep of the tongue. She offered, and he took.

His mouth was open, hot and demanding. It was fueled equally by the heat inside him, by the way she responded to his touch, by the smell of her. He pushed her back against the wall and kissed her until his head spun. Until he could barely breathe.

And then he kissed her again. With a groan, he tore his mouth from Rebecca, his hands greedily seeking out and releasing her right breast from her silky black bra. His mouth closed over the hard, pebbled nipple, and he used his tongue to taste the pink bud. He smiled savagely when she wiggled and pulled her bra all the way off and offered up both nipples. He'd always loved her breasts. So damn soft. Supple. Perfectly round. They were fuller then he remembered, but Hudson wasn't complaining.

He suckled harder, and she bucked against him.

He grinned. She groaned.

He found her mouth once more, his tongue going deep while his hand stroked its way down her stomach until he felt the edge of her panties. Impatient, all it took was one hard yank and he tore the material away, giving him full access. She trembled beneath his touch, and he didn't stop stroking until he settled between her legs.

He teased her, long fingers rubbing her outer lips. Then pulling away. Increasing the pressure, nearing the edge…and then pulling away again. All the while, Hudson devoured her mouth as if she was his last meal and he hadn't eaten in days. When her hips began to gyrate, he smiled wickedly and whispered against her mouth, "What do you want?"

A groan was his answer.

"I want to hear you say it."

She clawed at his hand and pressed it against her. "Touch me." At the sound of her voice, he sank his fingers deep inside her.

Christ, she was wet.

Hudson felt Rebecca freeze as her muscles clenched around him. He tore his mouth away. Her lips were swollen and red, and that damn pink tongue darted out and touched her top lip in a way that made his cock twitch. Slowly, he rotated his index finger inside her, while his thumb took care of her clitoris. The small nub bloomed beneath his touch, and her head fell back against the wall as he continued to massage and tease. Her eyes glittered, heavy with passion and pleasure. And that part of him, the one that had always belonged to her, roared to life.

It was possession. It was want and need. It was the knowledge that she was his. Always his. The thought echoed in his mind, and he couldn't take his eyes from her. Her head rolled to the side, and he increased the pressure on her clitoris while angling his long finger just so. He didn't have to think—he knew her pleasure points—and damn, but he meant to press every single one of them.

Her hands now clutched his shoulders, and her legs trembled so much, he knew she was close. The walls of her sex clenched hard against him, and her fingernails dug into flesh as she arched her back and cried out.

"That's it, darlin'. Come for me." He barely got the words out.

She shattered against his hand, and her head fell forward onto his chest. Her legs gave out, but Hudson had her. He picked her up and carried her to the bed, placing her in the middle, right there where the light from outside hit. It bathed her in a glow that lit her hair up like a damn halo. There was something insanely sexy about a woman who looked like an angel, lying in the middle of a bed with her mouth swollen, legs parted, and all that pink, shiny flesh on display.

Rebecca was silent as he climbed onto the bed. He bent low and kissed a knee, caressed the small strawberry birthmark just to the left of it. His mouth continued up her thigh, and when he spied the small scar on her lower belly, he kissed that too. Every little bit of it. He licked the tattoo on her hip, chest swelling at the sight, and then gave some attention to her breasts before reaching her face.

She was trembling again, and Hudson used his arms to hold himself up so that he could see her face. He nipped at her nose and dropped a light kiss to her mouth. Everything inside him raged. His body was tight and heavy with anticipation. Her eyes were luminous. Her skin soft as silk.

"You're so damn beautiful," he whispered, positioning himself between her legs, loving how her hips rose to meet him. Her hands crept up to his shoulders and she pulled him down to her. Her mouth was there, right near his ear.

"Now, Huds."

He sank into her fully, groaning loudly at the sensation of wet, hot skin on skin. Sweat broke out on his forehead, hell, it was a sheen that covered his entire body. If he had his way, he'd screw as fast and as hard as he could, because that was what his body was demanding. The need was that urgent.

Her hands were on his ass, and he clenched his jaw tight, trying to slow things down. Trying to build up something good for her. But his lady was having none of that. She slapped at him and gripped his hips with her legs.

"I don't want to play nice, Hudson." Her voice was throaty, and it struck a chord that set off all kinds of hot shit inside him.

"Good to know," he growled. "We'll go slow next time."

He stared down at a face that had haunted him, forever it seemed, and felt something inside him give. He was close, so damn close to the edge. He picked up the pace, his body giving in to the animalistic needs that took over. He loved the way she felt, so hot and tight. Loved the way her hair spilled across the bed. The way her lips parted. The noises she made.

He couldn't remember the last time sex had been this good. He rode them both to orgasm, and as he collapsed on the bed and pulled her close, Hudson kissed the top of her head. He listened to her breathing, to the sound of her fast-beating heart. Everything about her was the same, yet different.

His chest swelled and his throat tightened with an emotion he couldn't quite name. But the one thought that lingered in his mind long after Rebecca fell asleep was that being with her felt like coming home.

* * *

Hudson woke up because an alarm clock erupted right beside his head. Literally beside his head. He rolled over with a groan that quickly escalated into a bunch of expletives that would make a nun blush. They didn't stop until he located the damn clock, wedged between his right shoulder blade and the sheets. What the hell?

He sat up and turned it off, bleary eyes slowly allowing him to focus.

White sheets and white walls. Blue comforter and curtains. White furniture. Dark wood floors. He slipped from the bed and turned in a full circle. A black-and-white framed photo caught his attention. Rebecca and Liam.

He glanced back at the bed. At the tangled sheets and his clothes strewn over the floor. One boot sat on the table beside the bed. Who the hell knew where the other one was. Everything came back.

Every. Hot. Detail.

He let his mind wander as he thought back to the night before and, with a slow smile, glanced around the room. Where was Rebecca? The house was silent, and he was naked. Quickly, he found his clothes and got dressed, his mood light. He glanced around the room once more and was just about to leave when he noticed a piece of paper that had fallen off the bed. Most likely when he'd been wrangling with the alarm clock.

He picked it up, immediately recognized the handwriting, and scanned the note. It didn't take long for his good mood to disappear as he read Rebecca's words. There weren't very many of them.

I need you gone by the time I get home at noon.

That was it. All she wrote.

"You've got to be kidding me." Hudson shoved the piece of paper into the front pocket of his jeans and headed out of the bedroom. He was angry. Hell, he was more than angry. He was pissed off and insulted and there was a healthy dose of bewilderment thrown in. What the hell?

Hudson paused at the top of the stairs. The house was small, with only two bedrooms and a bath on the upper level. He glanced at his watch, curiosity getting the better of him, and took some time to peek into Liam's room. The kid was a die-hard Red Wings and Tigers fan, with signed jerseys on the wall opposite his bed. A typical boy's room, the bed wasn't made, his desk had a bit of clutter, and a lone sock peeked out from under the bed.

At the bottom of the stairs, Hudson sidestepped the sheets of drywall and paint cans he'd tripped over the night before. The walls in the living room were ripped down to the studs, and the carpet had been pulled out, exposing the original hardwood floors. The planks were wide dark oak and in need of some TLC. But, judging from the equipment in the corner, they were to be refinished. The hallway was about the same, empty of anything save the materials needed to bring it back to life.

He opened a door near the alcove by the stairs. It was a bathroom, though at the moment, the toilet was in a box, and so was the shower. There were samples of tiles, glass blocks, and paint chips.

The kitchen, however? He glanced around, taking in the new stainless-steel appliances, dark granite counters, gray slate floors, and refinished white cupboards. Red was the accent color of choice, and a trio of owls—the color of a fire engine—watched him from the countertop. A simple vase of red daisies sat in the center of the small table, and black-and-white photos sporting red frames were on the wall above it.

She still had a thing for owls.

The space wasn't large, but the design gave it optimum room. An island provided extra seating, and a large window brought in the outdoors—the river and the dam. The backyard was a good size, though the shed in the far corner looked like it needed some improvements, and the deck should be shored up.

He walked over to the table, his gaze moving over pictures of Liam, Rebecca, and a few of her brother, Mackenzie, who seemed to have landed a beautiful wife and a new baby. Huh. Never thought Mac would turn into a family man.

He hadn't noticed any of this stuff the night before, but then he'd been getting naked with Rebecca and the damn décor wasn't at the top of his list of things that mattered.

Hudson stood in the middle of the kitchen for a good long while, unsure how to proceed. He didn't give a damn that Rebecca had blown him off. There were things that needed to be discussed and addressed. Things he needed to say.

He might have stuck around for it too, if not for the timely alarm clock sounding once again. It echoed shrilly through the empty house, and he winced. It was as if Rebecca knew he needed a kick in the ass to get him out the door.

With a sigh, Hudson headed outside, taking note that the shutters needed painting and the railing needed to be secured. The porch floorboards, however, looked as if they'd been attended to and prettied up with a fresh coat of off-white.

He sat in hi truck, glaring at the house. He sure as hell hadn't seen this coming. Not Rebecca. Not the sex. Not waking up alone. Not any of it. Hudson turned the key, and the engine roared to life. With one final look at her place, he backed out of Rebecca's driveway and headed out to the lake.

She might have thought getting the hell out of Dodge before he got his ass up was a good way to get rid of Hudson.

"Not a chance," he murmured. She should know better. Seemed as if time and distance had made Rebecca Draper forget a few things. Like the fact it was going to take a hell of a lot more than a damn note to keep him away.

The sun glinted off the top of the hood as he sped down River Road, the town disappearing from his rear view mirror. He had some things he needed to take care of, but he'd be back. Now that he knew where she was bunkered down, Rebecca couldn't hide from him.

Hudson turned up the radio, and for the first time since he'd been home, found himself looking forward to what was coming next.

CHAPTER EIGHT

The door opened before Rebecca had a chance to knock.

"Hey." She barely got the word out before Violet reached out and yanked her inside, quickly hustling her over to the kitchen and plopping her onto a seat at the island. The open space was full of light, thanks to the bank of windows, and several vases of fresh flowers drank it in.

Rebecca watched Violet warily, noting the spiky hair, flushed cheeks, and…geez, love bites on her neck. The Grinch Christmas nighty was a little much and barely covered her shocking pink undies, but then, this was Violet. Her crazy-ass best friend. Her go-to person. The one woman on the planet who never judged.

And she'd at least made the effort to pull them on.

Rebecca cleared her throat and started to speak, but Violet shook her head and held her hand up for added emphasis.

"Nope. Not yet. We need to get this right."

Violet poured two large mugs of coffee and then grabbed cream from the fridge. She slid onto the chair across from Rebecca and then swore, jumping to her feet again.

"What the—"

"I said not yet." Violet reached into the cupboard beside the fridge and grabbed the bowl of sugar. She sat back down, fixed their coffees, and then, after taking a sip from her mug, nodded at Rebecca. Her face was eager. "Okay, I'm ready."

"Good to know," Rebecca replied, holding the mug between her hands for warmth. She'd been cold since she got up. Since she'd wriggled out from Hudson's arms and left him in her bed.

Naked. *In her bed.*

"Spill. I've been waiting since you called me an hour ago."

Rebecca swallowed some of the hot brew and set her cup back down. The words burned at the back of her throat where they'd been since the early hours of the morning. She had to clear her throat again and take a mental step back.

Violet's eyes widened, and she leaned closer. "I knew it. This is gonna be good."

"Where's Adam?"

Okay. Those weren't the words she'd been dying to share, but considering the fog Rebecca had been in since she woke up, it was a start.

Her friend gave her a look that said, *are you kidding me?* "He went to get the twins at his mother's. I told you that already. Shit, I had to make up the lamest excuse ever so that I could stay home and get the goods from you."

"What was the excuse?"

Violet snorted. "Becs, really? We need to do this?"

Rebecca nodded, the tension easing a bit. "We do."

"Well," Violet began dramatically. "I told Adam that the sex was so good and so hard, and *so* damn long last night that my girlie parts—"

"Okay," Rebecca cut in with a laugh. "I get it."

"Did you?"

"Did I what?"

"Did you get it last night? Because everyone in town is talking about it, and I want details."

Rebecca opened her mouth and then slammed it shut again. She felt the heat burn up her face and winced when Violet giggled. Everyone in town. *Great.*

"I knew when you disappeared, something was up." Violet leaned closer and lowered her voice, which was ridiculous considering they were the only two people in the house. "So was he good?"

"Everyone knows?" Rebecca croaked.

"I might have exaggerated a bit. Maybe not everyone." Violet shrugged. "I heard some of the guys talking, and then Melissa Davidson said something about you and Ethan."

Rebecca jerked back in her chair. "Ethan?"

Violet's wicked smile slowly faded, and she was silent for a few seconds. "You guys were pretty cozy on the dance floor, and then you both disappeared at the same time, so..."

Rebecca knew exactly when her girlfriend realized she'd gotten the story wrong. Violet's eyes nearly popped out of her head. "You didn't leave with Ethan last night."

Rebecca slowly shook her head and reached for her coffee cup. "No."

Violet watched her closely, and Rebecca could see the wheels spinning. Her friend's eyes narrowed, and then she was off her chair like a shot.

"Don't you say another word. Hold on." She rummaged through the cupboard above the fridge and returned to the table with a bottle of whiskey.

"Really, Violet? It's barely past eight in the morning."

Violet held the bottle in front of Rebecca. "Do you want some or not?"

Rebecca hesitated, for like two seconds, and then, with a sigh, held out her mug. Violet poured a generous finger or two for each of them and then grabbed a box of donuts from the pantry before she settled down. She shoved one of the sugared delights into her mouth and nodded.

"Okay. I'm ready."

"Hudson took me home."

"I knew it!" Violet grabbed another donut. "And?"

"I slept with him."

Violet had to take a good long gulp of coffee to wash down the donut, and she still sputtered and stammered when she found her voice. "You slept with him? What the hell? Last night, you made it seem like if he was the last man on earth, you wouldn't go there."

Rebecca almost choked on her coffee. "This tastes disgusting."

"Never mind that. I need the deets. What happened. How?"

Rebecca sighed. She picked up one of the donuts, but her stomach was full of nerves, and she knew she'd never get it down. She put the chocolate confection back and shrugged.

"I wish I could blame it on booze, but I can't." She paused. "I was having a good time, and Ethan was being so nice, you know?"

Violet nodded, her head bobbing up and down as she reached for her third donut. "I know."

"I didn't care that Hudson was there. Didn't care at all."

Liar.

"And then…"

"Then?" Violet prompted, mouth full.

"Shelli was all over him, and I don't know. Something inside me just…" She stumbled over her words, trying to think of the right ones to describe what she'd felt. "I wanted to scratch her eyes out. *For talking to him.*"

"This is Shelli Gouthro. She doesn't just talk to a man."

"Doesn't matter. I haven't seen Hudson in over ten years, so it's seriously screwed up to get upset because he was talking to a woman."

"Again. Not just any woman. We're talking about Shelli."

Rebecca shook her head. "It's still screwed up."

"Not really. You and Hudson have a complicated past. He was your first love. There's always going to be some kind of territorial thing going on."

A few seconds of quiet passed. "Well, we sure as hell got territorial last night. I saw him leave, and, I don't know what I was thinking. I followed him out to the parking lot and threw myself at him."

"I doubt that."

"No. I did." Rebecca winced at the memory. "I told him to take me home and then practically dragged him into the house."

Violet finished her coffee. "Hudson's a big boy, and I saw the way he looked at you last night. He didn't like you with Ethan. That was pretty obvious. Trust me. You didn't drag him anywhere he didn't want to be."

Rebecca waited while her girlfriend topped up her coffee, though she refused any more whiskey. When Violet plopped down beside her, a slow smile spread across her face.

"So," Violet began, that smile of hers widening. "How was it?"

How was it? Rebecca blew out a long breath, squirming a bit as she thought back to the night before. She was sore, but it was the good kind of sore that came from a long night of hot sex.

"It was good," she managed to say, avoiding Violet's eyes.

"Good?" Violet got to her feet. "It was *good?* Jesus, Rebecca. You have to give me more. Good is when the fettuccine noodles are done just right, or when you break a nail and Ramona at the salon can fit you in. Good is when you've made it through the week without overdosing on carbs." She shook her head. "Seriously. If you're telling me that sex with Hudson was good, then I'm taking back the donuts, because you so don't deserve them."

She reached for the box, but Rebecca grabbed it and held it up. "Okay. God, you're relentless." She snagged the last chocolate morsel and popped it in her mouth. "Sex with Hudson was amazing. Is that what you wanted to hear?"

Violet slid back onto her chair. "How amazing?"

"Better than chocolate."

"That's pretty friggin' amazing."

Rebecca was quiet for a few moments. "I thought after the second time, it couldn't get any better, but then…"

"Second? How many times did you guys get territorial?"

She blushed. "Three."

Violet dug in for another donut. "And what made door number three better than chocolate?"

How could Rebecca explain it? It wasn't as if Hudson had done something out of the ordinary. But the way he'd looked at her. The way he'd touched her when he was inside her. Something was different. It had been more intimate. More intense. It had been… More.

And that wasn't acceptable. That spelled trouble.

"I don't know. We just… It just was."

"Okay. I'll take that for now." Violet's eyebrows rose in question. "And then he left?"

"No. He was still there this morning." Tangled in her sheets. Every single naked inch of him. She'd taken the time to look him over—really look him over, and even now, her body reacted to the sight. His tattoos were intricate. Dangerous. Sexy. His body was perfection. It was muscular and trim. His face, relaxed in sleep, could make an angel weep. And those hands of his—large, male… The things they'd done to her.

"He's still at your place?" Violet looked surprised.

Rebecca glanced out the window, suddenly feeling very vulnerable. "I don't know. I left him a note and asked him to leave. Said I'd be back by noon."

"Wow. That's kind of harsh, don't you think?"

"No." Rebecca looked at her friend. "Last night shouldn't have happened, and I can't let it happen again."

"But don't you think maybe it happened for a reason? Obviously, there's still something there." Violet looked at her pointedly. "Maybe the two of you being back here at the same time means something. Maybe—"

"There is no maybe. There will never be anything between us. I had too much to drink and things happened and that's the end of that."

"Then what are you going to do?"

Rebecca reached for another donut. "I'm going to do what any other responsible, sane woman who had sex with someone they shouldn't have had sex with would do."

"And that would be…" Violet waited expectantly.

She nibbled the edge of her donut, mind made up. "I'm going to pretend it didn't happen."

CHAPTER NINE

Darlene was at the house when Hudson got home. The smell of coffee and bacon made his stomach rumble, and he headed to the back where the kitchen and great room overlooked the lake. A large, open space, it had always been the main hub of the Blackwell place and for good reason. It was big, bright, and inviting. And for a bunch of growing boys, more importantly, it was where the food was.

"There you are," Darlene said with a smile as she bustled about the kitchen.

He inhaled the mouth-watering scents. "You didn't have to do this."

She shrugged and smiled but said nothing.

Hudson took some time to appreciate his surroundings. The gleaming countertops and stainless-steel appliances were new, as were the cupboards. Gone was the oak that Hudson had grown up with. It been replaced by dark cherry, which was a smart contrast to the light cream-colored granite countertops.

"When did this all happen?" Hudson asked, sliding onto one of the stools at the island. This was the first chance he'd had to chat with her since he'd come back to Crystal Lake. Darlene handed him a cup of coffee, which he accepted with a smile, and he took a sip, watching as she prepared him a plate of food. Along with bacon, there were eggs, hash browns and—he smiled—fresh-cut pineapple, which was his favorite.

The woman remembered everything.

"Last year. Just before Christmas." She set the plate down in front of him and got busy cleaning up while he dug in. Shit. A guy could get used to this.

"This is amazing. Thanks, Darlene."

He watched as she tossed some plates into the dishwasher. After his mother passed, she'd appeared in their lives and had become as much a part of the Blackwell clan as any family member. She'd come in as a newly divorced woman in search of an income—she'd been hired to look after the boys—and had never left.

A few years younger than his father, she'd managed to age in a much more gentle, refined way. Her body was trim, though there were new wrinkles around her eyes, and her once jet-black hair was silver. It looked good on her. Dressed simply in jeans and a blue blouse, she was a striking figure, and not for the first time did Hudson wonder about the fact she never remarried. About the fact that she was always in their home. Even after the boys had left. There were several times his father had called, and he'd heard her voice in the background.

He finished his plate and sat back on the stool, glancing around the place and seeing it through new eyes. There'd been a lot of improvements since he'd been home last. New leather furniture sat in front of the fireplace. No longer were the walls beige; they'd been updated to an off-white with dark charcoal accents. The dark wood floors and rich leather, coupled with the fresh, crisp walls, was a good look for the room.

The new décor and furniture hadn't quite made it upstairs yet. At least not to his old bedroom. That particular space hadn't changed one damn bit, and Hudson had been pleased.

"I talked to Dad's doctor."

Darlene paused and then tossed the scraps from his plate into the garbage before leaning against the counter.

"What did Regan tell you?" she asked.

Suddenly restless, Hudson got to his feet. "It's not good."

"No," Darlene said softly. "I didn't think it was." She watched him closely. "When are Wyatt and Travis coming home?"

"I don't know. Wyatt is racing, and Travis is gearing up for a new season. Exhibition games right now, but he's the starting goalie, and that's something he worked hard to get, but it's even harder to keep. They just traded for a hotshot backup, and I know he's keeping Travis on his toes."

Darlene's lips thinned. "I get that the boys are busy. I really do. But for God's sake, Hudson, surely an exception could be made? He's their father." Her cheeks were pink and her nostrils flared. "He's *your* father. He deserves more than to be alone when he's so ill. Deserves more than to be ignored by his children."

Hudson loved Darlene. He really did. He knew she meant well and that her heart was in the right place. But in this instance, he had his brothers' backs. There were reasons things were the way they were.

"It's a hell of a lot more complicated than that, Darlene, and you know it."

Darlene put her hands on her hips, and all five foot three inches of her vibrated with anger. "I know your relationship with your father isn't ideal."

"That's putting it mildly."

"I know that it's been hard and tough and that he can be an absolute bastard. But Hudson, the man is dying. If you want to know the absolute truth, he's been dying for years. Alone here in this big house with no one to keep him company but regret and pain and pride."

"He had you." Hudson wasn't sure where that came from, and he sure as hell couldn't take it back.

Darlene was silent for a few seconds and in that small window of time, Hudson glimpsed an incredible sadness.

"I wasn't enough," she whispered. "I wasn't your mother."

"I'm sorry. I shouldn't have said that."

Darlene sighed. "Look, Hudson. Talk to the boys. That's all I'm asking. He's had a hard time these past years. He knows there are wrongs he needs to make right. But he can't do them on his own. He needs that chance. None of you have seen him struggle. With his health. His loneliness. With the business."

Hudson frowned. "Dad wants me to check in on things at the office. Everything okay as far as you know?"

Darlene shrugged. "As far as I know. But you know John. He worries about everything. Worries about the legacy he's leaving his boys." Her eyes hardened. "Boys who have no interest in him or his life."

"That's not fair." Hudson was starting to get ticked off. As much as Darlene had been a part of their lives, she'd never lived with them. She was the pretty woman who smelled nice. The one who showed up in the morning before they left for school and made sure they had lunches. She was there when they got home. There to make dinner. When John Blackwell got home from the office, she left. There was a lot she hadn't seen and a hell of a lot more she didn't know.

How could he make her understand?

"A parent's right to respect and love isn't just handed to them. Like anything else, it's earned, and sometimes it's lost. My father wasn't just hard on us. That doesn't come close to describing what went on in this house. There are things you don't know, Darlene. Things no one knows."

Hands clenched into fists he stared across the room at a woman who'd come as close to a mother as he'd known. He was angry. Pissed. And hurt.

Darlene walked over to him and gave him a hug. When she stepped back, her eyes shimmered. She slowly exhaled.

"I can't pretend to know what it feels like to be John Blackwell's son. I only know what I know." She attempted a smile, but it fell short. "None of the men in this family are happy. You're divorced. But then you never should have married Candace in the first place. Wyatt is trying his damnedest to prove something. I don't know what that something is, but I'm going to tell you that if he's not careful, it's going to cost him his life. He drives like the devil and takes chances none of those other drivers take."

Hudson couldn't disagree with her there.

"And Travis just seems lost to me. The last time I spoke to him, he told me about this fancy new house in LA he'd just spent ten million on. I asked him about the gardens. About what I could send him for his gardens." She shook her head. "That boy used to help me outside for hours. He loved getting his hands dirty. Do you know what he told me?"

Hudson shrugged, damn certain she was gonna fill him in.

"He told me he hadn't even been outside. He had no clue what was in his back garden. What kind of man buys a ten-million-dollar house and doesn't even know what kind of flowers populate his garden?"

"Darlene. He's busy."

"No. He's spoiled and lost and right now only cares about himself. His agent knows more about what goes on in his life than he does. It's not good for him. He's not grounded. None of you are."

"I don't know what you want me to say." Frustrated, Hudson ran his hands through his hair.

"I want you to talk to your brothers. I want you to do what you can to get them home so that they can make peace with your father. I want all of you to give him the chance to make things right. If you don't. If he…" She shuddered and swiped at her eyes. "If he passes without that happening, there will be consequences. Lifelong consequences."

He kept his mouth shut, because he didn't know how to respond, and because deep down, he knew she was right.

"I'll see what I can do," Hudson said, finally getting his thoughts together.

The relief in Darlene's face wasn't something she could hide. She nodded and headed back to the kitchen. "Okay. I'm off to the hospital. I told your father I'd bring him some real food, even though lately he's had a hard time keeping it down." She raised an eyebrow. "Are you going to pop in and see him?"

"Yeah. Later. I want to check out the boathouse. Dad said the dock was starting to rot. Thought maybe I'd take a shot at fixing it instead of hiring out the job."

"He would like that." She scooped her purse from the counter and took a few steps before she paused and looked back at him. "Where were you all night?"

Hudson's tongue tripped all over the place because suddenly he felt like a guilty sixteen-year-old who'd been caught doing something he shouldn't be doing.

"Never mind," Darlene said with a small smile. "It's none of my business. I'll be back tomorrow after a meeting at the church with some homemade soup."

"Darlene, you don't have to."

"No," she replied. "I don't. But you're home, and it's been too long since I've had the chance to spoil you."

She was almost to the front door when he heard her voice drift back at him. "Rebecca Draper is back in town. If you don't already know."

The door clicked behind her, and Hudson was left on his own. He stretched and walked over to the bank of windows, watching the water roll in from the lake. It was going to be another sunny day. Hot by the looks of it. His gaze swept the shoreline and rested on the boathouse.

How many nights had he and Rebecca spent out there, holed up in the room above it? Too many to count. Hudson backed away from the window, shaking off the melancholy that had claimed him, and headed upstairs. He needed a quick shower and a change. He'd take stock of the boathouse and dock, make note of what he needed for repairs, and then he'd head back to town to get them.

A few hours of good hard labor would help him think. Help him figure out how he was going to deal with Rebecca. Because they were going to have a conversation whether she wanted to or not.

Decision made, he got busy.

CHAPTER TEN

It was nearly four in the afternoon when Rebecca pulled into the parking lot at the hospital. Liam was with her, anxious to get inside and show Sal the new model car he'd convinced his pal Jason to trade a hockey card for. A gorgeous replica of a 1972 Corvette, it was shiny red, and the details were exquisite.

"Do you think he'll like it, Mom?" Liam pushed a chunk of blond hair away from his face and looked at her. As always, the sight of him made her heart hurt. Sometimes it was so full, she didn't think she could stand it.

"I think Sal will adore it." Her voice shook a little bit as she spoke. The elderly gentleman meant a lot to her and Liam. Six months ago, when he'd hired her, Sal had taken a shine to her son, and the two of them had hit it off. Sal even started referring to Liam as one of his own grandboys. It meant a lot to Rebecca, considering her own father wasn't grandfather material. Kind of hard to be there for your family when you were a mean drunk with a hard right hook, and in and out of jail.

"I hope so. I think it's the exact same car as the one he had when he used to be a badass."

"Liam. Language."

"What? Sal told me he was a badass. Besides." Liam shrugged. "That's not a bad word. Maybe when you were a kid it was, but not now."

She shook her head as the two of them slid from her car and headed inside. Crystal Lake Memorial Hospital was a bright, sunny place, and the design was such that there weren't many areas without natural light. For a hospital, as bleak as they could be, it wasn't so bad. They made their way through the main entrance and over to the elevators. She listened to Liam talk excitedly about some new video game he was playing with his pals, Michael and Ian. It had something to do with cars, and he was hoping Sal would be able to play with him when he got out of the hospital.

Again, her heart squeezed. Sal's prognosis wasn't good. His cancer had spread. And that was something she hadn't shared with Liam. Not yet anyway.

They reached the fifth floor, and she paused, spying Regan Thorne over by the nurses station. "Go on and see Sal. He's expecting you. I'll be there in a minute or two."

Liam ran off, the path to Salvatore's room one he knew well. She smiled as she watched his blond curls bounce. Not many boys would take time out of their Sunday afternoon, especially on fair weekend, to visit a sick elderly man. She had a good kid. Considering the toxic environment he'd been born into, it was saying something.

Turning quickly, she hiked her bag over her shoulder and headed to the nurses station.

"Working Sundays now?" she said, approaching the doctor. A white overcoat didn't hide the sleek black dress and elegant heels.

Regan glanced up from the chart she was reading and smiled. "I got called in to check on a patient, but I'll be heading out soon to dinner. You here to see John and Sal?" Regan knew her routine well.

"Yes. I thought I'd pop into John's room. That's if… Is he alone right now?" She was tumbling over her words and hoped that her cheeks weren't as red as they felt, because that would be embarrassing. She was thirty-three, for God's sake, not a damn teenager.

Something shifted in Regan's eyes. They softened with understanding. "Hudson isn't here, if that's what you're asking."

Was she that easy to read? "Okay." Rebecca started to back away. "Thanks."

"Hey, what's this I heard about you and Ethan Burke?"

Rebecca groaned. "Don't believe everything you hear, Regan."

"I know the way this town works." The doctor chuckled. "Still, it was a good story."

"I'm sure it was," Rebecca murmured to herself as she made her way toward the private wing known as Grandview. She pushed through the doors, and a few moments later, slipped inside John Blackwell's room.

He was sitting up, which surprised her, and she smiled when he glanced up at her.

"There's my favorite girl," he said gruffly..

"Hey." She walked to the bed and eyed the food tray. It was half-empty. Again. Another surprise. "I see your appetite has returned."

"Not really. Darlene brought me some soup and, well, the mashed potatoes weren't half-bad today."

His thick white hair was askew, and he ran his hands through it. The action was simple, but it reminded her so much of Hudson that she had to look away. He coughed, and couldn't seem to stop. She motioned to the oxygen mask, but he shook his head, and after a while the coughing eased.

"You look better," she murmured. And he did. There was color in his face, and his eyes seemed brighter.

"Hudson's back." He spoke bluntly—as was his way—and there it was, the thing they never talked about.

Rebecca poured some water into a cup and handed it to John. "I know."

Back when Rebecca had dated Hudson, she and John Blackwell had never been close. He'd been the aloof father, with the hard, stern face and a disapproving manner. He thought she wasn't good enough for his boy—being a Draper and all—and while never impolite, there was a noticeable lack of warmth when he was around. After Hudson left Crystal Lake, she'd had nothing to do with the man. It was by chance they'd reconnected several months earlier. He'd brought a dog into the clinic. The poor thing had wandered onto the Blackwell property, half-starved, flea ridden, and heavy with pups.

John had known Rebecca right away, and after that initial visit, he started coming by the vet clinic a few times a week. At first it was to check on the dog and her pups. But as time passed, Rebecca realized it was just an excuse to come in and talk. He started bringing her coffee on Fridays, and it became a regular thing, right up until he got sick.

They'd never discussed her past with Hudson, and the John she came to know wasn't anything like the one she remembered. This man carried a burden and seemed lost. Something inside her responded to his sadness, and here they were.

He took the glass of water. "That's all you've got to say? I know?"

"It is," she said, taking a step back.

"That's surprising. Thought there'd be more."

"There is. I just don't want to talk about it right now." She was more than a little hurt he'd not told her his oldest son was coming back to town.

He studied her for a few moments and then took a sip from his glass. "Did I ever tell you how Angel and I met?"

"No," she murmured, relieved he'd decided to move on.

John was silent for a few seconds, his forehead furrowed, as if considering things. His head dropped back to the pillow, and she inched closer, taking the glass of water from his hands. They shook a little, and she gently squeezed his fingers.

"I was home. On leave with a few weeks of nothing to do but drink and mess around with whoever was willing to mess around with me." A wry grin touched his mouth. "What else was a young man of twenty-two to do? I had no desire to get involved with anyone. No desire to put down roots. Much to my parents' dismay. And then I met Angelique the day before I was to head back to active duty. It was early spring, and the daffodils poked through the ground around the dock. I remember ice still clung to the edge of the lake, and mist rolled across the water as I headed out for a run."

He closed his eyes and smiled. "Nothing in the world will clear your head like air that smells of winter but feels like spring. I ran damn near around the lake and ended up in town. Decided to stop at a small café that had opened up in the heart of the square, right there beside the clock tower. I walked in, dripping of sweat and smelling of the previous evening's bad choices, and there she was."

His voice was so wistful, it brought a lump to Rebecca's throat.

"She was taking someone's order. Jeremy Levitz, if I recall correctly. Angel was small, with the tiniest hands I'd ever seen. Her eyes were as blue as the Caribbean, and her hair was so shiny, like spun gold. It was long, hung nearly to her waist. I'd never seen anything like it. Never seen anyone like her. She came over and took my order, and I could barely muster the courage to look her in the face. I went home and told my parents I'd met the girl I was going to marry."

"Really," Rebecca said with a soft smile.

He smiled. "Of course, Angel didn't make things easy. I managed to get her information from the owner of the café and went round her apartment that night, but her roommate told me she wasn't home. She was at the drive-in with that damn Levitz."

John started coughing but again shooed her away when she would have given him oxygen.

"I drove out there and found them. No way could you miss Levitz's bright red Chevy. I yanked open the door and told Angel to wait for me. Told her I'd be home in the fall. That my service would be over, and I was coming back to Crystal Lake to make my life."

John fell silent then, seeming exhausted. When he spoke, his voice was noticeably weaker. "She waited." He attempted a smile. "I loved her like I've never loved anyone."

"I know," Rebecca watched him closely.

"She gave me three boys, and I…" His chin trembled, and he paused. "I didn't take care of that gift. I did things I shouldn't have. And then when she was taken from me, I was hard on those boys. Hard on them because I felt sorry for myself. Sorry that I was alone. Sorry and…" He sighed. "Guilty." That last word was whispered, and she barely heard him.

There was such sadness in his voice, such self-condemnation, that Rebecca felt her eyes water.

"What kind of father does that? Takes out his shortcomings on his boys?"

"The kind of father who's hurting."

He looked at her then, eyes as clear as could be. "That's no excuse."

He was right. Of course he was. But Rebecca didn't have the heart to agree with him. Instead, she offered a small smile and filled his water glass.

"I need to go. Liam's with Sal."

"How's that old bastard doing?" His breathing labored, he finally accepted the oxygen from Rebecca.

"He's doing as well as can be expected. But it doesn't look good. The cancer's spread, and I don't think chemo is an option anymore."

John inhaled deeply and pulled off his mask. "Give him my best. Maybe if I'm feeling up to it, I'll take a walk down there to see him."

She nodded. "I will. You have a good night, John."

The elderly man nodded but didn't speak again, clearly exhausted. With one last smile, and a small kiss to his temple, Rebecca left John Blackwell's room. Preoccupied, she didn't bother to look around as she headed back to the main hospital.

If she had, she would have seen Hudson a few feet from his father's room, watching her closely, his expression unreadable. As it was, she pushed through the double doors and headed to Sal's room, while Hudson watched her go. His face dark, his eyes bleak, he stood there for a few more seconds, and then disappeared inside his father's room.

CHAPTER ELEVEN

Monday afternoon found Hudson down on the dock. He'd slept like shit—couldn't turn off his brain—and had been up since early morning working. His Sunday hadn't gone as planned. More determined than ever to see Rebecca, he'd swung by her place, but no one was home. He'd hung around for at least an hour before deciding the neighbor was either going to call the cops or come at him with a rifle. So he'd left.

What the hell had Becca been doing in his father's room? And why hadn't his dad said anything to Hudson about it?

It was a question that dogged him all day, and one he'd not been able to answer. The sun was low in the sky as he finished nailing the last board in place. He grabbed an old towel and wiped sweat from his forehead. He was dirty and tired and thirsty as hell. Tossing the towel back onto the dock, he trudged inside the boathouse and headed to the fridge.

He'd stocked up the day before and grabbed a cold beer, taking a long pull from the can before heading back out to take a look at his handiwork. The smell of freshly cut wood and sawdust hung heavy in the air, along with a healthy dose of fall. In the distance, the trees surrounding the lake were starting to turn, and he knew within a week the landscape would look much different. No longer would it be green, but awash in red, orange, and yellow.

Hudson took another drink and spied a bald eagle as it swept over the water before disappearing into the bush.

"Damn," he murmured. It had been years since he'd seen an eagle, and the sight brought a lump to his throat. In DC, he was too busy with work to get out much and enjoy nature the way he'd been brought up to. He'd been a guy who enjoyed hiking, sledding, boating, and biking. But his life was different. Right now, the only exercise he got was at the gym, and he'd forgotten how amazing the outdoors was.

Right now, standing on this dock enjoying the late afternoon sun, watching an eagle glide across the lake, DC seemed a million miles away.

Hudson crushed the can and tossed it in the pail of garbage he'd amassed during the last eight hours of work. His back was killing him, and he thought maybe thirty minutes in the hot tub would cure that particular ailment. He was just about to clean up his mess when he noticed someone heading down to the dock. He shaded his eyes so he could see better.

"Son of a bitch," he said, taking the steps two at a time. Hudson reached the top of the stairs and stepped onto the upper deck. He didn't hesitate and strode forward to envelope the man in a huge bear hug. Which was reciprocated—for exactly two seconds—and then the newcomer pushed Hudson away with a slap on the back as a wide grin spread across his face.

"Jesus, Hudsy. Don't get all emotional on me. When the hell did you turn into a girl?"

Hudson took a step and shook his head. Nash Booker. The guy was his oldest friend, and up until a few years back, they'd been in close contact, talking at least once a week. But then life got in the way. Nash had fallen off the grid, and Hudson's job became his number one priority.

He grinned, taking in every detail. Nash's hair was on the long side, and there were a few new tattoos, but on the whole not much had changed. Tall, with long lean lines, the guy had been a division one quarterback for Texas A&M, until he'd been kicked out of the program. As he was bullheaded with an attitude the size of Texas, no one had been surprised. What *had* been surprising was that he'd lasted long enough to win State. He'd always been the crazy one in their group, stubborn as hell with a wild streak that made most folks uneasy. But when your back was against the wall, Nash was the guy you wanted in your corner.

"It's been, what, two years since I've seen you?" Hudson asked.

"Three."

That surprised Hudson. When the hell had time gotten away from him? "Last I heard, you were thinking of going to Nepal to climb Everest."

"Buddy, that was last year."

Hudson's eyebrows shot up. "You did it?"

Nash grinned. "I did."

"You crazy-ass bastard." Hudson grinned. "So what are you doing here?"

Nash nodded toward the boathouse. "That, my friend, is a long story. You got any more Bud?"

"Absolutely."

The two men made their way back down to the dock, and once Hudson pulled a couple more beers from the fridge, they sank down on the low-slung Adirondack chairs.

"Shit, our names are still carved into these."

Hudson looked down at his chair. Saw the HB etched into the arm. His smile slowly faded when he spied RD right there underneath his, a small heart drawn between them.

"I stopped by your place in DC."

"Yeah?" Hudson took a sip from his can.

Nash leaned back in his chair. "Ran into Candace. She filled me in."

"Huh." That kind of surprised Hudson. "She's still at the house?"

"She answered the door." Nash gave him a side look. "You good with it? The divorce?"

Hudson nodded. "She deserved a hell of a lot more than I could ever give her.".

The two men were silent for a few moments, and then Hudson spoke. "Becca's here. Back in Crystal Lake."

Nash didn't answer right away. He fiddled with his beer, and, always the observer, Hudson sensed something was up. "You don't seem surprised."

"I'm not. Becca and I keep in touch." He shrugged. "It's been a few weeks, but we talk every now and then." Nash watched him closely.

"You seem surprised."

Hudson was more than surprised. Heat flushed through him. "You never said anything about Rebecca before."

"It never seemed like a good idea to bring up the past when we talked." Nash took a sip of beer and then leaned forward. "Truthfully, I didn't think I had to keep you in the loop where Rebecca is concerned. She was your girlfriend, but she was one of my best friends. That's nothing new." His eyes narrowed. "It's been years, Hudsy. You left her, remember?"

Hudson's jaw clenched, and he looked away, his gaze on the water once more. "You're right. I guess I'm just surprised." He was feeling a hell of a lot more than surprise, but right now, Hudson wasn't exactly sure what that other stuff was. He decided to ignore it and change the subject.

"So what's the story? Why are you back?"

The tension dissipated as Nash's face broke open in a wide grin. "You're not going to believe it."

"Try me." Nothing Nash Booker did surprised him. This was the guy who at seventeen entered a race at a track in Detroit, agreeing to drive his cousin's car even though he'd never driven stick before. He won the race, the trophy, two hundred and fifty bucks, *and* his cousin's girl. After his football fiasco, he'd been all over the world, working at whatever job he could find to fund adventure after adventure. It wasn't exactly a stable life, but then Nash had never been the kind of guy to lay down roots.

"You know Sal is sick, right?"

Hudson nodded. "I heard." Regan Thorne had filled him in the day before.

"He wants to sell his place, and I'm thinking of buying it."

"The Coach House." Hudson snorted, but his laughter died when he saw the look on Nash's face. "Seriously?"

Nash nodded. "Crazy, right?"

Truthfully, the notion of Nash working in a bar wasn't crazy. Hudson was pretty sure the man had done a ton of bartending in his day. But business owner? That was something else entirely. That was a commitment, and Nash Booker had never committed to anything more than a good time, and that only lasted as long as it felt good. He had a Gypsy soul. Hell, his own family knew it.

"So you're telling me that you coming back here is permanent."

"Could be." Nash tossed his empty can. "I know what you're thinking."

Hudson raised an eyebrow and chuckled. "I don't think you do."

"You think I'm not responsible enough. Not dedicated or grounded. You think I'll go nuts staying in one spot longer than a year."

"That's generous. Six months is what I would have said." Hudson eyed his friend. "Have you thought this through?"

"That's why I'm here. To think things through."

Hudson let things settle as he pondered Nash's words. "Where you staying?"

"Up the road. My grandmother left me the cottage when she passed on last year. It needs a bit of updating, but it's solid. Nothing I can't handle."

"If you need help with anything, let me know." Hudson looked down at his handiwork. "Feels good to get the hands dirty."

Nash got to his feet and stretched. "How long you plan on sticking around? I hear your old man isn't doing great."

"He's not. I took a leave from work to deal with things, and right now, everything is up in the air."

"You got plans tonight?"

Hudson got to his feet and followed Nash up the steps. "Hadn't thought that far ahead. What's up?" They reached the top steps just as a gust of wind rolled across the water. The air was definitely on the chilly side, and the sun had dipped behind the tree line.

"It's wing night at the Coach House. Thought I'd get a head start on the whole thinking-things-through thing."

The Coach House. Wing night. Shit. Had it really only been a week since he'd been back?

"Becca works there Monday nights," Nash said.

"I know."

Hudson took a moment to respond. He had to. Because his heart started up, beating something fierce, pushing something hard and almost…angry through him.

"You and her aren't…" Hudson's jaw clamped down because he couldn't verbalize what he was thinking. "You guys…"

Nash's eyes widened. "Are you kidding me?" He shoved his hands into the front pockets of his jeans and cocked his head to the side. "I told you already, Hudsy. Becca and I are friends, and we've kept in touch."

Hudson looked away from eyes that saw too much and wished he'd kept his damn mouth shut.

"What's up with you two anyway? You run into each other yet?"

Naked limbs. Delicate mouth bruised from his kisses. That tattoo on her lower hip. *His tattoo.* They were images he couldn't shake, and the reason he'd spent half the night in bed with a raging hard-on and a need to see her so bad, it left a bitter taste in his mouth.

"You could say that," he muttered.

"And?" Nash prodded.

That was the big question now, wasn't it? Where the hell did he and Rebecca go from Saturday night? They couldn't go back. Couldn't change what had happened between them.

The note Rebecca left made it seem as if Saturday night was a mistake. As if it was something she regretted. Hudson Blackwell didn't believe in regret. He believed in action and consequence. She'd opened the door for him, and he'd walked right on through. That was her action and his reaction.

As for the consequence? The consequence was still unknown. The consequence was buried in need and want and desire. They'd always been good together. Sure, the sex had been off the charts, but they'd had so much more than just the physical. Until he'd left and screwed up everything. For a long time, he'd blamed his father for making it impossible for him to stay in Crystal Lake. Eventually, he'd realized it was on him. Every decision. Every action and consequence was on him. He could use the excuse of being young and stupid and irrational, but again, it only held so much weight.

By the time Hudson figured it out, it was too late. Rebecca had left Crystal Lake and married some guy he'd never heard of.

And now what? Had Saturday night only been about sex? Just a connection with a woman who would always hold a special place in his heart? Or was it something more?

Seeing her at the hospital, in his father's room, kissing the old man tenderly as if he meant something to her, that had thrown Hudson for a loop. He didn't understand it, and he didn't like being off his game.

"Hudsy?"

Hudson turned to Nash, his brain running full steam ahead. "Give me fifteen minutes to shower."

"And?"

"Chicken wings and beer sound about right."

Nash nodded and followed him into the house. "That's good."

Hudson didn't know if it was good or not. He only knew that he had to see Rebecca again. That was his action. As for the consequences? Truth be told, he didn't give a goddamn.

CHAPTER TWELVE

"Table three needs a pitcher of beer and another five pounds of Dry Cajun."

Rebecca punched in the order and shot Tiny a frazzled look. "Where did all these people come from?" She glanced out at the boisterous room and shook her head. The Coach House was packed. Every single table was occupied and not a seat at the bar was open. Mondays were busy, but she hadn't seen it like this in months.

"Hockey game."

"Huh?" She grabbed two empty pitchers and began to fill them from the fountain.

"High school. First game of the season, and the boys started strong. A lot of folks think they're on the road to State this year. I hear the game was rowdy and the crowd pretty hyped."

"I bet." Rebecca watched as a table near the stage erupted in loud laughter, with a lot of backslapping and roughhousing. She placed the filled jug to the side and slid the empty one in its place, watching it carefully so as not to give it too much of a head before grabbing up the jugs and heading out to table three.

There were three couples at the table, and Rebecca knew them all. Margot and Pete Havershane, Jodi and Daryl McDougal, and Katelyn Davies practically sitting in Jason Bodemont's lap. Jason was a couple of years older than Rebecca. He was good-looking, she'd give him that, but he'd always been an arrogant, entitled know-it-all. From what little she'd seen since her return to Crystal Lake, he hadn't changed one bit.

He'd asked her out more than once over the last few months, but she'd always said no. She hadn't seen him in a few weeks, and Rebecca was guessing Katelyn was the reason.

Rebecca dropped the jugs in the middle of the table and stood back. "Your wing order is in. We're pretty busy, so the wait will be longer than normal."

Katelyn slipped her arms around Jason. "Hey, Becca." She dropped a kiss on Jason's cheek. "Since when do you work at the Coach House? I thought you worked at the vet clinic."

"I do work for Burke at the clinic, but wanted some extra cash. I started about six months ago."

Katelyn frowned and sat up straighter, reached for a mug. "I've never seen you here."

"That's 'cause Rebecca only works Monday nights." Jason winked up at Rebecca. "It's the only reason I come in."

Katelyn's smile was as frosty as the north wind that buffeted the outside of the building. "Really? And here I thought it was for the wings."

Jason laughed and smacked his lips together. He didn't take his eyes from Rebecca. "Those too."

There was an awkward silence, and Margot piped up. "I don't know what is going on, but I hear Ethan Burke is moving back home, and Hudson Blackwell is in town."

"Blackwell, huh?" Jason smirked. "Come back to count his daddy's money."

"John isn't dead yet," Rebecca said, indignantly. "And Hudson doesn't give a rat's ass about his father's money."

"That's right," Jason said. "He doesn't give a rat's ass about much in Crystal Lake. Isn't that right?"

Margot's eyes widened, and everyone looked uncomfortable, even Katelyn. They were all townies and well versed in the sad history of her busted romance with Hudson Blackwell.

"Is that all for now?" Rebecca asked tightly, taking a step back. She didn't wait for an answer and threaded her way through the crowd, motioning to the busboy to clean the booths at the back.

By the time she returned to her place behind the bar, a slow-simmering anger heated her cheeks. And to make matters worse, she wasn't even sure why. Jason was an asshat. She expected him to be rude. It wasn't as if he hadn't said anything that was untrue. Hudson had left. He'd broken ties, and that was the end of that.

She was over it. She'd been over it for a long time. Saturday night was just a… God, Saturday night. She bent her head, knowing that her cheeks were about as red as the label on the bottle of beer she'd just handed Tiny. Her hands were shaking, and she swallowed that stupid lump that had a bad habit of clogging her throat when it was most inconvenient.

"I'll take two Guinness."

She nodded but didn't look up, trying to clear the lump and get her nerves settled. It took a bit, but she was able to plaster a fake smile on her face when she finally managed to look up. The fake smile lasted all of two seconds.

"Nash!" Holy. Cow. Margot was right. There was something in the water. "What the hell?" she asked, grinning crazily. "What are you doing here?"

He chuckled. "I told you I might come home for a bit."

"I know, but I guess I thought you'd give me some warning."

He grinned cheekily. "And here I thought you'd love the surprise."

"I do…" Rebecca's smiled dimmed a bit. "You said two?"

Nash watched her for a few seconds before responding. "Yeah. Two. I'm here with Hudsy."

No shit.

"You okay with that?" he asked slowly.

"Yeah. It's fine." She shrugged. "We're fine."

"'Cause we can go somewhere else."

"There is nowhere else."

The man in question suddenly appeared, sliding up to the bar beside Nash, his dark eyes finding Rebecca right away.

For the longest time, the two of them stared at each other as if there were no one else in the place. As if the music wasn't blasting, or the two tables directly behind him weren't being rowdy and loud. It was as if the world melted away, leaving only Hudson and Rebecca.

He looked good. God, but he looked good. His thick hair was combed back, exposing every angle of his handsome face. Those high cheekbones and square jaw. The sexy beard that covered his chin and gave him a dangerous edge. The dark navy crewneck with white collared shirt.

And those eyes. A girl could get lost in them.

Rebecca glanced away. She'd gotten lost in them once. Considering all it took was a couple of vodkas and some nostalgic music to get her into bed, she was damn near close to losing her shit all over again. She grabbed a mug and angled it slightly; the first thing Tiny had taught her was that there was only one way to pour a Guinness and it was an art form she'd learned quickly. Once she topped it, she put it aside to settle and grabbed the second mug, repeating the same procedure.

"Hey," Hudson said softly. "I came by your place Sunday."

Rebecca stared at her hands. They were shaking slightly, and she had to work hard to keep them still. Tiny sidled up beside her. He reached over and grabbed a couple of limes, his gaze moving from Rebecca to Hudson.

"You got this?" Tiny asked, a small frown touching his lips.

Rebecca nodded and murmured, "I'm good."

Tiny lingered an extra second or so and then moved away to garnish the drinks he was making.

"Becs." Hudson leaned closer.

"We can't do this." She whispered the words and, not sure he heard her, looked up, shaking her head and speaking clearly. "Not now, Hudson."

His dark eyes were unnerving, but she managed to hold his gaze while reaching for the mugs and sliding them across the bar.

"We good here?" Nash asked, glancing between the two of them.

"We're good," Rebecca replied, that fake smile of hers back in place where it belonged.

"Okay." Nash leaned over and gave her a kiss on the cheek. "We're going to grab a table."

She focused on Nash and ignored Hudson. "So how long you around for?"

"That depends."

Curiosity piqued, she watched him closely. "On what?"

"A lot of things." He flashed that devilish grin of his. "We'll catch up. When are you off?"

"I don't know. It's busier than usual."

"Good to hear. Hudsy and I are in for the night."

Her smile frozen in place, she wasn't sure if she answered or just mumbled something or walked away without saying anything. All she knew was, by the time she ran a few more jugs of beer out to another table and then went to the kitchen to pick up several wing orders, Nash and Hudson had claimed a booth in the back.

They weren't in her section—which was a good thing—and Dee Jacobs looked pretty damn pleased they were in hers. The girl was barely in her twenties. Her body was young and tight and toned, her hair long and lustrous. And her ass... Ugh. Her ass was as perky as ever. Rebecca hated her.

Except she didn't.

Dee was a great girl, with an infectious laugh and more charm than she needed. So what if Hudson seemed to laugh every time the girl came to their table? Rebecca didn't care.

Except she did. And Dee was at their table *a lot*.

By the time things were winding down, Rebecca's jaw was sore from clamping it tight, and she was not in a good mood.

"Dammit!" She grabbed her finger and stepped back from the bar. "Shit."

"You okay?" Tiny shot her a look. He was a few feet away.

"I sliced my finger open prepping limes."

Tiny came over and had a peek, a concerned look on his face. "That's deep. Hell, you might even need some stitches." He glanced across the room. "We're about done here. Why don't you go and clean that up, and then we'll see how it looks. The first aid kit is in the office."

Finger throbbing, Rebecca grabbed a clean cloth from under the counter and wrapped it up good. She headed for the office and found the kit on the top shelf behind Sal's desk. Rebecca cleaned the cut quickly and, after checking it out thoroughly, decided a bandage was good enough. It hurt like hell, but the bleeding had stopped.

Once she was done, she opened the door to leave the office, only to find Hudson standing there with a strange expression on his face. He glanced at her hand and immediately reached for her.

"What happened?"

"It's nothing. A small cut."

"You okay?" His touch was warm, and her focus shifted to his long fingers and strong hands.

Mouth dry, she could only nod and carefully extract her hand from his.

"I saw you at the hospital the other day."

Her head shot up, and she wondered where Hudson was going with this. "Liam and I visit Salvatore when we can. I'm not sure if you know or not, but he's ill."

"Regan filled me in." He seemed to be considering something. "I saw you in my father's room. I didn't know you guys were close."

Rebecca watched him closely. Did he really want to talk about his father? "Why are you here, Hudson?"

"We need to talk about Saturday."

"Do we?" Her comeback was fast and sharp.

"You don't think we do?" he shot back just as fast.

"I think..." Tongue-tied, she licked her lips nervously and shuffled her feet. "I think this isn't the time."

Hudson swore and shoved his hands into the front pockets of his jeans. "You're not going to make this easy, are you?"

"Why should I?" Her chin jutted forward, and she squared her shoulders.

"I'm not letting this go, Becs. We need to talk about what happened."

Maybe it was the words he'd just said. Or the way his eyes held a dangerous don't-fuck-with-me glint. Or the fact that he blocked the only exit from the office. Whatever it was, some kind of fire erupted inside Rebecca, and she took a step forward, thumping him in the chest with her good hand.

"*We* don't need to do anything, because *you* aren't calling the shots. I'm not the same girl you left behind. I'm not going to sit in my room and cry for weeks over you. I've got a life, and a son to look after and things that matter to me. Things that you have no part of. Saturday night shouldn't have happened. End of story."

"But it did." He edged closer to her. "Happen."

"I..." Were they really going to do this now? "It did, and it was fine, and—"

"Fine?" He was silent for a few moments, and then a slow grin crept across his face. "Maybe the first time was fine. But not the second." He paused, head cocked to the side in that way that was all his, and the slow grin became a full-on wicked grin. "Definitely not the third. Remember we did that thing?"

"You're an asshole."

"I've been called worse."

"That doesn't surprise me."

Silence fell between the two of them, and by the time it passed, the anger inside Rebecca deflated, leaving her spent, tired, and way too emotional for her liking.

"Hudson," she began, hating the way her voice trembled. "I really can't do this."

A muscle worked its way across his cheek, and his eyes glittered in the dim light. He looked dangerous and edgy, and her defenses screamed at her to run.

"Okay." His voice was gentle, and she relaxed a bit, wincing at the pain in her finger.

"Can I come by your place tomorrow night?"

"I don't think that's a good idea." She shook her head slowly, almost afraid to ask the question. "What would it accomplish? We should move on and forget it ever happened."

"Why?" His question surprised her, and she didn't quite know how to respond.

"Because it's never going to happen again."

Nash suddenly appeared behind Hudson and, after a quick look between the two of them, patted Hudson on the back.

"We should head out. They're closing up." Nash nodded to Rebecca. "I'll call you, and we'll catch up this week."

"Give us a minute," Hudson said, eyes never leaving Rebecca.

Nash waited for Rebecca to nod. "I'll meet you in the parking lot. I called a cab."

"I will see you tomorrow night," Hudson said when they were alone again.

She started to shake her head, but he stepped forward and placed his index finger on her lips.

"That's a promise."

Rebecca took a step back, some of that fire back in her veins. "I might not be home," she responded, chin up.

Hudson's eyes glittered, and that damn smile touched the corners of his mouth once more. "It doesn't matter," he said, taking a step back. "I'll find you. No matter where you are."

His words were coated in silk, but there was an underlying current of purpose to them. Rebecca watched him walk away, almost in a fog, and realized she was breathing so hard, she felt light-headed and her stomach went woozy. There was a strange electricity in the air, and she dragged a big gulp of it deep into her lungs.

She watched him until he disappeared from sight and then sagged against the door. Her finger throbbed, and her body was hot, on edge. She knew there was no way to avoid Hudson Blackwell. He would show up at her home or hunt her down.

She should be pissed, and yet she wasn't. Sure, there was anger there, but there was something else. Something that thrived on all that electricity in the air. It was a strange exhilaration, and she kind of liked the way it made her feel.

She should be concerned, and yet, as she closed the office door behind her and made her way back to the bar, it wasn't so much concern that she felt. It was almost like...*anticipation*. But that would be crazy. She pushed all thoughts of Hudson to the back of her mind and headed home. It was the wrong thing to do, letting Hudson back in. And in her short life, it was one of many wrong choices.

Rebecca Draper was in trouble; she just didn't know it yet.

CHAPTER THIRTEEN

The next morning found Hudson downtown, sitting in his truck, gaze fixed on a large building that took up the entire southeast block. Several windows looked down over the busy town center, the black trim that boxed them in, crisp and clean looking against the aged gray stone. The surface had been recently sandblasted, and the windows were new. The plaque above the double doors was large and bold, featuring gold lettering encased in black granite.

Blackwell Holdings.

Hudson slid down in his seat and watched a bunch of leaves whip across his windshield, pushed by a gust of wind that shook his truck. The sky was overcast, a dull, gray start to a cool, and what promised to be a wet, fall day. Across the street, he spied a woman opening one of the many boutiques that filled the downtown core. Tall and thin, with white-gold curls and a sharp profile that was unmistakable. *Mrs. Martin.* She was older and a little slower, but it was definitely her. She'd been in business as long as Hudson could remember. She fiddled with her key, let herself in, and a moment later, the OPEN sign was face out. For just a second, she looked his way, eyes lingering on the truck, before she disappeared from view.

God, his mother had loved that boutique, almost as much as Hudson had hated being dragged into it. He smiled at the thought, a small, wistful sort of thing, and closed his eyes. The sun filtering in through the window made him warm and lazy.

"Hudson Zachariah Blackwell. Get your butt in that chair and don't move

until I tell you."

Hudson froze.

"If I ever see you peeking up a lady's skirt again, well, mister, it will be the last time. Trust me on that."

"But, Mom." Embarrassed, Hudson glanced over to Mrs. Martin, the rest of his retort dying at the look of disapproval on the woman's face.

"Women are not objects, Hudson. And when I say that, I mean the girls your age as well. They should always be treated with the same respect you show me."

He snuck a peek at Mrs. Martin. The woman looked at him as if he'd committed some sort of crime. His mother marched into the changing room, and Hudson was pretty sure the fact she spent a good half hour in there was her way of turning the screw. 'Cause really, after all that, she didn't buy anything. Not even the pink shirt with the white lace.

Geez. It was a stupid mannequin. And he didn't even like girls. What was the big deal?

Hudson sighed and climbed from his truck. He stepped onto the sidewalk and gazed up at the building that carried his family name. The Blackwells had been in the area since the early 1800s, though the Blackwell money was both Southern and old. His grandfather many times removed had come to the area to take advantage of the lumber boom, and Blackwell Holdings was born. Lumber gave it life, but diversification into construction, railways, and roads filled the family coffers.

Today, Blackwell Holdings included banks and investment firms, though the bulk of its money came from the construction empire built over the last couple of centuries. An empire with no prince to take over the helm, because sadly, he and his brothers were the last of their line and none of them was interested.

Hudson felt the weight of that hit him hard, and with a curse, he swiveled around and headed in the other direction. Sam Waters could wait.

He'd never wanted any part of the business, though in truth his father had made it easy enough for him to turn his back on the family legacy. Frowning darkly, he strode down the sidewalk, shoulders hunched against the wind as the first drops of rain splattered on the pavement in front of him. He crossed at the light, and before he knew it, he was inside Coffee Corner, a mug of hot java in his hand, a double-chocolate donut in the other, and sitting in a seat at the counter.

The place was busy and boasted a mix of local business owners as well as a good number of retired folk. Hudson nodded to several of them but made no effort to start up a conversation. He wasn't in the mood to talk and sipped his coffee in silence, glancing at the door now and again when the bell jingled, signaling a new arrival.

The owners were either new, or the Nelsons had hired staff to run the place, because he didn't recognize the middle-aged man behind the counter or the woman who worked alongside him. The other guy, though, the one who was sweeping up in the corner and moved in a peculiar way, that one tugged at Hudson's memory. Though the heavy beard and long hair did a lot to disguise his features, something about him was familiar. He was roughly six foot, with wide shoulders and long, lean legs. His faded blue sweatshirt was frayed, and his jeans had seen better days, but they were clean.

"Harry doesn't like to be stared at."

Hudson yanked his head back and found crystal-clear blue eyes on him. "What was that?"

The woman behind the counter frowned as she wiped up crumbs. She leaned on the counter, her gaze direct, and nodded at the man mopping the floor. "Harry doesn't like to be stared at."

Harry.

Hudson glanced at the man again. Now that he was turned, Hudson could see the writing on the back of the sweatshirt. Crystal Lake Cannons. Football.

"Harry Anderson?" Couldn't be.

"You know him?" the woman asked, taking his empty plate and depositing it under the counter.

"We played football together."

"You're from Crystal Lake, then."

Hudson turned back to the woman and accepted a fresh cup of coffee. "I am."

She nodded to the man at the till. "That's my husband, Milo, and I'm Beatrice. We bought this place a couple of years ago. Originally from LA."

His eyebrow shot up at that. "You're a long way from California."

She snorted. "And happy to be. Life is so much slower here. We love it." She paused. "I haven't seen you before. Must be a while since you've been home."

"You could say that."

"You got a name?"

He liked Beatrice. She was direct, and he was going to assume her bullshit meter was in fine form. "Hudson Blackwell."

"Blackwell?" She whistled and smiled. "I see it now. You look a lot like John."

Startled, Hudson took a sip from his coffee. "You know my dad?"

"He comes in every morning for his coffee." Her smile dimmed a bit. "That is until he took sick." She wiped up the counter once more. "How's he doing, by the way?"

"Hanging in there."

"Good. Glad to hear that."

Hudson glanced back at Harry. "What happened?"

Beatrice lowered her voice a bit. "Motorcycle accident, I think. At least that's what I was told. He's a sweet soul and, after his morning coffee, likes to sweep my floors. He has a hard time sitting still."

Jesus. Harry Anderson had been one of those guys who'd had it all. A popular guy, he'd had unlimited potential and a love of life that should have taken him far. He was a gifted athlete and had gotten a full ride on a hockey scholarship, if Hudson remembered correctly. And now he was mopping floors in a coffee shop.

Hudson was silent as he drank his coffee, his thoughts dark and his mood blacker. Sometimes life sucked, no way around it. The bell tinkled, and, lost in thought, he didn't bother to turn around. Someone slid onto the seat beside him, and after a few seconds, Hudson glanced over.

Mackenzie Draper ordered a coffee and bagel from Angie and nodded. "Blackwell. Heard you were back in town."

"Draper."

Rebecca's brother was dressed casually in old jeans, boots, and a plaid jacket more suitable for a lumberjack. He accepted his cup from Beatrice, took a sip, and then set it down.

"I hear the old man is holding his own." It wasn't really a question, and the green eyes that regarded him weren't exactly friendly.

"He is. How are your folks?" Hudson realized Rebecca hadn't mentioned them once, and as Mackenzie's eyes narrowed, he found himself curious. He'd always liked Rebecca's mother, Lila Draper. Her father, on the other hand, was a no-good son of a bitch with a mean streak that was well known.

"Not much has changed there. Mom's good. She keeps herself busy at church. I guess she thinks if she prays enough, some of that holiness might rub off on Ben. He's a bad habit she just can't give up. He's drying out again. We're all hoping he's gone for a good long while."

"Sorry to hear that." He knew firsthand how much of a bastard Ben Draper was. Most folks in town did. But back then, and even now, he supposed, most people turned a blind eye to problems of the domestic sort. Figured if they didn't get involved, the bad things they suspected might be happening, weren't.

Mac shoved his bagel into the pocket of his jacket and scooped up his coffee-to-go. When he turned back to Hudson, curiosity filled his eyes. "You've been in DC?"

"Yeah. For over five years now."

"FBI, I think I heard."

Hudson nodded.

"Huh. Never figured you for a lawman."

"No?" Considering he'd been a bit of a hell-raiser back in the day, not many folks did.

Mackenzie slowly shook his head. "No. I remember you and Becca talking about moving up north. You guys were always camping or on the water. I remember plans to own your own hunting and fishing lodge. Never saw you for a suit-and-tie guy living in the city."

Annoyed, and for no reason other than the man in front of him, Hudson barely kept his tone civil.

"Life doesn't always turn out the way we want it to."

Mackenzie took a step back, and gone was any semblance of warmth. "I hear ya there. Just ask Rebecca." He glanced to his right. "Harry. You ready?"

Hudson's hands balled into fists, but he made no move to get up or say anything else to Rebecca's brother. He watched Harry follow Mac from the coffee shop, and, with one last sip, finished his coffee.

"Can I get you anything else?" Beatrice asked softly. It was obvious she'd heard most, if not all, of his exchange with Mackenzie. No point in ignoring it.

"What's Harry doing with Draper?" He had to admit he was curious. Last he'd heard, Mac was some big shot architect in New York City. Now he was back in Crystal Lake with a kid and wife and living the life of domesticated bliss. Mac thought Hudson had done a one-eighty? Well, he could say the same about Draper.

"Gosh, that Mackenzie Draper is just the nicest man. He's involved in that development across the lake. The one with the big golf course.

I think he designed it. He's given jobs to folks like Harry. It's really a blessing. And I hear he's looking into developing low-income housing, which is so badly needed for the community. For folks like Harry and for families in crisis."

Shit. Since when had Mac Draper become the savior of Crystal Lake?

"The only problem is land."

"Oh?" Seemed as if Beatrice was a fountain of information.

"From what I understand, most of the land around the lake is privately owned or protected from development, and there's not much in town that's suitable or for sale."

"That would be a problem," he murmured. Hudson glanced at his watch. "I should get going. Thanks for the coffee, Beatrice."

"It was very nice meeting you, Hudson. Tell your father we said hello."

"I will."

Hudson left the coffee shop feeling pissed off, annoyed as hell, and just plain grumpy. The rain was falling in sheets, the sting of the cold drops sharp on his cheek. But it wasn't pain he felt. In fact, he liked the sting. It was exhilarating.

This weather. The cool, crisp air. The damp. The smell of the lake. He loved it. As he walked toward Blackwell Holdings, his chest tightened and his breathing sped up. There was a hole punched in his gut—a hole he'd forgotten about. A hole slowly breaking open. It wasn't just melancholy that settled across his shoulders. Or sadness.

It was loneliness. And regret. It was the mourning for the life he'd never lived.

The visual of Rebecca curled into his arms as they cuddled in front of a fire. A fire they'd lit in a place they called home. A place in the forest at the edge of a lake. Maybe a dog or two.

Damn Mackenzie Draper for reminding him of everything he'd lost.

Because as Hudson strode up the steps and entered the building that held his name, he knew he'd never get it back. No matter how much he wanted it. No matter how much he *needed* it. It was too late.

Twelve years too late.

CHAPTER FOURTEEN

Work had been crazy busy. Tuesday was blocked off for surgeries, but there were always a few emergencies that couldn't be delayed, and they added to the chaos. Then Ethan Burke decided to pay the clinic a visit. Talk about sending the office into a tizzy. Kimberly Higgins's eyes had nearly popped out of her head when Ethan stopped by reception to say hello to Rebecca.

"He wants you," Kimberly proclaimed after Ethan disappeared into his father's office.

Here we go.

"You think every single man in the area wants me." Rebecca couldn't help but grin. She didn't have to look far for an ego boost.

"They do."

"Sorry to burst your bubble, Kimmy. But I haven't exactly had men pounding down my door."

Kimberly had pursed her lips and set her hands on her hips in a way that said she was serious. "That's because you give off a vibe that scares most of them away."

"Oh? And what vibe would that be?"

"You know. The 'come near me and I'll break your balls' vibe." The woman clucked. Actually clucked. "Men don't like women who challenge their masculinity."

"Well, I don't want a man who can't handle a woman with balls."

Kimberly had just shaken her head and grabbed her purse from beneath the counter. "If you don't change your tune, you're going to end up alone."

That had annoyed the hell out of Rebecca. "Maybe I want to be alone. Not every single woman needs a man."

"I get that. And you obviously don't *need* a man. But there are some things you need a man for."

"Not really. A pack of batteries and my vibrator do just fine."

"Really?" Kimberly frowned. "I'm being serious, Becca."

"So am I."

But Kimberly wasn't giving up. "You're doing great on your own. You really are. I don't think I would have the strength to own my own home and raise my son alone. But I don't think that's the case here. I think you're afraid."

Okay. This woman was a coworker. *A coworker.* Where the hell did she get off?

"Kim, I don't want you to take this the wrong way, but honestly, my personal life is none of your business."

Kimberly just smiled and headed for the door. "I know. But I'm not sorry for pointing out the obvious." She paused, her hand on the doorknob. "Life's too short to be afraid, Rebecca. And wearing that crown of 'don't come near me' must be exhausting."

That last line had been a zinger, and it stuck with Rebecca all the way home. By the time she walked into her kitchen, she was in a crap mood, and not even the smells emanating from her Crock-Pot could put her in a better frame of mind. She grabbed a bottle of pinot grigio from the fridge, poured a generous glass, and flopped onto the sofa. Liam wasn't home from hockey practice yet, but her appetite wasn't exactly healthy anyway.

Wine before food was how she was gonna roll tonight.

She was onto her second glass when the door opened and Liam walked in, followed by her brother. Her son tossed his backpack onto the floor, but one look from Rebecca and he sheepishly picked it up.

"Hockey bag?" she asked.

"In the garage, and my equipment is airing out."

"Wash your hands," she said, eyes on his retreating back.

"Mom," Liam moaned before disappearing up the stairs.

"Smells good," Mackenzie said, dropping a kiss to his sister's cheek.

"Cabbage roll soup."

Mackenzie flashed a smile. "I'm impressed."

"Don't be. Liam did most of it this morning before I even dragged my ass out of bed."

Mac's eyebrow shot up. "The kid's a chef?"

"Perfect combination. I guess I did something right." She sank farther into the sofa. "You want some wine?"

"Nah. Can't stay long. Date night."

She smiled up at her brother. A knot formed in her throat, and she had to look away, because, dammit, there were tears forming in the corners of her eyes. What the hell was wrong with her?

"I ran into Hudsy today."

She bit her tongue. Had to. Anything to keep those damn tears from falling. God, she needed to keep it together.

"Did you?" she managed to say.

"You never told me he was back. I heard it from Edwards."

Rebecca was silent for a few moments. "Hudson has been out of my life for years, Mac. Why would I care that he's back?"

Mackenzie watched her closely. "I know how much he hurt you, Becca."

"Old news." But the knot in her throat told her something else.

"Yeah, well, sometimes the past has a way of biting us in the ass. Just be careful with Blackwell. Don't let him in again. I don't trust him."

Rebecca cleared her throat and set her wineglass down. If her brother knew what had transpired just a few days ago, he'd have a whole lot more to say. As it was, Liam appeared, and she was saved from further conversation.

"Uncle Mac. You gonna try my soup?"

Rebecca's heart swelled, watching her son. His clear green eyes and flushed, healthy skin—his exuberance and love of life—was something she cherished. He'd come a long way from the sullen, unhappy boy he'd been when they'd first come back to Crystal Lake.

"Can't, buddy. Lily is taking me out on a date."

Liam snorted. "Old people still date?"

"Hey. Who you calling old?" Mackenzie roughed up Liam's thick blond waves and winked at Rebecca. "Better get my butt in gear, or there'll be hell to pay."

"Who's watching the baby?" Rebecca smiled at the thought. Her niece was gorgeous and the sweetest little thing ever. And she'd had her father wrapped around her little hand from the get-go.

"Mom. I gotta swing by and pick her up."

"Tell her I said hello." It had been a few days since they'd talked, and a twinge of guilt made Rebecca squirm.

"Will do." With another pat on Liam's shoulders, Mackenzie headed for the front door. Before her brother made it there, however, the doorbell sounded, and Rebecca froze. Hudson hadn't been serious… had he?

"Liam, are you expecting anyone? Michael?"

"Nope." Her son was busy spooning out his cabbage roll creation into a soup bowl and didn't bother to look up. "He's grounded. He got caught looking at naked ladies on his dad's computer, and now his dad's computer has got a stupid virus. I told him it was dumb and that he'd get caught, but he didn't listen."

"Oh." Great. Naked ladies and computers. Was she already there with Liam?

Rebecca got to her feet and made her way down the hall. Her brother had opened the door, and his tall frame blocked her view, but there was no mistaking the voice. The sound of it was like a punch to the gut, and she hung back a bit, sweat beading on her top lip, breaths falling rapidly.

Jesus. He'd meant everything he'd said the night before.

Mackenzie glanced over his shoulder, but the look in his eyes was unreadable. "I'll talk to you tomorrow." He gave a quick nod to Hudson and stepped around him.

That left Rebecca staring down the hallway at the one man she wasn't sure she could handle right now. She ran a nervous hand through the loose hair at her nape and cleared her throat, not really knowing what to say.

Hudson closed the door behind him and stood there, his leather jacket damp from the rain that had been falling all day. He'd pulled on a black knit cap and hadn't bothered to shave. She thought of what her brother had said, and her heart lurched. Mackenzie was right. She needed to be careful. Hudson was her past, and she'd buried him years ago. Yet the man in front of her was very much alive. He was so damn masculine. So damn sexy. So damn dangerous.

She hated him.

Except she didn't.

"I told myself coming here wasn't a good idea," he said, that hint of rasp she'd always loved coloring his words. "I was headed home, but…"

A pause.

"You going to invite me in?"

She shouldn't. She should tell Hudson to leave and never darken her door again. She should tell him that a repeat of the weekend wasn't going to happen anytime soon. That whatever this was between them meant nothing. It was just left-behind residue. An echo from their past. An acknowledgment of a desire that still burned, but a desire that would do neither one of them any good.

"Are you hungry?" she found herself asking.

I'm crazy.

"Something smells good."

Certifiable.

"We've got lots."

Should be locked up.

Hudson stepped out of his boots and shrugged off his jacket. He hung it on the hook by the door, and Rebecca turned and headed for the kitchen, very much aware of the man who trailed behind her. Liam was sitting at the small island, spoon halfway to his mouth, when he spied them. He looked from Hudson to Rebecca and then set his spoon down, his curiosity evident.

"Hey, Liam. My friend Hudson is joining us for dinner. You remember him from the other day?"

Liam nodded. "Hello."

Hudson walked over to her son and offered his hand, which Liam took rather gingerly (wasn't often he shook hands with anyone).

"Smells good in here." Hudson smiled.

"I made it." Liam jumped off his stool. "I'll grab an extra bowl, Mom."

And just like that, her kitchen became a hub of domesticity. Hudson washed up while Liam filled two more bowls of soup. Rebecca grabbed rolls and butter, and the three of them sat down at the kitchen table to eat.

Rebecca's appetite wasn't anywhere near where it should be, and she couldn't even blame that on the wine. Hudson made her nervous as hell. She ate slowly, while in just under thirty minutes, Hudson managed to find out pretty much everything about Liam's life in Crystal Lake.

He knew that Liam played defense on a local house league hockey team, and that one of his coaches was his Uncle Mac. He also knew Liam loved fishing and boating and camping. That Liam loved math and science but hated reading, even though his mother made him read every night for twenty minutes. Something he agreed to do if she let him stay up for an extra hour.

"So what's your mom got you reading? The classics?"

Liam grinned. "Nope. She never said what I had to read." He giggled at his mother. "I read comics."

Rebecca shrugged. "You're still reading, and that's all that matters."

Liam pushed his bowl away. "What's your job, Hudson?"

Hudson leaned back in his chair as if considering his answer. "I work in law enforcement."

Liam's eyes widened. "You're, like, a cop?"

"He's FBI." Rebecca grabbed their bowls, not in the mood for small talk anymore.

"FBI?" Except that particular acronym lit a firestorm of questions, and while Rebecca cleaned up after dinner, she listened to Hudson patiently explain some of the duties he performed.

After at least the tenth question, Rebecca leaned against the counter. "Liam. Homework."

"But…"

"No buts. I happen to know you have a geography test tomorrow, and I haven't seen you study for it." She pointed to the stairs. "So get to it."

Liam sighed, an exaggerated sort of thing, and slid from his stool. "Maybe you could come for dinner again?"

Hudson nodded. "I'd like that."

"Cool." Liam grabbed the glass of milk Rebecca poured and headed for the stairs, leaving her alone with the man responsible for the butterflies causing havoc in her gut. Hudson got up from his chair and slowly slid it back into place. His intense gaze found her, and, mouth dry, she pretended to clean up an already pristine countertop.

"He's a great kid."

She nodded. "He is."

"His dad in the picture?"

Rebecca tossed her rag, and her voice rose, taking on a sharp edge she couldn't control. "I'm not discussing Liam's father with you."

Hudson shoved his hands into the pockets of his jeans and was quiet, as if measuring his words. "Fair enough. I didn't come here to upset you."

"Then why did you come?" She marched around the island until she stood a few inches from Hudson.

"I wanted to see you again."

And here they were, having the conversation she didn't want to have, with a man who still made her feel all sorts of things she shouldn't be feeling.

"Hudson. We're over. We've been over for years. What happened Saturday night… Well, Saturday night was just…" She swore and glanced away. "It was a mistake."

"Probably."

"It shouldn't have happened."

"But it did."

Exasperated, she hung her head. "It's not going to happen again."

She knew the moment he stepped closer, because the air around her did that funny electrical thing again. She thought it was hard to breathe a few seconds ago? It was nothing compared to what it felt like now. Dragging big honking gulps of air deep into her lungs, she made to step back, but her butt met the kitchen table.

"Becs."

Hearing her name on his lips made her stomach dip. She was hot. And cold. And it felt like her skin was pulled too tight.

"I can't get you out of my mind, and I can't stop thinking about Saturday. About how good it felt to hold you again. To breathe you in. To touch the curve of your cheek. Kiss that spot behind your ear. To be inside you." A groan fell from him, and she bit her lip in an effort to remain calm.

"You're right, Rebecca. You and me. Probably not a good thing."

Slowly, she looked up and held her breath.

"I know I should walk away." His eyes glittered. "But I can't."

"You didn't have a problem doing that twelve years ago."

His jaw clamped shut at her words, and a muscle worked its way across his cheek. "I was young and dumb twelve years ago."

"Can't argue with you there."

A ghost of a smile touched the corners of his mouth. "So where do we go from here?"

Rebecca slid past him and opened the door. She stepped out onto the porch, shivering in the cool night air, and waited for him to join her.

"There's no point in going anywhere, Hudson."

He bent lower, so low that she felt his warm breath on her cheek. "You can't tell me you don't feel this."

"I feel it," she admitted, turning around to face him. "Doesn't mean I should act on it." She thrust her chin forward, straightened her shoulders. "I'm not a teenager anymore. I'm not easily swayed. I know most things that feel good have a dark side to them. And you are definitely on the dark side. Besides." She shrugged. "I'm not looking for a relationship. I've been burned twice. I'm not going there again."

His eyes glittered. His nostrils flared.

Something inside Rebecca liquefied until she felt like she was coming apart. The air crackled with energy, and damn, but it was hot. A thought hit her then. One so crazy she didn't have time to think about it before the words fell out of her mouth.

"Not saying I wouldn't consider something casual."

Jesus. Did she really just say that? Rebecca didn't do casual. Hell, she didn't do anything these days.

"You and me and casual are three things that don't go together," Hudson said softly. *Dangerously.*

Rebecca came to her senses and stepped around him. She walked back inside and leaned against the door. She had started something, and that probably wasn't a smart move. But damned if she wasn't going to own it.

She arched an eyebrow. "Who said anything about you and me? Ethan Burke has a lot going for him."

That was the truth. And contrary to what she'd told Kimberly, Ethan was interested. He'd asked her to dinner; she just hadn't given him his answer yet. Maybe it was time she did. Maybe it was time she lived a little.

But Hudson Blackwell was never the guy to underestimate. He didn't hesitate. All it took was one step and he was in her face, his lips close to her ear.

"You've forgotten a few things, Becs. I don't like games, and I don't like to lose." He licked her lobe, and she gripped the edge of the door as he stepped back, eyes so intense, they made her knees weak. "But..." His gaze dropped to her mouth.

Keep it together.

"If you want to do this."

God, it's hot.

"If you want to play this game, I'm in."

So hot.

"But I want you to remember something."

Okay. Calm the hell down.

"What's that?" she managed to croak.
"I play to win."

CHAPTER FIFTEEN

It was still raining the next morning when Hudson headed to town. He'd slept like shit, was out of cream, and hated black coffee. The bitter taste was still on his tongue, and he grimaced as he drove through the downtown core and headed to the hospital.

He'd spent most of the previous day with Sam Waters, and by the time he'd gotten to the hospital, his father was asleep. He'd waited for nearly an hour, but when the nurse told him that John was most likely down for the night, he'd gone to Rebecca's.

His scowl darkened as he slipped from the truck and headed inside the hospital. Ethan Burke? The guy had no business being anywhere near Rebecca. And maybe it was a prick move on his part, but Hudson would make sure Burke took a step back.

"Jesus, Hudson. Who crapped in your cornflakes this morning?" Regan Thorne was at the nurses station, a bemused look on her face as she watched him get off the elevator. "Coffee?" she asked when he reached her.

"No. I'm good."

She tossed her own cup into the bin. "You look like shit."

"Is that your professional opinion?"

"Pretty sure anyone who crosses your path is going to say the same thing." She flashed a smile. "Cheer up, though. Your father is doing much better."

"Yeah?" Hudson glanced over to John's room.

"See for yourself. I just finished rounds and have some patients to check in on, but if you have any questions, ask the nurse on duty, or you can reach me later." She pursed her lips. "You have my cell number?"

At his nod, she grabbed her iPad and headed down the hall.

Hudson peeked through the window into his father's room. Regan hadn't been kidding. His father was sitting up in bed, looked as if he'd made good progress with the breakfast tray, and there was color in his cheeks.

Slowly, Hudson pushed open the door and slipped inside, so far undetected. John Blackwell was leafing through a book, a thick volume that looked much too large for his frail hands. A small smile swept across the older man's face, and Hudson sucked in a sharp breath. In that moment, the glimpse of the man he'd been, the father he'd been, was undeniable.

It was both bittersweet and painful.

He watched his father for several more seconds, and then, feeling like a voyeur, cleared his throat. Almost instantly, John looked up from the book, though the smile on his face never left. In fact, it widened. Hell, it even reached his eyes.

"There you are," John said, closing the book and setting it on his lap. "I hear I missed you last night."

Hudson strode forward until he reached the edge of the bed. "You were sleeping."

"Apparently, I slept the night away. Missed *The Bachelorette*."

"*The Bachelorette*?" Hudson couldn't be hearing right.

"Damn straight," John replied a little sheepishly. "Don't look at me like that. It's Darlene's fault. She watches all those damn reality shows. After a while, I kind of got sucked in." His eyebrows rose. "You ever watch it?"

"No. Can't say that I've ever been tempted."

"Stay strong, son. Or you'll end up like me. Usually Darlene and I discuss what happened. But I have no idea if that there bachelor, Brad, I think his name is, gave Tiffany a rose or not."

"Sorry," Hudson said, trying to hide a chuckle. "I can't help you there."

"No. I suppose you can't. I guess I could google it."

Hudson studied the man closely. "You're looking good, Dad."

"I feel pretty damn good today. Don't even need extra oxygen." He shrugged. "Not sure why, but I'll take it." He paused and settled back on his bed. "You get in to see Waters yesterday?"

"I did." Hudson pulled up a chair and sat down.

"And?"

"And things are running the way they're supposed to be. We've got a bid going in for roadwork in the next county, and I was told that phase three of the development across the lake is a go." Hudson paused, watching his father closely. "Sam told me you sold off the financial branch."

"I did. My heart wasn't in it anymore, and I knew you boys would never come around." There was no bitterness in his father's words. No blame. Just quiet acceptance. "I had Sam invest most of the profits into your individual portfolios." His father offered a weak smile. "Did it damn near a year ago. I see none of you boys check after your financials."

That was an understatement. Sure, Hudson saw the statements when they arrived in the mail, but years ago, he'd stopped opening them and shoved them into the bottom drawer of his desk. It was as if hiding them meant he didn't have to acknowledge a life that he'd given up. A name and a legacy he had no interest in. A community he was no longer a part of.

And yet…

Yet an idea had begun to percolate. One that he couldn't stop thinking about.

"Can I talk to you about something?"

John nodded. "Fire away."

"I ran into Harry Anderson yesterday."

"Ah." John's mouth tightened. "Damn shame what happened to that boy. Nearly broke his father's heart."

"I bet." Hudson splayed his hands over the tops of his thighs. Up until this moment, he hadn't been exactly sure what he was going to say or do. "Remember when Myrtle Winger's diner caught fire and all her kitchen equipment was ruined?"

"I do. She'd just closed up for the night. Thank God she wasn't inside with the children. That could have been a real tragedy."

"They lost everything. She had no insurance, no money, and they would probably have declared bankruptcy if not for the anonymous person who donated the funds to get her up and running again." He looked at his father pointedly.

John glanced away. "Anonymous means that no one knows who the donor was. It means no one can take credit. It means everyone can take credit. No one knows who that was."

"I do," Hudson said, leaning forward. His chest puffed up a bit, and he clenched his hands together. "I heard you on the phone with a company from out of state. Heard you ordering the equipment. All commercial. All the best of the best."

His father remained quiet.

"It's no different from James Denton. You payed his hockey and football fees for years. Everybody knew it."

John laid his head back and sighed. "His father was killed overseas. He served this country and gave the ultimate sacrifice. I did what I could. What any man of means would do. A man should help his fellow man when he can. It's good for the soul. Sometimes it was the only thing that soothed my pain."

A knot formed in Hudson's throat, and he had to work hard to clear it. "The money in my portfolio, the money from the sale of the financial branch of the business. It's a lot, and I don't need it. I'd like to use the money and reinvest it into this community. I want the money to matter. To make a difference."

John turned to his son and nodded slowly. "Go on."

"Do we still own that land along the river? By the old mill?"

"We do."

"I'd like to buy it. I'd like to buy it and build housing specifically for people like Harry. People who under normal circumstances couldn't afford their own home. Families who can't afford to buy but are putting money into their landlord's coffers instead of their own. I'd like to help them build a better life and not feel like they're being given charity in order to get it. I'd like them to help build their own community, in any way they can. People like Harry? He can be productive. He can work. He can build his life."

Hudson got to his feet and shoved his hands into his pants. He strolled over to the window and pretended to be interested in the view. But his mind was on the man behind him. Did his father think he was crazy?

"Nothing would make me more proud than if you did this, son."

Hudson turned back to his father. "There's a lot I haven't considered, and I know a project like this won't be a walk in the park, but I really feel we can make a difference."

"Well, you're right about that. If you take this on, Hudson, it's a commitment. What about your job? What about DC?"

Hudson frowned. "I'm on leave, Dad. Eventually, I have to go back to DC. But I have time to get things up and running. Time to get things organized. And once I'm back in Washington, I'll find a way to balance my life there and this project."

His father seemed to be considering Hudson's words. He slowly picked up the book and set it on the table beside his bed, his long fingers caressing the cover as he did so.

"This isn't a book I thought I'd enjoy."

Hudson took a few steps closer to the bed so that he could see the hardcover. "*The Bronze Horseman?*"

His father nodded. "A gift. From a young woman who's come to mean a lot to me." John looked up suddenly. "You've seen Rebecca?"

Startled, Hudson nodded. "Yeah. I've seen her."

"You never told her about that night. Or if you did, she never said anything to me."

Hudson sure as hell didn't want to talk about that night. He shrugged and looked away, his reply clipped and to the point. "No. It never came up."

A long, painful silence fell between them before John broke it. "She's an amazing young woman. Reminds me a lot of your mother."

Hudson's good mood vanished, and he glared at his father, not bothering to hide the cold hint of frost that touched his words. "We're not talking about Mom. I can't do that with you. Not now. Maybe never."

John looked weary and sank farther into his mattress. "I'll donate the land. Contact Mackenzie Draper. He's the best architect around. Talented. Hardworking. Comes highly recommended. I know the Edwards have used him for several projects, including the development across the lake."

Hudson nodded. "I'd planned on giving him a call."

"Good." John attempted a smile. "Better watch out, son. You're in danger."

"Danger?" Hudson asked. "Danger of falling in love with Crystal Lake all over again."

CHAPTER SIXTEEN

By Saturday night, Rebecca was more than annoyed. And the sad part? It was because Hudson Blackwell had once again managed to screw with her head, and then he'd pretty much disappeared.

Didn't matter that it was, in fact, what she wanted. What mattered was that he'd basically thrown down the gauntlet and then…

Then nothing.

She glanced down at her cell phone, finger running over the number that glowed in the dark. She hadn't picked up when Ethan called. But she should have. She should damn well have gone out with Ethan Burke when he'd asked her. Except, contrary to what Hudson had inferred, she wasn't into games either. No way would she go out with Ethan when she knew there was no point.

She'd never been that girl and wasn't about to start now. Though, truthfully, it would have been nice to have a plus one for dinner. Being the only single at a get-together hadn't bothered her before. But now? Now she felt like the odd girl out, and she didn't like it.

Rebecca grimaced as she pulled in behind her brother's truck.

She didn't like it one bit.

The dinner party had been on the books for several weeks, and she had no real excuse to back out except for the fact that she was dog-ass tired. She'd spent the day mudding the drywall seams in her front room. Her shoulders and back killed, and the thought of soaking in a hot tub had been enticing. But the thought of spending the night alone was not. She'd grabbed a quick shower and now here she was.

Rebecca scooped up the bottle of red wine from the passenger side and slid from the car, shaking out her long hair and shivering in the cold air because it was still wet. Out here, along the lake, the air was definitely cooler.

Her brother and Lily had never moved out of the quaint home they'd first shared together. A former carriage house for a much larger estate, the stone building was charming, with loads of character, and the lot was to die for. Situated on the lake, with plenty of forest on either side, it was private—the perfect spot to raise a family—and only ten minutes from town.

There were several cars in the driveway, and she recognized a few of them, her brother's, his wife's, and the Edwards'. Hoping the "quiet" dinner party she'd been invited to was indeed quiet, Rebecca made her way up the steps onto the porch and let herself inside.

Voices echoed from the back of the home, and she peeked into the kitchen, which was just off to her left, but there was no one there. The smells, however, were wonderful, and her stomach growled as she got a whiff of lemon chicken and roasted potatoes.

Rebecca shrugged out of her coat and hung it up, then smoothed out the black silk top she wore. She considered doing up one more button but promptly forgot about it, tightening her leather belt one more notch. Her jeans were soft and old and comfortable. This was about as dressed up as she got on a Saturday night.

Her brother suddenly appeared, a small bundle of blonde curls and giggles in his arms. Hannah Rose Draper was the light of her father's eyes, and who could blame him? The little girl, just over a year old, was gorgeous.

"Thought I heard the door," Mackenzie said.

"Hey," Rebecca said, a big smile on her face as she bent down to kiss her niece. Chubby hands rose up, grabbing at her, and, with a chuckle, Rebecca handed the wine to Mackenzie and scooped up the little girl so that she could hug her tightly.

"I've missed you, pumpkin."

Hannah Rose snuggled into her neck, and Rebecca's heart melted a little more. She gazed up at her brother. "Who's here? I saw Jake and Raine's car, but didn't recognize the others."

Mackenzie's smile faltered a bit. "About that. I meant to call you but got busy at work, and then I had to run to the grocery store for Lily because we ran out of diapers and milk. And ah, well, I just sort of lost track of time."

Okay. Rebecca wasn't feeling the warm fuzzies any longer. Her brother actually looked guilty. Well, this wasn't good.

"Mackenzie, please tell me you didn't invite Ethan Burke to dinner."

"What?" Mackenzie looked surprised. "No. I…why? Would you have wanted him here?"

"No. Forget it. What did you want to tell me?" Hannah Rose was squirming, and Rebecca propped her on her hip.

"Nash is here."

"Oh." She frowned. "That's great. I haven't had a chance to catch up with him since he's been back." She studied her brother in the dim light. Okay. Something was up. And the longer the two of them stared at each other, the more suspicious she became. She knew who was in the family room before he opened his mouth.

"Hudson." Mackenzie spoke quietly.

"Okay. Have we just slipped into an alternate reality? What the hell? You don't like Hudson Blackwell. At all."

Hannah Rose started to whimper, most likely sensing the tension between the two adults, and Rebecca shot daggers at her brother, all the while whispering sweetly into her niece's ear.

"I don't have to like him to work with him. Besides, I didn't invite him. Lily did."

"What the…" She was confused. "I don't understand. What kind of project would you and Hudson work on?"

"It's complicated."

"I bet." Her voice rose. She sounded like a shrew but didn't care.

"Look. You told me the other day you didn't care that he was back. If I'd known him being here would make you this uncomfortable, I would have happily told Lily to un-invite him. Trust me. I was looking for an excuse." Mackenzie's eyes narrowed. "You want me to tell him to leave? Because I have no problem doing that."

"No." Feeling like an idiot, she was silent for a few seconds. "I'm fine. I just wasn't expecting to see him is all."

Mackenzie gave her a quick hug and motioned to the back room. "Let's go. We'll fill you in. But Becs, if he makes you uncomfortable in any way, let me know."

Her brother headed down the hall, and once Rebecca got her heartbeat under control, she followed in his steps, cradling Hannah against her chest. The great room boasted nearly an entire wall of windows that looked out over the lake. To the right, a large stone fireplace was the focal point of the room, and the furniture was both functional, and comfortable. The space was leather and wood and stone, softened by pale gray walls and cream-colored accents.

Her eyes found Hudson right away, and her breath hitched in her chest. Painfully so. She forced herself to swallow. Seriously. Did the man not have a bad hair day? Did his jeans have to fit him like a damn glove? Did the color blue have to be his color?

He was in the far corner, head bent and listening closely to Lily speak. Lily St. Clare, her brother's wife. Lily, a modern-day Marilyn Monroe, and that was no exaggeration. The woman had curves, looks, intelligence, and wit. Rebecca would have loved to hate her, but she was also the nicest, most genuine woman she knew.

The heat that pulsed in Rebecca's veins was sharp and fast and fueled by an emotion she wasn't used to. One she hadn't felt in a good long while. No, that was wrong. She'd felt it the week before when Shelli Gouthro had been all over Hudson.

Jealousy.

Lily turned just then, pleased to see her. "Rebecca! I see Hannah has managed to find you already."

Rebecca nodded and attempted a smile. It felt forced and tight, and she hoped like hell it at least looked normal. No way would she give Hudson the satisfaction of knowing his presence was enough to throw her off her game. She jiggled the baby, and Hannah's laughter eased the tension inside her. Hudson stared across the room, a strange expression on his face, and she looked away, glad to spy Nash a few feet from her.

Nash gave her a hug and a quick kiss to the cheek. "That's a good look on you," he whispered.

At first, Rebecca's mind went blank, but when she realized what Nash was getting at, she shook her head. "Yeah. No. Not gonna happen. I couldn't imagine being single and pregnant."

He squeezed her shoulder, a gentle touch. "Hey, I'm just teasing. She looks good in your arms."

Rebecca glanced down at the baby. Her robin-egg-blue eyes shone, the little bow mouth glistened, and those chubby cheeks were to die for. Hannah reached for her again, her small hand tugging on a piece of Rebecca's hair, and the gibberish that fell from her lips was adorable.

Something shifted inside her, something sharp and a little bit painful. She turned to her brother. "I think she wants her daddy." She handed off the baby just as Raine and Jake Edwards walked into the room. Seemed as if Hudson being here wasn't the only surprise.

"Raine," Rebecca said, walking over to the woman and offering a congratulatory hug. "I didn't know…when are you due?"

The small dark-haired woman glowed, and the man at her side looked so damn happy, it brought tears to Rebecca's eyes.

"We wanted to wait before letting people know. I mean, after the last time." Raine's voice wobbled a bit, but her husband, Jake, slid his arm around her waist, and she found strength in that. They'd suffered a stillbirth late into their last pregnancy. It was heartbreaking, having to bury a child Raine had carried nearly to term.

"I'm about five months along, and things are perfect." Raine trailed her fingers across Jake's forearm—a simple, intimate gesture. One that tugged at Rebecca's heart.

She needed to be away from all this happy. It was suffocating.

Drawing in much-needed air, she smiled and congratulated the couple once more, then turned to her brother. "I need wine. Where's the wine?"

With that, she pushed past him and grabbed a glass off the side table and let Nash fill it. "More," she said when he would have stopped. Hudson was still on the other side of the room, and he and Lily had resumed their conversation. What the hell was she going on about?

"So," Nash murmured before he obliged her with a generous amount of vino. "It's gonna be that kind of night."

Rebecca took a big gulp and winced as the wine flooded her taste buds and found its way down her throat. The pinot noir was smooth, a Californian, but still, wine wasn't meant to be gulped.

Hudson laughed.

Lily followed suit.

Rebecca tried like hell to keep her cool.

"What kind of night would that be?" she asked Nash.

"You tell me." He stood beside her and followed her gaze.

Rebecca took another drink and held her glass up for a refill. "A long one."

Nash nodded and reached for the bottle. "That's what I thought."

CHAPTER SEVENTEEN

It took Hudson about thirty minutes after dinner was over to get Rebecca alone. She'd hardly spoken to him, and if not for Nash, Lily, and the Edwards, the evening would have been a bust. As it was, the undercurrent that ran through the room wasn't exactly pleasant, and Hannah Rose obviously picked up on it. The little girl was no longer a bundle of happiness and had been fussing for the last half an hour or so.

Hudson watched Lily take the little one to her bedroom, followed by Raine, and while Mackenzie, Jake, and Nash opted to head to the deck for a cigar, he'd held back. As soon as the boys disappeared outside, he headed to the kitchen and Rebecca.

She was at the sink, rinsing a pot, and for the moment unaware of his presence. Hudson was fine with that. He drank her in like fine wine. The black shirt she wore clung to her curves, the soft, silky material gliding across her breasts as she lifted the pot and turned it over. Her hair was loose, long silky waves that tumbled across her shoulders. In the muted light, it looked so damn soft. God, he loved her hair. He used to spend a lot of time untangling it after a dip in the lake.

Rebecca suddenly glanced up, and their eyes met. She didn't look away—which was encouraging—and Hudson pushed off from the doorframe. A few steps brought him to her, though he kept the island between them because he had a feeling she'd bolt if he tried to get closer.

"You need help?" he asked.

"I'm good," she replied, placing the pot on the drying rack. She reached for a towel and dried her hands.

"Lily putting the baby to bed?" she asked, politely.

He nodded.

"The guys were heading out for cigars." She watched him, expression unreadable.

"I know."

Her chin jutted up a bit, and her cheeks darkened. "And you're not joining them because…"

"Because I want to talk to you."

She tossed the towel and leaned her palms onto the counter. "I'm all ears." Her words were clipped, and it was obvious she was pissed at him.

"You gonna tell me what's got you so riled tonight?"

"You do," she fired back at him. Her directness surprised Hudson, and he stood a little straighter.

"What the hell did I do? We've barely spoken."

She glared at him, and if looks could kill, well, Hudson would be a dead man. She opened her mouth to speak, but then must have thought better, and snapped it shut. She grabbed the wineglasses she'd rinsed and got up on her tiptoes to put them away on the top shelf in the cupboard next to the fridge. It wasn't intentional, but man, it gave Hudson an unfettered look at an ass he was dying to touch. She closed the door but didn't turn around.

"Becca."

"Don't," she said, shaking her head.

Hudson ran his hands through his hair. He was frustrated as hell. "Becs. You gotta let me know what's wrong."

He rounded the counter and stopped a few inches from her. The air was hot, and he yanked on the edge of his navy-blue Henley.

"Why are you here?" She turned her head to the side, giving him a view of a profile he could have traced in his sleep. After all this time. The intensity was still there.

"I was invited."

"No." She shook her head. "I mean, why are you *here*? Why are you still in Crystal Lake?" She turned around and faced him.

Hudson shoved his hands into the pockets of his jeans. It was that or put them on Rebecca and pull her close. He inhaled sharply.

"Vanilla."

"What?" She was confused. He saw that. He got it. Because his mind was working in a way even he didn't understand.

"You still wear vanilla." Her hand went to her neck, there where her pulse beat erratically. It was an unconscious gesture, but it drew his gaze to all that creamy, soft skin.

"God, you're beautiful." He couldn't help himself. Hudson took that last step until he was so close, only a whisper separated them.

"You're avoiding the question." Her eyes fell, those long lashes of hers sweeping the curve of her cheek. "I thought you'd be gone by now. Back to DC."

"I'm not going anywhere."

Her head shot up, and he was nailed by those incredible blue eyes.

"At least, not in the next little while. I'm not sure when I'll head back. I'd like to get the housing development up and running. I'd like to get Harry looked after. I'd like…" Hudson sighed and shrugged. "I want to spend time with you."

"You want to sleep with me."

"No." He frowned. "It's not just about sex."

She gripped the edge of the counter with her fingers. So tightly the knuckles whitened. "Then what is it about? What's the point of any of this?"

Her lips parted, and damn if that tongue didn't dart out to touch the corner of her mouth. He knew Rebecca. Knew she wasn't a cock tease. But the sight of her tongue gliding along the edge of a mouth that drove him crazy set off all sorts of things. Hot, wild, *sexual* things.

And here they were in her brother's kitchen. Hudson needed to get a grip on himself. He took a step back—*physically* took that step—and ran his hands over the back of his neck. He was so damn tense, he felt like at any second, it could snap in two.

"Does there have to be a point? Can't we just acknowledge that there's something still here? Something that never died?"

She shook her head. "No."

"You're saying there's not?"

"I'm saying…" She swore and thumped him in the chest. "I'm saying that I have no idea what to think or say or do." She threw her hands up, eyes now closed. "How did I end up here again? With you?" Her voice ended on a whisper.

He saw she was upset—knew he should probably back off—but his mind couldn't seem to communicate that to his body. He slid his hand along her jaw, his fingers cupping her while his thumb caressed her. Hudson stared down at Rebecca for what felt like minutes, but in fact was mere seconds. She leaned into his palm, and his heart caught up to the pulse that still beat at her neck.

"When you left, that last time, I thought I would die, Hudson." Her bottom lip quivered, and everything inside him stilled. "I *wanted* to die."

"Becca."

Her eyes flew open, and she made no effort to keep her pain from him.

"I kept thinking that it was a mistake. That you would turn around and come back to me." She swallowed and inhaled a shaky breath before slowly disengaging herself from his touch. Rebecca walked around him and stood at the window. She shuddered, and he took a step toward her, but Rebecca held her hand up and shook her head violently. "Don't."

Hudson held back, hands clenched at his sides, and in that moment hated himself more than he had on that night twelve years earlier.

Time stood still and the only sound he heard was the muffled cry of Hannah Rose. Rebecca took another step and leaned her cheek against the window. He watched as her breath came alive on the cold glass. And as every wave of warm air spread across the surface, the weight on his chest got heavier.

"The first time you noticed me, I was fifteen. It was summer, the Fourth of July weekend. My father was locked up, so it was easy to sneak out of the house with him gone. There was a big party out at Pot-o-hawk Island, and all the older kids were going. Somehow I convinced Nash to let me tag along. I think he felt sorry for me." She paused and glanced over her shoulder. "Do you remember?"

Did he remember? Hell, it was burned into his brain.

The water was calm, the air humid with the heat of July, and the party was going full tilt. Up the beach, a bonfire lit up the sky, and Hudson could see the sparks crackle against a sky full of stars. He grabbed up his cooler and stepped out of his boat. He'd taken two steps before a voice cut him short.

"Did you forget something?" The sarcasm was heavy, and he made a face before turning back to his date. "Sorry. Hands are full." Amber hopped off the boat straight into the water, her boobs nearly falling out of the black bikini top that barely covered them. Not that he cared. He'd have them out in a few hours. It was the only reason he'd brought her. Amber put out, and he was in the mood to get laid.

Except that about five seconds after he got to the bonfire, he spotted her. At first, he wasn't sure who the girl was, but he sure as hell liked what he saw. Long, tanned legs. Jean shorts that were loose but hung on hips just the way he liked. A simple white T-shirt. And all that hair. It hung in golden ropes halfway down her back.

She stood beside his buddy Nash, and something about the tilt of her head, or maybe the way the starlight lit up her hair like a halo, drew him to her. Who the hell was she?

Hudson set down his cooler, grabbed himself a beer, and tossed one to Amber before making some lame excuse to head over to Nash. It took him a bit—they were on the other side of the fire, and there were a lot of kids to wade through.

By the time he got to them, he felt strangely exhilarated. And when she turned to him, and shyly smiled up at him to say hello… He was gone. So. Fucking. Gone. It was a punch to the gut, those blue eyes.

He ignored Nash completely. Wild horses couldn't drag him from this girl.

"Hey," he said, voice a little hoarse. "I'm Hudson."

Her lips were parted, and a blush stole over her cheeks. "I know," she replied. The wind picked up and tugged the ends of her hair. Her long, delicate fingers tucked the strands behind her ear.

He wanted those fingers on him. Wanted that hair in his fists.

Hudson took a sip from his beer, calculating the fallout that would occur when he blew off Amber. Even though it was a dick move, he was going to blow off Amber. No way was he leaving this angel's side.

"I'm Rebecca."

He smiled at her then, liking the way her cheeks flushed even more.

"Rebecca," he said slowly, with a wink. "Mind if I call you Becca?" She nodded but remained silent.

Nash snorted and, with a hard pat to Hudson's shoulder, leaned close and whispered, "She's not like Amber. Just so you know." He took off and disappeared into the shadows, leaving the two of them alone. And that night, under a blanket of stars, surrounded by at least one hundred kids, Hudson felt as if he and Becca were the only two people in the entire world.

And in a way, they were, because after that night, and in spite of the fact he was barely seventeen, he knew she was the only girl for him. And she was. Until he broke what they had.

"Hudson?"

Jerked out of the memory, he yanked his head up and cleared his throat. Rebecca was looking at him, a strange expression on her face.

"I'm sorry," he said slowly, voice so rough and low, he wasn't sure she heard him.

"For what?" Her eyes were luminous, shiny, and full. Yet he saw the wariness there. The pain that still lingered.

Hudson had to take a moment. He needed to get this right.

"For everything. For being too young to know better. For leaving you like I did. For handling things badly. For throwing away the only good thing I had because I thought it was the only way. I know none of that makes sense to you, because there are things you don't know. Things…" He exhaled and bowed his head. "Things no one knows. But I need you to understand, Becs."

Hudson glanced back up. "When you say that you felt like dying. I get it. It killed me to leave."

"Then why did you?" she asked, her voice quivering.

"It's a long story." He waited a heartbeat and then said something he was either going to regret, or something that had the potential to set him free of a past that haunted him. "Come back to my place, and I'll tell you."

Silence. Silence so big, it was loud. And crushing. It sucked the air from the room, and he had a hard time breathing. And hot. It was so damn hot.

"Okay," she said abruptly, sliding past him and heading for the door. Stunned, he watched as she grabbed her coat and slipped her feet into her boots. "Let's go." She was all business, and the fire in her eye was fierce. She swept by him without another word.

It took a full five seconds for Hudson to get his shit together. He didn't bother with her brother. Or Nash. They'd figure things out. He followed her out into the cold air, and it pinched his nostrils as he struggled to get his breathing under control. She was by his truck, arms wrapped around her body for warmth, small puffs of air falling from her lips as she exhaled.

He unlocked the truck and waited, but instead of climbing inside, she walked to his window, and he was afraid she was going to bail.

"You getting in?" he asked, quietly.

"No." Rebecca motioned to her car. "I'll follow you."

She didn't give him a chance to respond, so Hudson waited until she was in her car, and when she was ready, they headed out along River Road. He was following her—she knew the way—and eventually, the darkness swallowed them whole.

CHAPTER EIGHTEEN

Rebecca was crazy. *Obviously.* She concentrated on the road as it curved, palms sweaty, her headlights cutting a swath of illumination across the quiet country road. On the left, thick trees stood tall and silent, lining the road like silent soldiers, while the lake glistened to her right, the stars reflecting off the top like diamonds. She'd cracked her window a bit, grateful for the crisp air. She needed it to clear her head and maybe find some kind of sanity again.

Because really…heading back to Hudson's? Had she lost her ever-lovin' mind?

She glanced in the rear-view mirror. What the hell was she thinking? The sad truth was that any semblance of common sense she possessed had fled the second he'd stepped foot back in Crystal Lake. But she couldn't seem to help herself. His orbit was too damn strong, and every time she was near him, he sucked her right back in.

To make matters worse, it didn't matter if she was pissed, because she'd had one hell of an anger on tonight, and in the end, it did nothing to prop her up. Never had she had such dark thoughts about her sister-in-law. She loved Lily. Trusted her implicitly.

Apparently not when Hudson was around.

"Jesus, Becca. Get your shit together."

The Blackwells' stone entrance came into sight, and she turned into the driveway. It wove through spruce and pine, and then their house came into view. It was impressive—always had been—stone and brick and windows. And nestled on an incline that gave an impressive view of the lake, one that was hard to find anywhere else.

As she cut the engine, Rebecca's stomach took a dive and she broke out into a cold sweat. She hadn't been here in years, but really, if she closed her eyes, it felt like only yesterday. She glanced up at the house, aware that Hudson had pulled up beside her. His headlights went out, and only the muted pot lights that accented the main entrance shone down on them.

Potted mums in rust, yellow, and deep burgundy lined the path that led to the wide entrance, and on either side of the double glass doors stood tall slate-gray pots filled with greens and berries. A soft smile crossed her face. Darlene.

Rebecca sat there for a good long while, wrestling with the thought that she should just fire up the engine, turn around, and head home. But that orbit… It was hard to ignore, and with a small sigh, she got out of her car.

Hudson was leaning against his truck, watching her. Shadows fell over him, and she couldn't see his face, but she felt the intensity of his gaze and shivered in the damp, cold air. An owl hooted in the distance, and she turned toward the lake. She'd forgotten how much she loved it here. The forest. The water. Surrounded by the kind of pristine nature that was hard to find in town. Only the rich lived out here. Other than Mackenzie making a name for himself in New York City, the Drapers had never had deep pockets.

The owl hooted once more and flew overhead, its wings cutting through the stillness and quiet with great big swoops. Melancholy stole Rebecca's breath, and with a start, she took a few steps toward the house, but then paused, eyes on the boathouse. Water lapped against the dock, shimmery as silk. The sound was gentle, and something about it soothed her—made the jitteriness melt away.

She headed for the steps that led to the dock and was halfway down when she heard Hudson's boots behind her. She kept moving and hopped onto the dock, walking to the edge so that nothing obscured her view of the water.

Her breath vaporized on the breeze, and she knew when Hudson stopped—she felt him inches from her back. Right then, a need so strong rolled through her that Rebecca almost leaned back, wanting the feel of his arms around her. She bit her lip and closed her eyes, listening to the gentle waves, letting the sound wash over her.

After a while, she was able to breathe easier.

"Do you remember the first time I brought you here?" His voice was low, husky, and intimate. It rolled over Rebecca like warm spiced whiskey. And along with it, so many memories.

She nodded and whispered, "Yes." A smile touched her face. "I was terrified."

"Terrified?" Hudson moved to the side. She felt his eyes on her. "Why?"

She glanced up at him. "You were Hudson Blackwell, and I was just…" Her gaze fell away. "I was Rebecca Draper. You lived here on the lake, and I lived in a little house off Burwick Street, filled with a bunch of kids, a mother who acted like a Stepford wife most of the time, and a drunk father who was mean as hell."

"I'm sorry. I never knew how bad it was. Not until a few years ago when I was home and heard Ben had beaten your mother so badly, she was in the hospital for over a week." His voice caught. "If I'd known…"

"If you'd known?" She cut him off sharply and took another step toward the edge of the dock.

"I would have done something about it."

Rebecca sighed and shook her head. "There was nothing anyone could do. Kind of hard when your mom is in denial and your dad looks like freaking Brad Pitt. He was the most charming man in Crystal Lake. Hell, probably the entire state of Michigan. No one stood a chance when he leveled those eyes of his on them. And the line of bull he came up with to explain shit? He should have been a writer. He was that creative."

Silence fell between them again, but it wasn't a comfortable sort of thing. Rebecca felt the tension like a band of steel coiled around her midsection. She shook out her arms, and they fell loosely to her sides. A splash sounded on her right, and she wondered what animal had decided to venture into the cold water.

"You took me out on *Glory*."

"What?" He took a step closer to her.

"Your boat," she replied softly, glanced over to him. "*Glory*."

Hudson nodded. "It was hot as hell. The sun was a bitch, and there was no breeze." He chuckled. "I couldn't wait to get you alone. Couldn't wait for you to ditch your shorts and T-shirt and let me see you in that white bikini."

"Didn't take long."

"No," Hudson said quietly. "It didn't."

God, he'd been so handsome. A young man on the cusp of adulthood—one whose dark good looks and confident personality made him one of the most sought-after boys in town. His height made him appear older, but it was the breadth of his shoulders, the fact that he'd already begun to fill them out that made him irresistible. Not only to the girls Rebecca's age, but the older ones as well. That summer they met, he'd been dating a girl named Amber, and she'd been almost twenty.

"We ran out of gas," she said, eyes on the horizon, there where the lake met the tree line.

"That's right."

"And you forgot to put oars in the boat."

"We were holed up in the cove just past Moody's Point. Which was fine with me. It was the best make-out place on the lake. Stole my first kiss from you there."

Rebecca didn't reply. Her mind was filled with images. He'd backed her against the side of the boat, wrapped his hands into the tangle of wet hair at her neck, and kissed her. She remembered how soft and hesitant his touch was, as if waiting for her to give him permission to be more aggressive.

Which she'd done without much of a fight.

It was the first time she'd let anyone take her top off. The first time she'd ever slid her young body along a bare-chested boy, one whose touch set her skin on fire. Her heart hurt. Remembering was painful sometimes.

"I had to swim over to the DeLucas' cottage to get gas, and it was near dark by the time I got back to you."

"Yeah. I got home late. Dad wasn't happy."

"Becca." Hudson reached for her, but she sidestepped with a shrug.

"It's a long time gone, Hudson. No use thinking about it now." She was shivering again, and her teeth chattered as a violent shudder hit.

"Let's go inside. I'll make you tea." His eyebrows shot up. "You still like tea, don't you?"

"I do."

He stood aside and indicated he'd follow her back up the steps. The entire way, she felt the weight of his gaze on her. And by the time she reached the house and he let them inside, her body tingled with an awareness. She knew being here wasn't a good idea. She should go home.

But she didn't.

"Wow." Rebecca turned in a full circle. "Darlene must have been given the platinum card and told to use it." The main level had been thoroughly updated since she'd last been here. She followed Hudson into the kitchen. It opened to the great room, and he flicked a switch that ignited the gas fireplace.

"My room is still the same. Hell, even my sporting trophies are still up on the shelves. Diplomas. Artwork."

"What about that stupid goalie helmet?"

"Yep. Still hanging in the same spot."

"Really?" For the first time, Rebecca laughed. "I hated that thing. It hung from the ceiling over your bed, and every time we were in there, I felt like Jason from *Friday the Thirteenth* was staring at me."

"Hey, that guy put Crystal Lake on the map."

"Whatever. It's creepy."

"I guess seventeen-year-old me thought it was cool," Hudson replied. "And if the thought of him made you want to snuggle some more, I was totally fine with that."

Rebecca slid onto a stool and waited for the water to boil. Once done, Hudson handed her a cup of tea, and she sipped it while he grabbed himself a beer and claimed the stool beside her. For the longest time, there were no more words, but she felt them. They were just beneath the surface. She wasn't so sure she wanted to hear them.

After a few more minutes, Hudson set his beer down onto the counter and turned to her. His face was serious, and his dark eyes claimed hers with an intensity that matched the pounding heart inside her—the one that suddenly took off like a jackhammer.

"About that night," he said, clearing his throat. "That last night. The night I left Crystal Lake. I want to tell you what happened."

Something broke apart inside Rebecca. It burst wide open and disintegrated into nothing. It was painful and then...not, like an awakening. Slowly, she shook her head. In that moment, she realized a few things, and sat a bit straighter.

"It doesn't matter anymore."

"What?" He looked confused. She got it, because she didn't exactly know where she was going with this.

"It's the past, Hudson. It's done." She had to wait a bit, the emotion inside her was that strong. "It's over. The weight of the past is unbearable. It's so heavy that it makes it impossible to live. I'm sick of that weight." She exhaled and looked away.

"I'm sick of trying to live a life that's weighed down by the sins of my past. By the mistakes I've made and the choices that followed. I'm done giving the past that much power over my future." When she glanced back at him, the look in his eyes made her mouth go dry.

"So where does that leave us?" he asked.

Rebecca slid off the stool and slowly pushed it back into place. "I don't know you anymore, Hudson, and you don't know me. Not really. You've lived a life for over twelve years that I know nothing about, and I..."

How much was she willing to share?

"I've had a child and been married to a man I didn't love. A man who made things...difficult."

"What do you mean by that?" He stepped closer, the look in his eyes intense.

"It doesn't matter what that means. What matters is that the last twelve years have changed us. We're not the same kids we were. We're not even close." She paused. "We can be friends. Old friends who get to know each other again."

Rebecca stepped away and headed for the front door. She reached for the handle and froze at the sound of his voice. "I don't know if I can just be friends."

"It's all I'm willing to give you, Hudson." A pause. "It's all I *can* give you."

Rebecca slipped outside and shut the door behind her. She didn't wait but ran down the stone steps and didn't stop until she reached her car. She fired up the engine and turned the vehicle around. Just as she began the trek down the long driveway, she glanced into her rearview mirror.

He watched her from the front window. And something about that solitary figure made her sad. And angry. Conflicted. She eased up on the gas pedal as she approached the road and, with a lot of effort, let go of it all.

She settled back in her seat and headed for home.

CHAPTER NINETEEN

"Are you sure this is a good idea?" The sun was just coming up over the lake, and frost touched the ground, turning the still-green grass to a silver hue that sparkled. Hudson zipped up his jacket and yanked down on his cap before turning to Nash. He'd slept like shit and had been up for hours. After thinking hard about a few things, he'd stopped by his friend's place to grab some tools before heading to town. *Before heading to Rebecca.*

It was brisk, the temperature not much above freezing, yet Nash stood in nothing but his boxers and an old pair of rubber boots. His hair was a mess, and by the looks of the red marks on his shoulders and the scratches across his chest, Hudson was guessing he wasn't alone.

Ignoring his pal's question, Hudson nodded to the house. "How in hell did you manage to pick up a lady when you were at Mackenzie's last night?"

"That's privileged information."

"Don't give me that crap. Did you go out?"

Nash snorted. "You and Rebecca killed the mood with your disappearance. Christ, couldn't get two words out of Mackenzie." He frowned. "That guy doesn't like you."

"No shit."

"Well. At least you didn't pull your disappearance until after I had my cigar. He had a box of Romeos."

"Good to hear. So. Coach House?"

"Where else."

"Shelli?"

Nash smiled. "Who else?"

Hudson shook his head. "Some things never change."

"True. But I gotta say she was pretty damn entertaining last night." Nash rolled his shoulders and grinned. "I should get back to it."

"Thanks for the ladder. I have no idea where ours disappeared to."

"Just don't fall off the damn thing." Nash stepped back toward his house. "Hey. You never answered my question."

Hudson opened the truck door. "What was that?"

"You and Rebecca. Are you sure this is a good idea?"

"We're doing the friend thing. That's all. What can go wrong?"

"Well, I'm pretty sure her definition of friend isn't exactly what you have in mind."

"Jesus, Nash." Hudson's eyes narrowed. "You're making me sound like a cold bastard with only one thing on his mind."

"Look. She's..." Nash went all quiet on him. "Be careful with her, Hudsy."

Hudson scowled, his good mood all but gone.

"I'm serious. She's strong like Superman, but you're her kryptonite. You always were." There was a warning underlying Nash's words, a warning Hudson didn't exactly appreciate. What the hell did Nash think he was going to do? Hudson would never hurt Rebecca.

But he had.

With that sobering thought, he climbed into his rig. By the time he got to town, the sun had nearly climbed to its perch in the sky, and the fall colors were a sight to behold. He pulled into Rebecca's driveway, cut the engine, and sat there for a good ten minutes, trying to decide if he should get out or head back home. In the end, he thought, *screw it*, and climbed from his truck, grabbing the ladder and a pair of work gloves before he headed to the back of her house.

It was early, barely seven in the morning, and he knew she was most likely sleeping. So, without bothering to knock on the door and letting her know he was there, Hudson got to work. He'd noticed her eaves needed clearing the week before and set about getting it done.

That was what friends did. They helped each other out.

Hudson started at the back of the house, and by the time he reached the front, he was sweating like a son of a bitch. He yanked off his jacket, tossed his hat, and was just about to climb back up the ladder when a blond head poked out the front door. Liam's eyes widened as he stepped onto the porch, a glass of milk in one hand, a piece of toast in the other.

"Morning," Hudson said with a wave.

"Hey."

"That peanut butter?"

Liam nodded. "Yep. Coach says I need protein before a game." "Ah. Smart man." Hudson stepped up a rung. "Hockey?"

"Uh-huh." Liam chewed off a corner of his slice of toast. Once he swallowed, he gulped down a swig of milk. "What are you doing up there?"

"I'm cleaning all the dead leaves and gunk that's collected in your mom's eaves."

"Oh." The boy frowned. "Why?"

"Because if they're full, they can't drain properly."

Liam frowned, and his eyes followed the eave trough across the roof and down the side of the house. He seemed to be considering the situation. "That would be bad for the basement. The water would collect there if it just came over the top."

Surprised, Hudson smiled. "You catch on quick, kid."

"My uncle is an architect, and I helped him this summer at one of his job sites. I want to be one when I grow up." He shoved the rest of his toast in his mouth, and Hudson could barely understand him when he spoke. "But why are you cleaning my mom's eave trough? Did she ask you to?"

"No." Hudson climbed up another few rungs until he was level with the eave. "I'm just helping her out."

"Why?"

Jesus, the kid asked a lot of questions. "Because your mom and I are friends. And that's what friends do for each other. They help out."

Liam scratched his head and frowned. "Are you her boyfriend?"

Shit. He was going there?

Just then, the door opened, and he was saved from answering. "Liam! Who are you talking to? Your hockey stuff is in the garage, and you need to get it into the car right now, or we're going to be late. And the last time you were late, Mackenzie gave me an earful." Her voice trailed off, and damn if meeting her eyes wasn't like a clobber over the head.

Unlike him, she looked as if she'd slept just fine. Her eyes were round and shiny, those cheeks of hers a soft pink. And her mouth, well, hell, she'd taken the time to put on some pale gloss, which emphasized the generous, round curve to the bottom lip. Dressed in a baby-blue turtleneck, faded jeans tucked into aged brown leather boots, and her hair falling in soft waves halfway down her back, she was a sight for sore eyes.

And his eyes were sore. On account of the no-sleeping thing.

"Hey, Becs," he said slowly, not wanting to spook her. Because she looked more than a little spooked. In fact, if he were to guess, he'd say she was more than a little *pissed*, something he hadn't considered. "You're wondering what I'm doing up here."

"I…" She pursed her lips in that way that told him he was in for it, and then turned to her son. "Liam, get your hockey stuff into the car. We need to leave."

"See ya." Liam waved to Hudson and finished his milk. He put the glass on the small table by the door, hopped down the steps, and headed to the garage. That was pretty much when all pretense of being polite vanished from her face. "Hudson, you can't just show up here."

"Why not?" He leaned on the ladder.

"Because it makes no sense." She blew a strand of hair off her face. "I don't need a man to clean my eaves. I don't need a man to shovel my driveway or salt it when it freezes. I don't need a man to take out my garbage or tell me when the water bill is due or rake the lawn or change the fuses in the fuse box. I've got all of that covered, thank you very much."

"But the eaves—"

"I planned on doing them tomorrow." She was lying, he could tell. That little tic near her right temple started to throb.

"Becca."

"Seriously, Hudson. People are going to talk, and I don't need that either."

"There's nothing for them to talk about," he said, smiling widely and winking. "We're just friends."

"I don't know what we are, but it's not even eight in the morning, Hudson. I can't deal with this right now."

"Don't worry about me. Liam's gonna be late for his game if you don't get your ass moving."

She swore under her breath, but his hearing was spot-on, and he knew she'd just come up with a new way to tell him to go screw himself. "You better not be here when I get back."

"Well, that depends now, doesn't it?"

"On what?" she snapped, stomping down the steps. She paused on the last one and glared up at him.

"On how long it takes me to rake your lawn when I'm done with your eaves." He hid a grin, because he was pretty damn sure Rebecca was going to lose it on him.

"Hey," he said as she clenched her purse in her hands, those baby blues of hers narrowed on him like lasers. "I don't know why your panties are in such a knot. Seems to me this whole friends thing is a little tougher on me than it is on you."

She opened her mouth to reply—no doubt tear a strip off him if she could—but he didn't let her get a word in.

"I don't mind though, Becs. I really don't. And don't worry. I won't ask you to take it to the next level." He was teasing and loved how her cheeks blushed.

"Next level?" she asked through clenched teeth.

"Yeah." He reached inside the eave trough and scooped out a bunch of wet leaves and debris. "The benefits level. We're not there yet." The devil had him by the balls, and Hudson was okay with that. He hadn't had this much fun in ages.

Rebecca's mouth dropped open.

"It's cold as hell in this morning, darlin', but you could still catch flies in your mouth if you don't watch out."

"I'd forgotten," she muttered, turning from him and heading toward the car.

"What was that?" he shouted after her.

She gave him one last look. "I'd forgotten how incredibly arrogant you are."

"I've been called worse."

"I know." She yanked the door open. "By me."

Liam chucked his hockey bag in the trunk and hopped into the car. Hudson watched them until the car disappeared down the road and chuckled. He could do this. This friend thing. The benefits thing would be nice, but for now, the friend thing worked. He inhaled a big gulp of fresh Michigan air, gave a wave to the neighbor who'd watched their entire exchange, and got to work.

CHAPTER TWENTY

The hockey game was a nail-biter. They gave the number one team in their division a run for the money and nearly pulled out a win, but ended up with a loss. With only one goal to break a two-period tie, the boys should have been happy. But it was a long line of glum faces that emerged from the changing room, and Rebecca was only too happy to agree to brunch as a cheer up.

But brunch only lasted an hour. After a trip to the hardware store to pick up sandpaper, a stop at the grocery store to grab fresh buns to go with her chilli, she was out of ideas and Liam was begging to go home. She had no choice and drove across the bridge, her fingers gripping the wheel a little too tightly. She was anxious. On edge. And still pissed at Hudson for showing up at her place and throwing a wrench into the whole let's-be-friends thing.

Who the hell was she kidding? With her and Hudson? It was all in or nothing. She didn't see how a happy medium would work.

A red light caught her a few blocks from home, and she relaxed a bit, fiddling with the radio, trying to find an upbeat song to calm her nerves.

"Is Hudson your boyfriend?"

Surprised, she turned to her son, only to find Liam watching, his expressive green eyes curious.

"Why would you ask me that?"

"I don't care if he is." There was something in his expression that tugged on her heart. "Addie Taylor's mom has a boyfriend, and she even likes him. Says he's kind of cool, like for a boyfriend."

A honk from the vehicle behind her made her start, and she accelerated through the intersection. "He's not my boyfriend, Liam."

"Why not?"

She glanced at him again with a small frown. "Where is this coming from?"

Liam shrugged and looked down. "You're so pretty. The prettiest mom in Crystal Lake."

Again, her heart melted a little bit.

"All the guys think so. And then Addie said…" He glanced up suddenly, just as they turned into their driveway. "Well, Addie said her mom didn't want a boyfriend for a long time because she thought it would make Addie mad. But she didn't care." Liam's chin jutted out. "And she even likes her dad."

"Liam."

"What?" he said, a hint of belligerence in his voice. "I don't like my dad, and you can't make me. No one can."

She slowly brought the car to a halt, noting Hudson's truck was still in the driveway. With a small sigh, she cut the engine and turned to her son. They hadn't talked about his father in a long time, and while she supposed they were way overdue, she wasn't so sure the time to have that conversation was this exact moment.

"Liam," she began.

"I just wanted you to know that I wouldn't care if he was your boyfriend."

Just then, Hudson rounded the corner, ladder in one hand, a hammer in the other. He hadn't bothered to shave, and the old ripped jeans and faded black T-shirt only made him that much more masculine. She scowled. As if Hudson Blackwell needed any help when it came to that.

"But if you don't like him, Zach told me his dad thinks you're hot. You could go out with him if you want."

Wait. What?

"Liam." She leaned across the car and dropped a kiss to his cheek. She supposed there would come a day when he wouldn't like such displays of affection, but right now he did, and she'd take it.

"I want you to know that I'm perfectly, amazingly, one hundred percent…" She shook her head. "No. I'm one hundred and fifty percent happy with our life here. With just the two of us. You're all I need right now, got that?"

Even as she said the words and smiled at her son, there was an emptiness that rocked her to her core. She was happy. She'd finally moved in the right direction, gotten away from an unhealthy situation. She loved her home. Her job. Her friends and her family.

But she was lonely.

Liam climbed out of the car, and she looked up to find Hudson's gaze on her. As always, her body reacted on an organic, basic level. Her heart sped up. She felt the heat flush her cheeks.

He didn't take his eyes from her until Liam walked up to him. It was then that she got it. Really got it.

There would be no one else for her. Not today. Not tomorrow. Not ten or twenty years from now. He still had her heart and soul. Still owned every piece of her, even the ones she kept hidden.

It was a depressing thought—knowing she would never have that kind of love again—and it meant a lifetime of being alone. Because she would never settle again. Not for anything less than what she'd had. And what she'd had wasn't sticking around Crystal Lake.

She grabbed her bags and slid from the car, feeling the weight of her future settle on her shoulders. As she approached Hudson and her son, she heard Liam excitedly replay one of his assists. Her boy had Hudson's full attention and she was able to watch the two of them unnoticed.

That is until Hudson glanced up, and she almost stumbled over her feet. She collected herself, straightened her shoulders, and tried to keep an even keel. She took the last few steps until she reached them and ran her hand through Liam's tousled blond locks.

"You're still here," she said after a few seconds.

"I am." He set the ladder down and nodded toward the house. "I got your eaves done and raked the backyard for you. The old oak tree, the one close to the house, needs to be trimmed. There's a couple of limbs that will land on the roof if a good wind takes hold."

Damn. Something else she'd noticed but had done nothing about.

"I was on my way to Nash's to grab his chain saw. That's if you don't mind."

Rebecca was silent for a few moments. This was her chance. She could turn him away. Thank him for all the work he'd done. Tell him she was good with everything else and she'd like him to leave. A smart woman bent on self-preservation would do that. Hell, that woman wouldn't even think twice.

But thing of it was, as she stood there looking up at a face she'd never forgotten, she wasn't so smart. She knew it was all kinds of wrong to play this friend game with Hudson. Who the hell were they kidding? They could never just be friends.

No way in hell would that work.

So the fact she was contemplating what it was she was contemplating told her just how far left she'd strayed. No longer was she on the road called self-preservation. She'd hopped the median and was headed in the other direction.

"I don't mind," she replied softly. "That would be great."

She headed into the house, very aware that he followed her movements until she disappeared inside.

"I'm going to regret this," she whispered to herself, trudging down to the kitchen. Her chilli was just starting to bubble in the Crock-Pot. She set the buns aside and changed into her work clothes. Mackenzie had put up the drywall in her front room and she'd done a damn good job mudding the seams. She had the afternoon to sand them and get cleaned up before Violet and Adam came for dinner and a movie.

Exciting times for Rebecca.

Liam headed outside to play road hockey while she changed into a pair of old jeans and a U2 T-shirt that had seen better days. She grabbed her earbuds, set her phone on the pile of leftover drywall, and got to work.

For a girl who'd grown up working at the local Dairy Queen, it was a surprise for Rebecca to find out how much she enjoyed working with her hands. She loved doing renovations, and as she got into a groove, she began to relax and enjoy the physicality of it.

She cranked the tunes, and the hours flew past. She forgot about everything but the job at hand, and as she finished the last seam, the ache across her shoulders tightened. She tossed the sandpaper to the floor and groaned, stepping back so that she could admire her work.

Beyoncé was up next, and she sang along, walking the room and inspecting each seam. It was important to get the surface smooth for when she painted them. She ripped out her earbuds, checked her watch, and realized she had less than an hour to vacuum the dust and grab a shower.

"I'm impressed."

Whirling around, she spied Hudson leaning against the doorframe.

"You're still here."

"Just finished piling the wood behind your shed." He glanced around the room. "Not many women I know would spend an entire afternoon sanding down drywall."

"I guess you know the wrong kind of women."

"You're probably right."

Suddenly hot, Rebecca yanked on the edge of her T-shirt, which only managed to draw his gaze from her face to her breasts. The problem? The T-shirt was an oldie, and the thin material stretched tightly across her breasts.

Hudson's eyes darkened, and the temperature ramped up even more.

"I should..." she began, voice cracking a bit. "I need to vacuum before Violet and Adam get here. And I still need to shower."

"I can run your shop vac. Go shower, and I'll get this cleaned up for you."

"No." She shook her head. "You've done a lot, Hudson."

"I don't mind." There was that smile again. That wicked. Sensual. Knowing smile. "It's all part of that—"

"Friend thing. I know." She blew out a hot breath, not believing she was going to say what it was that was currently sitting on the tip of her tongue, but why stop now?

"I've got chilli in the slow cooker, fresh buns, and Caesar salad. If you want to join us for dinner." Did she really just invite him to stay longer?

He seemed as surprised as she. "Are you sure?"

She found her backbone and nodded. "Don't read anything into this, Hudson. I just... I made a lot of food," she said in a rush.

Hudson walked toward her, each stride long and measured. By the time he crossed the room, she felt faint because her heart was pounding like a crazed drum machine, and she was pretty damn sure he knew it.

He stopped a few inches from Rebecca, and silence slid around them. She noticed the pulse at the base of his neck—knew he was just as affected by their close quarters as she was.

"Sounds good." Hudson reached for her, and she froze, her breath caught in her throat, her eyes as wide as saucers. She might have squeaked or groaned or *something* when his fingers grazed the side of her cheek.

"You've got some dirt here." He carefully rubbed just beneath her earlobe, and by the time his hand dropped away, she ached for more.

"I'm going to shower," she managed to say.

"You do that." Hudson paused. "Friend."

Rebecca practically ran to her room. She closed the door behind her and locked it. Silly, really, because it didn't keep him out. As she climbed into the shower and let the hot water roll over her, he was right there with her. Her eyes slammed shut, but she could still see him. Feel him. Smell him.

Her friend. Her buddy. Rebecca swore. She was so screwed.

So. Damn. Screwed.

CHAPTER TWENTY-ONE

"Dinner was great."

Adam and Violet had just left, their boisterous twins in tow, while Liam had gone up to bed. It wasn't late—just past ten—but the kid had spent most of the day outdoors, and the fresh Michigan air had pretty much done him in.

"Thanks for inviting me," Hudson continued, taking a step toward the front of the house where his boots and coat were.

"You're leaving already?" Rebecca seemed surprised, and truth be told, so was Hudson. They'd reached that awkward post-dinner and pre...*something*. He'd been thinking about this moment since before dessert and wasn't sure what that *something* was. Hence the awkwardness.

"It's been a long day, Becs."

"Jesus, Hudson. What are you, like ninety?"

"Hey, I'm just trying to be polite here." His smile slowly widened. "Don't want to overstay my welcome."

"Trust me. If I wanted you gone, you'd know it."

"I don't doubt it." She was full of fire. He kind of liked that.

She set aside the folded tea towel she'd been holding. "What about a movie?"

He'd been trying to read her all night and still wasn't sure where they were headed. The only thing he did know was that wherever they were going, it was down a road called Complicated. He wasn't so sure either one of them was ready for that.

"Are you sure that's a good idea?" he asked, watching her closely.

"I'm not sure about anything." She waited a heartbeat as if considering her words. "But it's just a movie, Huds." She cleared her throat and looked as jumpy as a jackrabbit. "We're friends, remember? We can do a movie."

Hearing his name come from her mouth like that did some crazy things to his insides. He resisted the urge to grab her and show her how *it's just a movie* didn't mean much where they were concerned.

"I think I can do that." As soon as the words came out of his mouth, he felt like taking them back. How the hell was he going to make it through an entire evening of being just friends? But he'd already given in, so he'd have to take it like a man.

She laughed. "Didn't take much to get you to cave."

Just five foot six inches of you.

He followed Rebecca to her dining room. With the renovations still underway in the front, she'd converted this space into a temporary entertainment area. The only problem was there wasn't a whole lot of room. Just enough for the television, a coffee table, and the sofa.

Hudson grabbed the right corner of the faded blue sofa and settled in while Rebecca dimmed the lights and searched for the remote.

"*Steel Magnolias*?" she asked in a tone that wasn't really asking, so he was guessing he had no say in the matter.

"Sure. That a superhero deal?"

"You're kidding me, right?" She gave him a look that told Hudson he was definitely wrong. "It's an old Julia Roberts movie."

Well, shit. "Does anyone die?"

"Not in a hail of bullets."

A guy could hope.

"No explosions?"

"Not the kind you like."

She was killing him.

"So it's a chick flick."

"One hundred and fifty percent." She bent over and grabbed a blanket from beside the coffee table. Hudson had just enough time to drag his eyes from her butt before she sat down beside him. "I can look for something else if you really don't want to watch it."

"Nah. This is good." Hell, he'd endure a chick-flick marathon if that was what it took to spend the night with her.

Rebecca relaxed and snuggled into the sofa, though he noticed she kept a few inches between them. It was probably for the best, and after a while, Hudson put his feet up and began to watch the movie—which wasn't as bad as he thought it would be. That is, the hour or so he managed to watch. His stomach was full. He was warm and content and more relaxed than he'd been in days. He wasn't exactly sure when he fell asleep, but he obviously dozed off, because when he woke up, the television was off, the room was full of shadow and silent as a graveyard.

He sat up, and it took a few seconds for his eyes to adjust to the gloom. Rebecca stared at him from her perch on the sofa. She'd drawn her legs up and tucked them under her. The light from the hall fell across her features, bathing them in a soft glow. Her eyes were huge, and they glistened as she slowly blinked and exhaled, while loose hair tumbled down her shoulders in soft golden ropes. He could just make out the lace edge of her bra strap because her blouse yawned open.

"I guess I missed the end of the movie." He found his voice and sat up straighter.

"Uh-huh." There was a husky quality to her voice, as if she'd nursed a tumbler of whiskey, and man, something about the tone brought to mind all sorts of wicked things.

"Anyone die?" he asked lightly.

A small smile flickered across her face and then vanished as quick as it had come. "Not in a hail of bullets."

"No explosions?"

She shook her head, and Hudson decided he liked this flirting thing.

"Not the kind you like," she replied.

"I figured as much. Next time, I get to pick the movie."

He watched her and time sort of stopped. They stared at each other, shadows sliding across rapid pulses and overheated skin, while Hudson's head went south—way south—and he fought the erotic images that assaulted his brain. He needed to get the hell away from her before he ruined things.

He jumped to his feet, actually made it to the door, when she spoke. "Stay."

This woman was going to kill him. Literally kill him.

"I want you to stay." Her voice sounded different, and he was pretty sure Rebecca was no longer on the sofa but close to him. He closed his eyes and inhaled that sweet vanilla scent that was all her. Definitely close to him.

"We decided to be friends, remember?" He was trying to do the right thing. God, was he trying. "I think I should go."

"Fuck the friend thing."

She moved quickly then, and a second later, he stared down into the one face he would never forget. Not ever. Rebecca Draper was in his blood like a fever, and he had a feeling he would never be cured. Not if he lived to be one hundred. Even then, she would manage to get his blood boiling.

"Becca, you don't mean that. Just the other day you told me—"

"I know what I told you." She shook her head. "And I'm taking it back."

"You can't take it back."

She made a face. "I can take it back if I want to. And I want to."

The air between was electrified. It curled around them both, embraced them with a primal energy that was hard to ignore. But Hudson had to get this right. No way was he going to be responsible for causing Rebecca pain. Not again.

"This right here, Becs, is not a good thing."

She stepped closer, and he clamped his mouth shut, when her hand reached for him. Not for his face. Or his chest. Or even his hand. Her palm swept across the hardness between his legs, and he bit back a groan when she settled there and caressed him through his jeans.

"You don't think this is a good thing?" she murmured, her voice sexy as hell, her eyes wide and open. Her lips wet and sultry from her tongue.

"You're not playing fair," Hudson bit out as she went for his belt buckle. He grabbed her hands and held her tightly. Both of them were breathing heavily, and his gaze fell to her chest as it rose and fell. He had to take a moment because he was riding the edge and way too close. If he wasn't careful, he'd fall over, and who the hell knew what that would bring.

"Let's do the adult thing and think about this."

She made a clucking sound. "Tell me you haven't been thinking about this all day." With that, she wrenched her hands from his and undid the buttons on her blouse, letting the sides fall free and giving him a peek at the sexiest pink lace bra he'd ever seen.

"Thinking and doing are not the same thing." He dragged his gaze up from her breasts, and, flush with desire and anger, he took a step back. He didn't like feeling as if he wasn't in control. He ran his fingers through his hair and regarded her warily. "What the hell, Becs?"

She looked so damn fierce staring up at him, all that hair and those eyes. His gaze dropped. And that barely there, pink bra just itching for his fingers.

"I've changed my mind. I want the benefits thing." Her eyes were defiant, and there she went, licking those soft lips again. "But we do this my way." She took a step closer. "My rules."

Okay, that got his attention, in more places than one.

"Rules." He practically growled the word.

"Yes." She took a step closer to him. "See, I got it wrong before, Huds." The little jezebel had the audacity to smile. Her tongue darted out and touched the edge of her mouth. She had to be doing it on purpose. Had to know it was killing him. "I don't think I can do the friend thing. Not with you. It just won't work, and we'll end up hating each other again."

"I never hated you, Becca."

Rebecca made a sound, almost like a soft sigh. "Well, I did, Hudson. I hated you. There were times over the last twelve years that my hatred for you was the only thing that kept me going."

It hurt him to hear that, and he wanted to say something, anything to make her understand, but the words escaped him. As it turned out, she wasn't interested in anything he had to say.

"So I propose an arrangement that suits both of us. The friend thing is off the table. I mean, what's the point? You'll be leaving here eventually, and I might not ever see you again. But why not give the benefits thing a go?"

He couldn't be hearing this right. "You want to use me for sex?"

"Why not?" She squared her shoulders, which only pushed her half-exposed breasts directly into his line of vision. "Men do it all the time."

She was unbelievable.

"You can be my booty call. What do you say?"

And obviously enjoying herself.

"Jesus Christ, Rebecca. This isn't you."

Her eyes narrowed at that. "You don't know me anymore, Hudson." She glanced away, and for a few moments, silence fell over them again.

"No," he said eventually. "I guess I don't."

He ran his hands over his chin, studying the woman in front of him. He was still hard as a rock, and he couldn't lie, he wanted her more than he wanted to take his next breath.

"Are you seeing someone in DC?" she suddenly asked. "Because I draw the line at that."

"Sorry to burst your bubble, darlin', but we already jumped over that line, remember?"

"Don't be an asshole, Hudson."

She was right. He was being a dick. "No," he said watching her carefully. "I'm not seeing anyone."

Her eyes dropped to his crotch, and a slow grin spread across her face. She took that last step until she was in front of him and reached for his cock.

"What do you say?" She breathed the words. "You in?"

There was power in her eyes. In the way she held her head, tilted her chin, and looked up at him. It was in the bold strokes of her fingers across his aching cock. In the tongue that darted out to lick along her bottom lip. That power and strength was hot as hell. And when Rebecca reached for Hudson's belt buckle, he didn't push her away.

He was probably crazy. Hell, they both were. But if there was gonna be hell to pay, they'd both have to cough up the dough.

At least there was that.

CHAPTER TWENTY-TWO

Early on in life, Rebecca learned that friends were as important, if not more important, sometimes, than family. The good ones were there for you when life seemed hopeless. They listened to the things you didn't dare tell your siblings. Things you couldn't share with your mom. Things only your best girlfriend could hear, because your best girlfriend never judged. Not ever. That is, if she was a keeper. Luckily for Rebecca, Violet was a keeper.

Thank God.

Right now she needed a nonjudgmental, sympathetic ear, because she'd either screwed up big-time, or… Shit. Rebecca sighed and sat back on the stool. She'd opened a can of worms the night before, and while at the time it had seemed so right, in the harsh light of the day after, she wasn't so sure.

She'd been in the Coach House for about twenty minutes, and the place was pretty much empty. That would change when the band started up in an hour or so. The regulars would come out even though it was raining buckets outside.

"You want another?" Tiny pointed to the empty glass in her hand.

"No," Rebecca replied, pushing the glass toward him. "I'll have a water until Violet gets here."

She watched the burly man get busy and hid a smile. Tiny's massive shoulders strained the T-shirt so badly, she was certain it would rip. His bald head shone beneath the overhead lighting, and his thick, fuzzy beard hung nearly two inches past his chin. He looked intimidating as hell but in reality was the one of the kindest men she knew. His heart was as big as his shoulders. Just the previous month, he'd adopted two kittens that needed round-the-clock care, and had spent several long nights bottle-feeding the little guys.

"How are Batman and Robin doing?" she asked, accepting the cold glass.

Tiny laughed, a full-on belly chuckle that lightened Rebecca's mood instantly. "You mean Batman and Diana. Turns out the little orange one is a girl."

Rebecca took a sip of water and frowned. "Diana?"

Tiny nodded as he shoved a pitcher under the tap and began to fill it with light amber draft. "Yeah. Wonder Woman was just too much of a mouthful, ya know? So I thought I'd go with Diana since, you know, Diana Prince is her name and all."

"Makes sense," Rebecca murmured, smiling at the thought of the big guy cuddling the small kittens.

"What's the kid up to tonight?"

"Tomorrow's a teacher work day, so my brother, Mac, and Cain took the boys to the cabin for some fishing before it gets too cold. They left around noon and won't be back until dark tomorrow."

"Nice!" Tiny grabbed the jug and two mugs. "I'll be back in a second."

"I'm good."

She watched Tiny deliver the draft to a couple of old guys deep in conversation near the stage, and was just about to check her cell phone when Violet kissed her cheek and slid onto the stool beside her.

"Man, I need a drink." Violet untwisted the long beige argyle scarf from around her neck and doffed her black leather jacket. "Twins OD'd on sugar after lunch and have been bouncing on the ceiling all day. Your phone call was the excuse I needed to leave them with Adam."

"What can I get you, darling?" Tiny was back behind the bar.

Violet winked at him, and Rebecca hid a smile as Tiny's cheeks heated up to a dusky red. "How about a large glass of your best pinot grigio."

"Really? We're going to do this again?" Tiny put his hands on his hips and shook his head. "You know we don't have any of that pinot stuff. I got some sparkly or cider."

"Well, you should get it," Violet said, eyeing up the bottles on the shelf behind the bartender. "I'll have a gin and tonic."

"Right. Coming up."

Tiny had barely moved out of earshot when Violet pressed her hands down onto the bar. "Okay. Spill."

Rebecca choked on her water and pushed the glass away. Her stomach flipped, and her eyes darted pretty much everywhere else except where her friend sat.

"Becca." Violet paused as Tiny handed her a glass, then took a big gulp. She waited until Tiny moved down to the end of the bar. "You're the one who wanted to meet me here, remember?"

"I know," she replied, meeting her girlfriend's gaze.

Violet's eyes narrowed. Her lips pursed, and she shook her head. "You slept with him again."

No use denying it. "I did."

"What the hell, Rebecca?" Violet reached for the bowl of nuts and shoved a bunch in her mouth before offering some to Rebecca. "I thought you said you weren't going there again. If I remember correctly, you said that if you even came close to going where you did fair weekend that I could shoot you with my dad's old rifle."

"I know." Rebecca hunched her shoulders and played with the condensation on her half-empty glass of water. "It's Julia Roberts's fault."

Violet's mouth fell open. Literally open. "Okay. You're going to have to explain that one to me, because right now, I feel I'm looking at a crazy person."

How in hell was Rebecca going to make Violet understand? On what planet did any of this make sense? She fingered the edge of her glass, tracing lazy patterns as her mind replayed the events of the night before. And then, with a soft sigh, decided to do her best.

"Maybe not so much Julia Roberts. But definitely *Steel Magnolias*."

"The movie?" Violet's eyebrows shot up in disbelief, and all Rebecca could do was nod.

"The movie."

"This is going to be good." Violet downed her gin and tonic. "You're driving me home, right?"

"Sure."

"Thank God." Violet shouted at Tiny, "Hit me up with another," and turned back to Rebecca. "Okay. I'm listening. Can't wait to hear how Julia Roberts and *Steel Magnolias* made your legs fall open."

"That's crude."

Violet giggled. "But totally one hundred percent correct, right? I mean, I'm impressed how you went from watching a sad, sappy movie to banging."

Rebecca sighed. "Violet, seriously."

But her friend wasn't giving up. "I'm listening."

Rebecca glanced around, just to make sure no one was within earshot. It was a small town, after all, and people liked to talk. Once she was satisfied her privacy was protected, she began.

"After dinner—"

"Why was Hudson at dinner again?" Violet interrupted, obviously curious.

Rebecca waited a beat to answer and realized this was going to be a long-drawn-out process. "Because we decided to do the friend thing. Remember?"

"Right." Violet blew a kiss at Tiny when he handed her another drink. "You and Hudson, just friends. Because that's such a good idea."

Rebecca decided to ignore the shot. "After you and Adam left, we decided to watch a movie."

"And you thought a tearjerker was going to put you in the mood?"

"No." Rebecca counted to three. "I wasn't looking to get in the mood."

"Uh-huh." Violet didn't look convinced. "So, *Steel Magnolias.*"

"Yes."

"With Julia Roberts."

Rebecca glared at her girlfriend. "Will you just shut up and listen?"

"Sorry." Violet giggled. "I'm enjoying this."

"I couldn't tell," Rebecca said dryly. She finished her water and wished she'd asked for something a little stronger. "Anyway. Hudson fell asleep after, like an hour or so, and I finished watching it myself. I forgot how good it was."

Violet made a face. "Um. It's about a girl who dies. You want to watch a really good chick flick? Try *Bridget Jones's Diary.* It's got it all. Sex. Laughs. Sex. Some bad language. Sex."

"We're not here to nitpick about what is or isn't a good chick flick." Irritated, Rebecca glared at her pal. "*Steel Magnolias* is so much more than just a movie about a girl who dies. It's about life and love *and* death. It's about realizing how quickly things can change. How life can change. And I…" Her voice trailed off as she tried to gather her thoughts.

"You?"

"It made me think." Was she even making any sense?

"About what?" Violet inched closer, her hands wrapped around her gin and tonic.

"I'm thirty-three years old. I'm divorced. A single mom. I don't do anything for myself. Not really. And up until last week, I hadn't had sex in three years."

"Three years?" Violet's eyes looked like they were going to pop out of her head. "You..." She sat back on her chair. "You and David didn't have sex for the last two years of your marriage?"

Rebecca shook her head, hating the hot tears that pricked the corners of her eyes. "No," she whispered. "It caused a lot of fights, but I couldn't." She cleared her throat, aware that she was going to share something she never had before. With anyone.

"The last time I had sex with David, it was just..." She blinked rapidly and looked down at her hands. They were fisted on her lap, the knuckles white, the nails digging into the soft flesh of her palms. "I hated every minute of it. I mean, the few years before that, the sex wasn't good. It had never been amazing or anything, but in the beginning, at least, I enjoyed it. But after a while, I wasn't in love with him. Wasn't attracted to him at all. In fact, I think I hated him. But whenever he rolled over in bed and touched me, I would do it, just to get it over with. Just to make him happy. Because when David was happy, he didn't hurt me." She glanced back up at Violet. She needed to clarify. "He didn't hurt me as much."

"Shit, Becca." Her friend grabbed her hands and waited.

"So that last time, I turned my face to the wall and tried not to cry. But he... After he was done, he saw the tears, and it enraged him. That was the first the time he put me in the hospital."

Violet looked shocked. Utterly shocked. "Rebecca. I didn't know. I hate that you lived so far from me. Why did you never tell me this?"

She shrugged. "I was ashamed. Embarrassed. I couldn't believe that I'd ended up just like my mom, which was something I'd promised myself would never happen. It was bad, but something happened that night. I remember lying in my hospital bed. I'd just sent the police away. Told them I'd tripped over one of Liam's toys and fallen down the stairs." She grimaced at the memory. "I told myself that I would never have sex with a man again unless I wanted to. And it didn't matter if that man was my husband or not. I wouldn't do it."

"Becca. I don't know what to say." Violet frowned. "But you stayed with him for two more years."

She slowly nodded. "I did. And every time he tried to have sex, I refused him. He got so angry, and I ended up with a lot of bruises. I don't know why I didn't leave then, but it was like I was stuck. Like I was waiting for something to happen. Something to make me act. When he hit me in front of Liam, that's when I finally got my shit together and came back here. I knew Liam was next."

At first, neither one of the girls spoke, and then Violet leaned forward and hugged Rebecca so tight, she could barely breathe. "I love you," Violet whispered in her ear.

"I know."

Rebecca pulled away and offered a small smile. "It feels good to talk about it. To finally say the words that have been trapped inside me for years. To finally acknowledge that I'm a grown-ass woman with needs, and right now, I need to feel wanted. Desired." She looked up at the ceiling. "I'd forgotten how good sex with Hudson is. Forgotten what it felt like to feel sexy, and I…"

"There's nothing wrong with wanting to feel that, Becs. Nothing wrong with a woman taking what she needs, but Jesus, Hudson Blackwell? He nearly killed you before. You didn't leave your room for days and days after he left."

"I know. But that was twelve years ago. Things are different this time. We're different."

"How so? Aren't you afraid of getting in too deep with him? Aren't you afraid he'll hurt you again?"

"No." Rebecca sat up straight. "This thing that we're doing is just about sex. That's it."

"This *thing* you're doing?" Violet looked as if she was going to explode. "So this is an ongoing *thing*? You're not just pals anymore?"

"We've decided to skip the friend part and just concentrate on the benefits thing."

Violet opened her mouth and then clamped it shut. She paused. "You're driving, right?"

Rebecca nodded.

"Good." She ordered a third gin and tonic, and when Tiny brought it to her, she took a big gulp and then slammed the glass down on the bar.

"I hope you know what you're doing. I mean, if it's just about sex,

Ethan Burke would be all over that."

"Ethan Burke is going to be my boss one day. So, that's not happening."

"Okay," she said, eyeing Rebecca warily. "If you say so. But please, Becs, please promise me you won't let yourself fall in love with him again."

"What?" Rebecca made a face. "Never."

Violet didn't look like she believed Rebecca.

"I'm serious." Rebecca lifted her chin defiantly. "This is strictly about sex. Nothing more. Hudson broke my heart once. I'm not letting him anywhere near it again."

Violet remained silent for a few seconds and then, with a shrug, scooped up her nearly empty glass. "Okay." She lifted it into the air, motioning toward Rebecca's water.

"It's empty."

"Doesn't matter. Pick it up."

Rebecca held up the glass and eyed her girlfriend warily.

Violet winked. "To you and Hudson and sex. May you have many orgasms and zero complications."

CHAPTER TWENTY-THREE

Hudson wasn't a man to keep idle hands, especially when he had something on his mind. And man, did he ever have something on his mind. Among other things such as the ever-changing state of his father's health, there was a certain five-foot-six-inch blonde who currently had him by the balls.

It was Friday, end of the week and nearly the end of October. The relatively warm fall had given way to a cold, nasty wind from the north. The rain had stopped—thank God—though the immediate forecast called for three inches of snow. Most of the folks in town had already hauled out their winter tires, bought up bags of salt, and the local hardware store was sold out of snow blowers. It had been a while, but he had memories of trick-or-treating in his snowsuit and boots and mittens. Nothing like trying to pull Superman tights over thick winter gear.

He'd spent the morning in meetings with Sam Waters and then had lunch with his father at the hospital. John Blackwell was something of an anomaly to his doctors and staff. A month before, he'd been on his deathbed. But now? Now he was eating, had even gained some weight, and a week earlier had been declared strong enough for the surgery needed to unblock his arteries. The surgery had been a success. He was still confined to Grandview, at least for the time being, but his doctors were impressed.

Hudson's cell phone pinged, and he scooped it out of his jacket pocket while crossing the street to where he'd parked his truck. It was nearly four, and he'd agreed to meet Nash out at his place on the lake. Something about a fridge and stove that needed to be moved. He glanced down at the number and, with a frown, picked up while he climbed into his rig.

"Blackwell?" The Bluetooth kicked in, and Charlie Woodard's voice sounded in his truck, a mix of Southern drawl and raw edge. FBI, the two men had worked together on a few projects in the past, but Hudson hadn't heard from the man since the previous winter when they'd taken down a terrorist cell in the heart of their capital.

"What's up?" Hudson eased his truck into traffic and headed across the bridge. He couldn't see Rebecca's place from here, but that didn't stop him from craning his neck to have a look as he sped by.

"Just checking in. Wondering when you're coming back. No one here seems to know shit."

"I'm not sure," he replied. "I'm on indefinite leave. Family thing."

"You got an expiration date for that?"

"Not yet." Hudson turned right and headed up River Road. "What's this about, Woodard?" Outside of work, he and Charlie weren't tight, so that meant the reason for the call was FBI related.

"Dartmouth is active again."

Hudson pulled over, ignoring the loud honk from the car behind him. "You sure about that?" he asked harshly.

"Last night, we picked up chatter on the West Coast. We're still verifying, but so far, the intel looks good." There was a long pause as that information sank in. "I thought you'd want to know."

Hudson's jaw ached because his teeth were clenched so tight, and he cursed again, slamming his hands against the steering wheel. Dartmouth was the bastard that got away. It was the second case he'd worked on and the only one he hadn't been able to close. There'd been a time when Dartmouth had consumed him. A time when he couldn't close his eyes without seeing the faces of his victims. The case still haunted him, but he'd learned to move on.

"You still there?" Woodard's voice jerked him back to reality.

"Yeah." A snowflake drifted on the breeze and landed on his windshield. It glistened in the late afternoon sun and then slowly melted. Hudson cleared his throat and, after checking the road, headed back along the river. "Let me know when that intel pans out. If Dartmouth is planning something else, I want in."

"Okay." Woodard sounded pleased. "I'll be in touch."

By the time Hudson reached Nash's place, he was in a foul mood. He parked his truck and sat in it, eyes on the lake and the dark water. Small whitecaps dotted the surface, moving quickly toward shore from the force of the wind. And in the distance, the once-vibrant shades of fall had given way to bare trees and a dull palette of gray and brown. There was something almost desperate about the scene, and yet it was one that had always invigorated Hudson.

Until now.

He scowled and hopped out of his truck, taking the stairs two at a time until he reached the screen door on the porch. He spied an old fridge and stove shoved up against the wall and walked into the house, but Nash wasn't inside. A quick look around told him the new appliances had already come and were in place, and he headed back outside, this time toward the boathouse.

He found Nash inside, cursing up a storm as he fiddled with some wiring, and when his friend glanced up, he could tell he was frustrated.

"Damn outlets aren't working," Nash grumbled. "But hell if I can tell what the issue is."

"I can't help you there."

"No shit." With another curse, Nash tossed a pair of pliers onto the floor and got up. "You're late."

"I got held up in a meeting with Waters. Sorry." Hudson nodded toward the house. "I see you got the appliances out of the house."

"I managed." Nash grimaced. "Might have pulled one or two muscles, but I got it done. Thanks for driving out, though. You want a beer?"

"Nah. I'm good. I'm supposed to meet up with Rebecca in an hour."

Nash moved past Hudson and grabbed himself a cold one from the fridge. "You and her are still…hanging out?"

"Yeah." His answer was gruff, and Nash gave him a curious look.

"You not liking the arrangement?"

He'd told Nash everything. How Rebecca had practically attacked him a few weeks back. And not that he was complaining or anything, the sex had been red-hot. Hell, it had been off the charts most every night since; it was just that he was starting to get pissed off at their arrangement. Something about the "benefits" thing was rubbing him the wrong way. He just wasn't sure what that something was.

"I don't know," he admitted, rubbing the stubble on his chin. "I'm just tired, I guess. I've got a lot going on."

"I heard you and Mackenzie are partnering on a new development in town."

That surprised Hudson. Nothing had been announced, and he hadn't said a word. Nash must have noticed the expression on his face, because he shrugged. "Nancy Davis."

Ah. Enough said. The woman worked for the county and had looked after the permits for him. Apparently, she had a knack for talking about her work.

"The permits should be approved, and then we can move forward."

"That's a good thing, Huds. Let me know how I can help out."

Hudson nodded. "Okay. I appreciate it." He sighed. "So, we're good? You don't need me for anything else?"

"We're good. There were three guys delivering the new appliances. I got them to help me move the old ones out. They're coming back tomorrow to take them off my hands." A sly grin touched Nash's face. "What do you and Becca have planned tonight?"

"Hell if I know. She just told me to be come over for five. Said Liam had hockey practice after school and then would be at Cub Scouts until eight."

Nash gave a low whistle. "Shit. That gives you three hours, and we both know you only need fifteen minutes."

Hudson didn't respond. His mind was on other things. Dartmouth. His father. Rebecca. The development. *Dart-fucking-mouth.*

"Hey." Nash slapped him on the shoulder. "You look like that, and I can pretty much guarantee you, Rebecca will slam the door in your face. Fifteen minutes won't matter at that point.

"Seriously." Nash's eyebrows rose. "Are you okay?"

Hudson rolled his shoulders and gazed out at the water. "You ever feel like you're just a piece of driftwood? Like you have no control over where the tide will take you? No control over where you'll end up or how you'll even get there."

"Every damn day, brother." No longer were Nash's eyes laughing. They were dead serious. "That's the thing about life. There are no guarantees. You've got to fight for what you want and then fight not to lose it. The hard part is figuring out what it is you're fighting for."

"You might be onto something." Hudson slapped his buddy on the shoulder. "I should get going."

"Okay." Nash stepped back. "Let me know."

Hudson was at the door and paused. "Let you know what?"

"Let me know when you figure that shit out."

Hudson headed back up the steps and climbed into his truck. He checked his phone and saw that it was nearly five. With a quick turn of the key, his truck roared to life and he headed back to Crystal Lake. Back to Rebecca. And his allotted three hours.

By the time he reached her place, dusk was falling, brought on early by the heavy clouds in the sky and the endless wind that buffeted the town. Her car was parked in its usual spot, and soft light fell from the windows. Rebecca hadn't bothered to install blinds in the front room and he could see she'd spent a night painting the walls. It looked good. She'd become one hell of an independent woman.

She'd become the woman he knew she would. Hudson slid from his truck and took the stairs two at a time. He didn't bother to knock. He reached for the doorknob, but before he could grab hold of it, the door opened.

And his brain pretty much exploded.

"Jesus, Rebecca."

Her hair was loose, slightly damp from the shower. It rippled over her shoulders in waves. Makeup free, with bright eyes and a soft mouth, she looked hardly a day over the eighteen-year-old from his past. Though her body had changed. She had more curves, more *everything*, and she'd grown into one hell of a woman.

She stood not more than two inches from him, naked as the day she was born.

He didn't think. He reacted.

Hudson took that last step and buried his hands in her hair, taking the mouth that was offered to him. He held her so that she couldn't move. So that every delicious naked inch of her was pressed against him. His tongue dove in, and he ravaged her mouth while moving her back so that he could close the door behind him.

He didn't break contact, because he needed to feel her. To touch and taste her. Hudson breathed her in, her scent inflaming his cells, infusing them with a need older than time. As his hands found their way down her body to settle at her butt, he had to take a moment.

"Hold on," he managed to say. "Or this might be over before we get started."

"No can do," she said, wiggling from his grasp, a sexy-as-sin grin on her face. "I've been waiting for this all day."

"Becca." He barely managed to get her name out before she

dropped to her knees and went for his zipper. "Jesus."

Within seconds, his cock sprang free, and with one last glance up at him, she opened wide. The feel of her hot, wet mouth on him made his head spin, and he slammed back onto the door, spreading his legs and giving her as much access as she needed.

"Hello," she murmured, grabbing his balls with one hand while holding firm to his cock with the other. She licked the tip and slowly slid the entire length of him into her mouth, not stopping until he felt the back of her throat.

"Becca," he said hoarsely.

But she wouldn't listen. She began to move her head and used her hands, her mouth, and her tongue to drive him crazy. His balls were tight, and he wouldn't last long. And if he died tomorrow, the sight of her naked, vulnerable, on her knees in front of him, was a picture he'd gladly take to his grave.

Hudson broke out in a sweat, and his fingers wove their way through her thick waves of hair. He closed his eyes and tried to control his breathing, but it was no use. Five minutes in and he was almost done.

With teeth clenched, he looked down at her again. His gut was tight, his balls even tighter. And that exquisite pressure began to build. He tried to tug her away even as his hips began to thrust, but she shook her head.

"Babe, I'm gonna come." His voice sounded hoarse, and he knew he was nearly there.

She made that sound—the one that drove him crazy and their eyes locked.

Fuck. Me.

She suckled him, kneaded his balls, and worked him over until he couldn't help himself. As his orgasm ripped through his body, Hudson couldn't take his eyes off Rebecca. Those lips. That face.

His angel.

He came, and with a loud groan, he watched from beneath half-lidded eyes as she took everything he had. As she milked him and rocked back on her heels to smile up at him. It was the most erotic thing he'd ever seen.

A slow wicked smile crept over Hudson's face. They were just getting started.

CHAPTER TWENTY-FOUR

Early on in her marriage, oral sex had become "that thing you did when you dated." So much so, that it became a bone of contention between her and David. The last time she'd gone down on him had been for one of his birthdays, a few years after Liam had come along.

She wasn't exactly sure why it had become something she loathed doing. Maybe it was because to Rebecca, oral sex was somehow more intimate than intercourse. It was all about trust and giving, rather than receiving. For whatever reason, it had become a nonexistent part of her sex life, before the sex life had become nonexistent.

She'd forgotten how exhilarating it could be. How sexy and fulfilling…to give rather than to receive.

Hudson's eyes were as dark as midnight, and they regarded her closely as she slowly got to her feet. Her chest rose and fell rapidly, and she licked her lips, enjoying the taste of him.

"Come here," Hudson said, his rough voice hitting all kinds of targets inside her. Targets that zigged and zagged, creating balls of heat that rapidly spread from the top of her head to her toes.

Breathlessly, she inched closer and groaned when his lips hit the side of her neck. "You're so damn hot," Hudson growled, trailing his mouth down to where her pulse beat like a frenetic drummer. He kissed her there, his tongue sweeping across the area, until his teeth nipped at her.

He pulled her closer, his mouth latching on, and she threw her head back, grinding her hips into his upper thigh. The ache between her legs was hot and intense, and it throbbed. She might have whimpered, or maybe groaned, but whatever sound she made had Hudson drawing back. He looked savage. Primal. So damn male that her knees went weak.

He reached for his jacket and tossed it aside before moving her down the hall and into the converted family room.

"Bend over the sofa."

Her mouth went dry at the look on his face. He tore off his shirt and stepped out of his boots before ridding himself of his jeans.

"Now, Rebecca," he said with a growl, pointing to the sofa.

She took an extra second just to drink him in. God, he was magnificent. Tall, muscled, with those long legs and wide shoulders. The tattoos that ran down his arms gave him a dangerous edge, and good Lord, but she loved them. Rebecca licked her lips in anticipation as she bent over the sofa. She spread her legs and smiled to herself when she heard him swear.

"You're the one who said bend over," she whispered, though she nearly ate her words when she felt his hands on her ass. She held her breath as his fingers slowly kneaded every inch of her and slid down the middle, teasing with his fingers. Slowly. Methodically. She bit her tongue.

He wouldn't…

She felt the heat of him behind her. Felt him spread her cheeks. Would he?

Every muscle in her body was tight, and with a groan, she stood on her toes, presenting her back end to him in a way that left no mistake—she was surrendering. One hand slipped around her, and she cried out when his fingers grazed the edge of her clitoris. Once. Twice. Again and again.

She began to writhe, her hips automatically finding a rhythm all her own, and when she felt pressure at her other opening, when his fingers began to play with her there, she rolled her head to the side, breathing heavily.

It appeared that he would.

"Huds, I've never…"

"Shshshsh, darlin'. Let me show you how amazing this can be."

She gripped one of the throw pillows with both hands and relaxed as he began to stroke the wetness between her legs, his expert fingers playing her clitoris as if it were an instrument. All the while his other hand gently massaged her from behind, his thumb and forefinger teased, pushing inside her with just enough pressure…to make her tingle. Arch her back for more. Lord but it was amazing.

She rocked against him, swollen and wet with need. All she heard was their labored breathing, the sound so basic, so raw. Both of his hands working in tandem, and she shuddered, moaning as the muscles in her stomach clenched. That beautiful pressure began to build, and her hips moved along with Hudson's hands. Faster and faster until she shattered.

"Oh God." Limp, she rested her cheek on the pillow, sides heaving. "That was…" Her mouth was dry and she began again. "That was…"

"It's not over." Hudson's face was near hers, and he kissed the side of her face, the touch gentle—so gentle it brought tears to her eyes. He eased inside her, the thick length of him stretching and filling her in a way that made her sigh.

"That's it, babe. That's what I love to hear." His voice was rough, his breath warm against her cheek as he slowly began to move. The sofa fabric was rough against her nipples and each time she pushed back to meet his thrust, the erotic sensation added to her pleasure.

The light from the hall filtered into the room, washing their bodies in a soft glow that reflected in the window. It drew her gaze, and she watched as Hudson's huge body covered hers, a primal male taking what was his. His muscles strained, his large hands spanned her hips as he thrust into her.

He was beautiful.

His thrusts increased, and he brought her ass up a bit more, the angle allowing him to go deep. To hit that spot that drove her crazy. Sweat shone on his body, emphasizing the absolute maleness of him, and when Hudson hunched over her to bite her shoulder, she thought that it was the most erotic thing she'd ever seen.

"I can feel you tightening," he said, his voice deep and husky. "Feels good."

"Don't stop," she said. "Not yet."

"Becs, I've got maybe two minutes left in me."

"Okay." She smiled to herself, eyes slamming shut as the first twinges of her orgasm began to build. "That's all I need."

* * *

At some point, they'd ended up in her bedroom. It was after Liam called to ask if he could spend the night with his Uncle Mac, and before Hudson had done that thing with his…

Rebecca blushed and rolled over. It was a bloody miracle she could still blush considering all the sex she'd been having. 'Cause there'd been a lot. Had to be some kind of record.

"Here."

She rolled over again and brought the blanket along with her, wrapping it around her midsection as Hudson strolled into her room. He wore only his boxers. Slung low on his hips, they left little to the imagination. She dragged her gaze upward and arched a brow at the satisfied look on his face.

"What?" she asked, making room for him on the bed. The mattress gave way as he settled in beside her, a tray of food on his lap.

"Nothing," Hudson replied, offering her a grape.

Her stomach rumbled, and she grabbed a napkin. "You did a good job." The tray was filled with kielbasa, aged cheddar, grapes, crackers, and… "Hey," she said, reaching for an orange wrapper. "That's my Halloween stash."

"I see you still like Reeses."

"Is there anything better?"

Hudson chuckled and got busy with the important task of eating. After a busy few hours, they were in desperate need of fuel, and it didn't take long for them to annihilate the tray. Even the crumbs were scavenged.

"Wow. It looks as if we licked this clean." Rebecca took the tray from Hudson and slipped from the bed. Aware that his eyes were on her, she let the sheet drop and made a big show of placing the tray on the stool next to her desk. You know, the stool she needed to bend over to reach.

He didn't give her a chance to say or do anything. His arms were around her before she could blink.

"Not fair," he growled, pulling her back to him.

"There is no way that you can…" She shook her head and giggled. "Not possible."

Hudson turned her around, his eyes glistening and wide with laughter. The sight took her breath away, and just for that moment, she forgot to breathe. Just for that moment, it felt as if the past hadn't happened. As if the life she'd envisioned when she was young and in love, a life with Hudson, had been hers.

She blinked it away, and when his mouth reached for her, there was a new desperation in her touch. A subconscious reckoning that this, this thing they were doing, couldn't and wouldn't last.

Hudson scooped her into his arms and carried her to the bathroom. There beneath the hot spray, he took her again. His body finding new ways to make her scream his name. New ways to claim what had always been his.

They made love with a heated passion that was sparked by something neither one of them wanted to dwell on. It gave their lovemaking an edge and filled their souls with something fierce, something with substance.

By the time they crawled into her bed, both of them were exhausted. "You can't stay," she said softly.

"I know. But, woman, let me have a few hours."

As Rebecca curled into Hudson's chest, she thought that maybe he felt too good. Maybe Hudson was too comfortable. It startled her, and as his breathing slowed and he fell asleep, she thought that maybe she'd made a mistake. Because the simple fact was that what they'd shared tonight wasn't just sex.

It was a lot more complicated than that. It was an uneasy thought, and it stuck with Rebecca, sinking into her brain until she finally gave in and fell asleep.

It was quiet when she woke up. The sun was high in the sky, and the threat of snow was gone. Dead leaves blew by the window, and she rolled over with a groan, wincing at the aches and pains that told her she'd been well and truly looked after the night before.

A quick glance at the clock told her it was just after ten in the morning, and she jumped to her feet. *Shit*. Liam would be home soon if he wasn't already. He had a game at one, and she'd promised him a trip to the comic book store.

Humming to herself, she slipped on an old pair of track pants, and a bulky sweatshirt that had seen better days. She pushed her feet into her slippers, made a face at her reflection in the mirror when she brushed her teeth, and tried her best to tame the wild waves that curled around her head. She gave up and clipped the entire mess on top of her head.

Rebecca took exactly one step downstairs when she heard voices. The next step confirmed that one of them was Liam's. By the time she reached the third step, she knew that Hudson was still here.

Frozen on the stairs like a teen who'd been caught doing something naughty, it took a few seconds for her to get her feet moving. And it was with a sense of dread that she made her way down the hall. What the hell was she going to tell Liam? And why was Hudson still here? He knew the rules. He should have been gone before the sun came up.

Heart pounding and more than a little scared of the impending scene, Rebecca exhaled and peeked into the kitchen.

Her heart skipped, and she felt light-headed. She made a strangled sound as she gulped in a deep breath, but it didn't matter. Liam and Hudson didn't notice. They were much too busy.

Hudson was peeling potatoes, tossing them into the frying pan while Liam was chopping onion and garlic. Sausages were on the go in another skillet, and a plate of freshly scrambled eggs was on the warmer.

Her son was chattering away about his upcoming game and some big kid named Gavin all the kids were scared of.

"Is he fast?" Hudson asked, grabbing another potato.

"He's pretty fast."

"Can you beat him?"

"Yeah."

"Well, just skate around the kid. Play smart and don't let him catch you in the corners. Remember, the bigger the guy, the harder he falls. If you give him a good, clean hit, you can take him out. Use the momentum of your skates."

Okay. She needed to nip this in the bud. "Liam's only eleven," she said, walking into the kitchen.

Her son whirled around and Rebecca tried to ignore the butterflies in her stomach. What did a person do when caught red-handed with a lover in the house? Just a few days earlier Hudson had hidden in her closet when Liam woke up in the night and knocked on her bedroom door. Liam had complained of a sore stomach and with Hudson in the closet, Rebecca had been more stressed than her son.

Seriously. She was too old for this stuff.

"Mom! Hudson was just coming over when I got home, so I asked him if he wanted to stay for breakfast, and he said that he was hungry because he did a lot of work last night."

Her eyebrow shot up at that. "Did he?" Rebecca didn't quite care for the grin on Hudson's face.

"I didn't think you'd mind because you're friends." He looked between the two adults. "Right?"

"Oh yes," she replied, heading for the coffee machine. "We're friends." Her words were laced with sarcasm.

Liam looked from his mother to Hudson and then back to Rebecca. "Is it okay? Hudson said because he'd worked up such an appetite, we should make a big breakfast."

"That's fine." She leaned against the counter and did her best to avoid Hudson's gaze.

"He's going to come to my hockey game too."

Her head whipped up at that. "I'm not sure…" She began, though the rest of her sentence died slowly at the earnest look on Liam's face. "I mean, Hudson's probably busy."

"I'm not," he said, moving alongside her and grabbing his own mug from the cupboard. His hard thigh pressed into her—only for a second—but it was enough to send electric pulses dancing across her skin.

"Busy," Hudson continued, shooting her a glance while pouring himself a coffee.

"Great." Rebecca downed her coffee and smiled at her son. "Just great."

"I know, right?" Liam grinned from ear to ear and turned back to his task.

It would seem that her fears the night before were coming true. Hudson in the kitchen with her son wasn't part of their program. Coming to his hockey game? Not in their program. This thing had become complicated.

The question was, what the hell was she going to do about it?

CHAPTER TWENTY-FIVE

The kid had skills.
It had been a long time since Hudson attended a hockey game, and he was impressed at the level of play Liam and his teammates possessed. The big defender on the opposing team, Gavin, had been successfully neutralized, and the boys pulled out a win. Only by one goal, but a win nonetheless.

It brought back a lot of memories, being here, and he was glad he'd come, even though it was obvious Rebecca wasn't exactly happy about the idea. He'd driven himself and had watched the game from a solitary perch high up in the stands. He knew enough to know that if he sat with Rebecca, that is, if she'd let him, tongues would wag.

As it was, he was getting more than his fair share of looks from the parents gathered in the main foyer of the arena. Hudson wandered over to the large glass display cases, one of which was devoted solely to his brother Travis. There were numerous photos spanning a career that had started at the tender age of three and ended with a framed shot from Travis's rookie year.

Hudson smiled. At one time, he and his brothers had practically lived in this arena. The smells, the fried food, and popcorn were still the same.

"You came!"

Hudson turned and spied Liam a few feet from him, hockey bag and stick in tow.

"I didn't see you watching."

"I was there. You guys worked your butts off."

Liam dropped his gear and walked over, peering around Hudson at the display case. Hudson saw the moment when realization hit. Wasn't hard to miss. Liam's eyes grew as big as saucers, and he began mumbling, "No way, no way."

"Is that..." Liam pointed to the rookie shot, his mouth open, expression pretty much priceless. "You guys have the same last name."

Hudson nodded. "Travis is my younger brother."

"Holy crap. How come no one said anything?" The kid was practically dancing. "Mom." Liam was so loud several people turned. "Travis Blackwell is Hudson's brother."

Hudson spied Rebecca just behind Liam, chatting with another mother. She nodded, her gaze not quite meeting his before she turned back to whatever it was the woman was saying. She was putting on her public face. He couldn't take it personally.

"He's like, amazing. Like a ninja between the pipes." Liam stood beside Hudson, his face full of awe.

Hudson looked back at the photo. "Yeah. He's kind of great."

Something hit him square in the chest. Something harsh and painful. The photos of Travis reminded him of everything he'd lost. Of a mother taken much too soon and a father who'd retreated from the world, brought down by guilt and pain. Of brothers he'd lost touch with and a community he'd been entrenched in. They'd been a family once. They'd been happy. They'd been everything he wanted for himself.

Hudson was thirty-five years old, and while a lot of folks would look at him and see success...all he saw was failure. He had no family. No wife and kids. He had a career he was damn good at, but did it make him happy?

He used to think so. And maybe at one point, it had. Maybe back then, it was all he needed. But now? Now he wasn't so sure.

"What do you think?"

Startled, he glanced down at Liam.

"What was that?"

"I was just wondering if, like, he ever comes home? Like maybe for Thanksgiving?"

Hudson slowly shook his head. He knew what Liam was getting at. "No. I don't think it's going to happen."

"Oh." Liam was disappointed. "That's too bad."

"Yeah," he murmured. "It is."

"Liam?"

They both turned as Rebecca approached them. As always, Hudson was struck by her natural beauty. By the clarity in her eyes. The soft curve of her cheek and the gentle swell of her lips. She'd pulled her hair back into a simple ponytail and was makeup free. Dressed in jeans, brown boots, and a thick cream-colored turtleneck, she looked younger than her years.

She cleared her throat, avoiding Hudson's eyes, and patted her son on the back. "We need to get going, hon. If you want to get to the comic book store before it closes."

"Okay." Liam turned back to Hudson. "Thanks for coming to my game."

"You guys did good."

"Come on, Liam."

Rebecca didn't look at him. She grabbed her son and offered a wave before shepherding him out of the arena. Just like that, he'd been dismissed. This was what they were, he and Rebecca. Two people who fucked and had some fun, but under the cover of darkness. In the harsh light of day, he didn't belong.

His mood dark, Hudson left the arena. He nodded to a few people he knew, but didn't stop to chat. He wasn't in the mood, and he didn't have time. Regan Thorne had left a message on his cell, and he was already five minutes late for a meeting at the hospital.

Snow began to fall by the time he reached Crystal Lake Memorial. It melted as soon as it hit his windshield, but still, it signaled a turn of the season. He hunched his shoulders against the wind and headed inside. The now-familiar path to his father's room was littered with people he'd come to know, nurses, porters, and clerks, but he ignored them all. He didn't have it in him to make polite conversation.

He spied Regan at the nurses station. She was on the phone and indicated she'd meet him in his father's room. When he got there, he was surprised to find Darlene at his father's side, though John was fast asleep. Instantly concerned, he crossed the room.

"He okay?"

Darlene's smile was as wide as the Grand Canyon. She nodded, her eyes shimmering. "He's great. He's doing wonderfully." She slid off the bed. "I need to get out to the house and get some things prepared."

"Oh?" Puzzled, he looked from Darlene to his father.

"He's coming home tomorrow."

The door opened just then, and Darlene gave him a quick hug before sliding past Regan Thorne on her way out.

"Does Darlene have it right? He's well enough to come home?"

Regan nodded and chuckled. "I don't believe in miracles, but honestly, if someone had told me a month ago that I'd be releasing John Blackwell, I would have told them they were full of crap." She looked down at her notes. "He's still not one hundred percent, but I'm encouraged by his recovery from surgery, and he's been asking to go home. We were able to clear his blockages, his heart is functioning much better, and his lungs are responding as well. I don't see a reason to keep him." She flashed a quick smile. "We'll have home care come in a few days a week, but as long as he follows my instructions and takes his meds, he should do okay."

Hudson waited until she left the room and then wandered over to his father's bed. The family photo was still there. He reached for it and walked over to the window where the lighting was better. Just as before, the image of his much-younger father and all the earnest faces of him and his brothers tore at him.

The past was something he couldn't get away from, it seemed, and ignoring it wouldn't do anyone any good.

"What you got there?"

His father's raspy voice brought him back, and Hudson returned to his bedside, carefully placing the photo back on the table. John sat up, his color much improved from only a few days before. His father's eyes softened. "That was a good day."

"It was." Hudson nodded. "I hear you're coming home tomorrow."

"That's what the doctor said. Darlene's been fussing about. You know how women get." John paused. "You sticking around for a while? Now that I'm not dying?"

Hudson shoved his hands into his pockets. He heard the hope in his father's voice. "I've got some things to take care of, so I'm not leaving just yet. Not real sure what my immediate plans are."

"One of those things happen to be Rebecca Draper?"

Hudson frowned. "What's that supposed to mean?" How the hell would his father know anything about what he and Rebecca were doing?

"She say something to you?" Hudson asked, curious as hell.

"Who?"

"Rebecca."

"No, son. She didn't have to."

Hudson studied his father. "I know she comes to see you."

"She does."

"Why?" And there it was. The burning question that had been buried inside Hudson ever since he'd seen Rebecca in John's room several weeks earlier.

John relaxed onto the double pillows behind him and sighed. "I suppose a part of her feels sorry for an old man looking down the road and seeing nothing but the end of his days here. She's got a big heart and a huge capacity to forgive. I can see why you love her."

"I don't..." Hudson was brought up short. Love? He clamped his mouth shut, his eyebrows furrowed in a deep line. "We're not in love, Dad."

"I didn't say anything about the two of you in a plural sense. I'm talking about you, singular. You're in love with that girl. Probably have been all along. You're just too dumb to know it." He shook his head and sighed. "Something you come by honestly, if you want the truth. Sometimes the good is right there for the taking, but we don't see it because the past is too overwhelming."

Hudson didn't know what to say, so he kept his mouth shut.

"Sometimes a man has got to say, fuck the past. Leave it behind and never dwell on it again."

If Hudson was shocked at the vulgarity of his father's words, he didn't show it. But as he stood there staring down at a man who'd influenced so much of who Hudson was, of how he'd gotten to this place in his life, he wasn't willing to let John off the hook. All that shit he'd buried was still there. The anger. The hurt. The blame. In that moment, he realized that not only did the past shape a person, its fingers took hold and never let go. It walked beside you every single day of your life.

A man couldn't say, fuck the past. A man had to embrace it, he had to own it, learn from it and then move on.

"That's the coward's way out."

"Maybe," John replied, offering a small sad smile.

The door flew open again, and a petite, bubbly nurse appeared. Her scrubs matched her appearance, boasting pink piglets and purple rainbows. "Time for a few tests, Mr. Blackwell."

Hudson took a step back. "I should go," he said, eyes on his father.

"What time do you think he'll be discharged tomorrow?"

The nurse glanced down at the chart in her hand. "Probably before eleven. We'll give you a call once we know for sure." She frowned. "Doctor Thorne has your information?"

Hudson nodded.

"Good." She bustled over to the bed.

"Okay. I'll be here tomorrow."

John Blackwell watched his son leave the room, and while the nurse got busy with her task, he thought ahead to his homecoming and all that it meant. After the nurse was done and he had the room to himself, he reached for the large book on his table and thumbed through it until he saw what he wanted. Next he picked up the phone.

"Hello?" The voice was clear, and the sound brought a smile to his old, lined, and tired face. He had a reprieve. A small window to fix something he should have a long time ago.

"Hello?" Rebecca's voice sounded uncertain.

"It's John."

He settled back on the bed and got to work.

CHAPTER TWENTY-SIX

The last Sunday of each month was designated as family day. Rebecca and Liam, along with her brother Mackenzie, his wife, and the baby, usually attended church with their mother. It was a simple gesture—one that made their mother happy—and truth be told, Rebecca loved the sense of family it evoked. It was a far cry from the household she grew up in. One ruled by fear because their father was a bullish, mean-spirited man with a fondness for whiskey and physical violence.

There was a time when Rebecca had believed none of the Draper kids would survive the darkness that existed inside the four walls of the small bungalow on Inverness Street. But they had. And while her other siblings were scattered across the United States, she and Mackenzie had found their way back to Crystal Lake. Back to their mother. And they'd managed to create a new life.

It helped that Ben was locked up, because when he was out, things weren't the same. Rebecca would go weeks without seeing her mother, because there was no way she would allow Ben to get anywhere near her son. The sins of the father weren't forgotten, and damned if she would let him sink his claws into Liam.

It was early afternoon, and the sun filtered in from outside to light her mother's kitchen in a soft glow. It was forgiving, the light, and the tired paint on the walls, the chipped cupboards and worn linoleum weren't as pronounced as usual. Mackenzie had been after their mother for the last year or so, wanting to update the place, but she would not hear of it.

Or rather, she knew Ben would hit the roof. He'd call it charity, and it would gall him to accept anything like that from a son who'd pretty much denounced him.

Rebecca watched her son playing with his cousin Hannah Rose, and her heart squeezed tightly. He was trying to get the baby to laugh and it sure as heck didn't take much. Hannah Rose was at an age where you could do almost anything and get a giggle. Each time the little girl's laughter and squeals filled the room, Rebecca's heart squeezed even more.

Her mother walked into the kitchen and immediately went for the children. The older woman was looking frail these days, and her clothes hung loose. Rebecca knew it was hard for her—loving a man who didn't deserve it. A man who never failed to disappoint. A man who, lately, spent more time in jail than out. The hard life Lila Draper had led was written across each and every line on her face. It was a constant reminder to Rebecca of all the things she didn't want. Of why she'd left Liam's father.

Her mother glanced up just then, and her expression of joy warmed Rebecca's heart. There was light, even amid all the darkness in this home. That was something.

"Mackenzie and Lily will be back for dinner. I was thinking of ordering Chinese. What do you think?" Her mother scooped up the baby and set the girl on her hip.

A memory rolled through Rebecca's mind. Hip Girl. That was what her mother used to call Rebecca when she was little.

"I… What was that?" she asked, clearing her throat as she reached for a coffee cup.

"Dinner." Lila Draper jiggled the little girl, and another round of squeals filled the kitchen. "I was thinking Chinese. Mackenzie loves the new place in town, but I haven't tried it yet."

"Sorry, Mom." Rebecca poured herself a coffee. "Liam and I can't stay for dinner."

"Oh?" Surprised, her mother leaned against the table, arms still firmly wrapped around Hannah Rose. "You have something else on?"

Rebecca took a sip and nodded. Okay. How to put this in a way that wasn't going to send her mother around the bend? She took family Sunday seriously, and so did Rebecca, but how could she refuse John?

"Are you going to share it with me?"

There was no way around things other than the truth. Suddenly cold, Rebecca cradled the warm cup between her hands. "John is coming home from the hospital." She glanced at the clock on the wall above the fridge. "Actually, he should be home already."

"John?" Her mother's puzzlement slowly gave way as she studied her daughter. "You mean John Blackwell?"

Rebecca nodded. "Yes."

Her mother was silent for a few moments, and then she cleared her throat. "Liam, come take the baby, will you? Put her in the playpen in the front room. The lighting is so much better there. And grab her little dolly. The soft one with the orange hair. She loves it."

Rebecca sighed inwardly. She knew what was coming, and there was no sense in trying to stop it. She thought she was prepared for it too, but when her mother folded her arms across her chest and nailed her with a look that said, *are you kidding me*, a bit of the air escaped the balloon, so to speak.

"Let me get this straight." Her mother's eyes were hard, and her lips were pursed tightly.

"You're missing a family dinner to go out to the Blackwell place because all of a sudden, John has decided he needs to see you at his homecoming? I thought that man was on his deathbed."

"Mom, that's not..." But her mother was fired up and didn't give Rebecca a chance to finish her sentence.

"When did you and John Blackwell get so damn cozy anyway?"

"I—"

"Or is it Hudson you're going to see?"

"No." Rebecca stood straighter. "No. Why would you think that?"

Lila rubbed her temples and sighed. "I saw him at the arena yesterday. He was up in the bleachers. I didn't notice him at first, but you kept looking over there, and finally I had to try and see what was so damn interesting. I think you spent half the game watching Hudson instead of watching your son play."

That got Rebecca. It got her hard. She set her mug down and squared her shoulders. "That's a shit thing to say and totally untrue."

"That's what I saw."

"Well, then you saw wrong. Hudson came to watch Liam play because Liam asked him to."

Her mother's eyebrows rose dramatically. "Liam asked him? When would Liam have the chance to ask Hudson Blackwell to come to his hockey game? Why would Liam ask Hudson to?"

"I'm not discussing Hudson Blackwell with you." Defensive, Rebecca took a step back.

"That's it, Becca. Do what you always do when things get tough."

"And what would that be?" Her voice rose, but she didn't give a rat's ass.

"You run."

Her eyes widened at that, and she sputtered. "Run? What the hell are you talking about?"

"Not more than two months after *he* left, you ran off with David."

"I didn't run off, Mother. We got married."

"You didn't love him. You didn't want to deal with the pain, so you took up with the first boy to make you forget."

"Wow." Rebecca was speechless. "You're giving me advice on relationships? On love?" She laughed, but it was a harsh sound. "I might have left town, but I'm sure half of Crystal Lake wonders why you're still here. Still with Ben."

"I know you don't understand what your father and I share."

"Understand?" Something big let go inside Rebecca. Something hot and nasty and filled with a rage that came from nowhere. "You have the most dysfunctional relationship I've ever seen. He's awful. He's selfish and nasty and hates all of us—"

"Don't you ever say that about your father. He doesn't hate you. Or me. Or Mackenzie. Not everyone loves the same. He's just…"

"What?" Rebecca stepped toward her mother, her hands fisted at her sides. "What the hell is he?"

"He's lost."

"Oh. Is that it? Lost." She sounded hysterical. "How could I not see that? Was he lost when he stumbled home from Deb Martin's every weekend? Was he lost when you called him out on it and he'd reward you with a black eye or a broken arm? Was he lost when we'd make too much noise and he was hungover so the back of his hand was what he used to silence us?" Tears pricked the corners of Rebecca's eyes, and she wiped at them, her hands shaky. "Was he lost when he punched me in the face for wearing mascara to the dinner table? Or when he beat the ever-lovin' crap out of Mackenzie for no reason at all, other than he was piss drunk and in a shit fucking mood?"

Her mother turned away, shoulders hunched, body trembling. She looked so small and fragile, and all the fire inside Rebecca died.

"I wanted better for you," her mother whispered. A sob escaped, and Rebecca took another step toward her mother, hot tears making tracks down her cheeks. "Hudson broke your heart, Rebecca."

Rebecca could have stayed silent, but that voice inside her, the one she'd buried for years, couldn't stay quiet.

"Ben breaks your heart every single day."

"That he does." Lila's voice wavered. "And it's my cross to bear."

Her mother exhaled and slowly turned around. For the longest time, the two women stared at each other in silence. They could hear Liam and Hannah Rose, and Rebecca hoped like hell her son hadn't heard their raised voices.

Lila walked toward Rebecca and grabbed her fiercely in a hug that spoke volumes. "Promise me you won't let Hudson break yours again."

"You don't have to worry, Mom." But even as the words left her mouth, Rebecca heard the hollow ring to them, and she was pretty sure her mother did as well. She couldn't shake the sense of gloom that settled over her, and by the time she and Liam reached the Blackwell home, she wished she'd never agreed to come out.

It was close to five in the afternoon by this time, and with the sun hidden by heavy clouds, the landscape looked cold and bare. Gone were the leaves that had painted the lake in rich fall colors, and she knew that sooner rather than later, the area would be heavy with snow. She cut the engine and sat back, wanting a few more moments before they went inside.

"Wow." Liam gazed up at the large house. "They must be really rich."

"It's impressive," she murmured. She remembered the first time she'd come back here with Hudson. She'd been scared silly.

"I think I should go home, Huds."

"What?" He slid closer to her. "My dad's going to love you."

They sat in the front seat of his car, where they'd been sitting for the last ten minutes. She was pretty sure he thought she was a wuss. Or crazy. Or both. Sometimes she wondered just what it was Hudson Blackwell saw in her.

The front door opened, and she shot up straight, heart in her mouth as John Blackwell slowly made his way down the front steps. The man was as handsome as a movie star, and she saw where Hudson got his good looks from.

He stopped just outside the car, and darn it if that cat didn't still have her tongue.

Hudson rolled down the window, and his father didn't bother to lean in. His voice was deep and cultured. Nothing like Ben's.

"You two coming in, or are you going to sit in the driveway all afternoon?"

"We're coming in, Dad."

"Don't take all day."

And with that, he headed back into the house. Rebecca spied two heads at the front window. "That Travis and Wyatt?"

"Yep." Hudson reached for her and dropped a kiss on her cheek. "Come on. They're not so bad."

She reached for the door handle but turned back to him as a thought suddenly struck. "You ever bring a girl home before?" She kept her voice neutral and tried to sound like she didn't care all that much. It was hard to do considering her heart was beating a mile a minute.

Hudson looked at her. A direct gaze that set her heart fluttering all over again.

"Never."

Turned out, Rebecca did care. She cared a whole lot.

"There's Hudson!"

Liam climbed out of the car and ran up to the man who stood on the front steps, staring down at her. He was dressed simply. Faded denim clung to his long legs, topped by a white T-shirt and a blue-and-white plaid. The sleeves were rolled up on the shirt, exposing his muscular forearms and those tantalizing tattoos. His hair was combed back and looked fresh, as if he'd just come out of the shower, and every single thing about him called to that part of her she'd kept locked away for so long.

Hudson broke eye contact and leaned close to hear whatever it was Liam was saying. He ruffled her son's hair and then pointed to the front door.

The time to retreat had passed. Rebecca hadn't gotten through the last year and a half by hiding in the shadows. Maybe her mother was right. Maybe she had been a runner, the keyword being *had*. But no more. It was time for her to figure this out. Whatever *this* was.

She opened the car door and headed for the house.

CHAPTER TWENTY-SEVEN

"So Liam tells me he's away next weekend at a hockey camp."
"He is," Rebecca answered slowly, moving around Hudson so that she could lean against the counter and watch her son. Her boy was in the family room with Hudson's father and Darlene, trying to explain the intricacies of some virtual game all the kids were playing. He was pointing his phone at the window, and Hudson grinned because, clearly, the older two were at a total loss.

"He's good with the old folks." Hudson moved closer to Rebecca. "Not many kids his age would interact with them the way he does."

"He had a bit of a rough patch last year, acting out, being disrespectful. For a while, I was worried about him." Rebecca folded the towel in her hand and placed it on the counter. "But Liam's got a big heart, and age doesn't matter to him. If you treat him kindly, he's all in. He doesn't discriminate."

He watched her closely. Saw the love and pride. "You did good, Becs."

She turned to him then, but he couldn't read her. Hell, he'd been trying to all night. Ever since she'd shown up for dinner. No one had been more surprised than Hudson to find Rebecca and Liam in the driveway. He'd figured it was Nash swinging by to see the old man.

"What about you?" she asked, head cocked to the side.
"Me?"
"Kids. Do you want them?"
"Yeah," he answered slowly, nodding. "I do. Some day. With the

right person."

They'd suddenly strayed into heavy territory, and she shuffled her feet a bit, though she never took her eyes from his.

"You and Candace never had that conversation?"

"Candace and I weren't married long enough to have that conversation. But maybe that was because we both knew a kid for us would have been a huge mistake."

She glanced back to Liam. "My marriage was a disaster. Pretty much from the beginning. But I wouldn't trade any of the bad, because at least I have Liam."

There were so many questions Hudson wanted to ask Rebecca. So many damn things he needed to know. Things he needed to say. But it wasn't the right time. Not here in his dad's kitchen. They needed to be alone. Needed to be in a place where there were no distractions. This thing between them was no longer simple, and he needed some clarity.

I want her back.

The words whispered through his mind. They hit him like a punch to the gut. He took a step toward her.

I want her back.

She looked up, a bit startled by his close proximity.

"Come away with me next weekend."

The look on her face was priceless. "Are you high?"

"No."

"Well, you sound crazy. Why would I go away with you for the weekend?"

"Because you know there're things we need to figure out."

"I…" She shook her head. "We…" And then slowly stopped. She stood there looking up at him, her face a myriad of emotion, and it took everything in him not to put his hands on her and stake his claim. When she spoke, her voice was low, with that throaty rasp that told him she was ruffled. "It's probably not a good idea."

"Probably not."

"Where would we go?"

"Leave it to me."

Liam laughed, a shriek that got both their attention. Rebecca couldn't help but smile when she spied her son practically standing on his head in an effort to prove some point to John.

"You know John thinks we're involved again." She spoke quietly now.

"No one ever accused my old man of being dumb."

"He called me yesterday and threatened to come get me himself if Liam and I didn't show for his welcome home dinner. I didn't think this was a good idea."

"But you came."

She turned back to him, her soft lips parted, those big blue eyes of hers luminescent. "I did," she whispered.

"Come away with me." He pressed forward, so close to her now, he could *feel* her.

A heartbeat passed. Then another. She leaned forward and whispered close to his ear, "I'll think about it."

* * *

I'll think about it.

After that parting shot, Rebecca had left him in the kitchen. She'd kissed his father good night, thanked Darlene for a wonderful meal, and then she and Liam had gone home. She'd put Hudson through three torturous days and nights without a word, and then finally, Wednesday evening, she'd sent him a simple text.

Okay.

It was now Friday afternoon, and he was ready to head out. He'd just come from a meeting with Mackenzie Draper. Rebecca's brother was donating his skills and company and would be drawing up the plans for the development. Once they were up to snuff, they'd be presented to the town council for approval. They were hoping to have everything in place for a spring start.

The meeting had gone well, and Mackenzie had been easy to work with and professional. Other than a warning not to dick around with his sister, Hudson was going to call it a success.

He left his father's office and headed back across town to catch River Road to the other side of Crystal Lake. Rebecca's car was in the shop, and she would have had to wait until five for a ride home, so he'd been more than happy to get her from work. Of course she'd told him to get there at four thirty. On the dot. Not one minute before. And then she'd proceeded to tell him not to bother coming inside because she'd meet him in the parking lot.

He smiled as he parked his truck. He was early, and damned if he was going to wait in the parking lot. Sure, there was going to be hell to pay for violating the terms of her agreeing to go away with him, but he was fine with that. He was curious about how she spent her days. He wanted to know everything.

Hudson strode across the lot just as an elderly woman reached the door. A large red-plaid coat nearly dwarfed her small frame, while a fluffy, saucy white hat sat on her head. Golden-white curls peeked from underneath the fluff, and her overly pink lips smiled up at him. Shiny black rubber boots made squishy noises as she trudged along, and a long red scarf billowed in the breeze. She gingerly held on to a small carrier with both hands, and he was going to assume the hisses and growls belonged to a cat.

"Would you like me to carry that in for you?"

"Oh, would you, dear?" She sounded winded. "My husband was too sick to come with me but I'm afraid I've not the strength I used to."

"Not at all." Hudson grabbed the carrier and held the door open for her. She looked familiar, and it hit him as he as followed her inside. "Mrs. Anderson?"

The woman turned around and a slow smile spread across her face as recognition hit. "Hudson Blackwell. Bless your heart. Harry told us what you're fixing to do in town. He's been so excited." She came at him and hugged him. "You don't know what this means to our grandson. His parents are thrilled. It's been a long, hard road for all of them."

"I think I do." He spoke a bit gruffly and set the carrier up on the counter. A large tank took up the entire middle of the waiting room, and it was filled with colorful fish. A cage in the far corner held four kittens up for adoption. And behind the counter was a lady who regarded him closely.

Mrs. Anderson shuffled past him. "Hello, Kimberly. I've got Bootsie here for her shots."

"I see that." The woman smiled, but her curious gaze fell back to Hudson. "I'll let Doctor Burke know you're here."

It was a few more minutes before Kimberly returned, and while Hudson waited, he wandered back to the cage. He'd never been into cats. As a kid, he would have killed for a dog, but as an adult, he'd never had the time to devote to a pet. Or a kid. Or, as it turned out, to a wife.

It was saying something that his head was thinking things. Things he'd never considered before. He stuck his finger in the cage, wiggling it like an idiot at the smallest bundle of fur. A light golden tabby with big blue eyes. It wandered over and took a swipe at him.

"Little shit," he murmured. He kind of liked his spunk.

He heard Rebecca's voice just then and straightened, his smile fading a bit when he spied her chatting with Ethan. She turned, as if sensing his presence, and he walked toward them, liking the way her cheeks darkened, the way her eyes widened.

"Hey," he said, aware that everyone in the clinic was watching them. She cleared her throat and darted a look at Ethan. "You're early."

"I am." Hudson tore his gaze from hers and offered his hand to Ethan. "Mind if we leave now?"

"No," Ethan replied. "Not at all."

"But I've got some things to look after." Her eyes were spitting fire and, holy hell, was Hudson looking forward to putting out the flames later.

"Don't worry about the filing," Kimberly said with a grin as she sat back down behind the desk. "I've got things covered. You two skedaddle off to wherever it is you're going." Kimberly ducked and disappeared under the counter, but they had no problem hearing her muffled words. "I was wondering what this big weekender was here for." She popped up, face red from exertion, and blew a long strand of hair from her face. "Here's your bag, Rebecca, and your winter coat." She winked. "Have fun."

"I've got it." Hudson reached for the bag and stepped out of the way so Rebecca could pass. She grabbed her jacket along the way.

"Are you sure?" she asked once more, only to have every single person in the clinic, including Mrs. Anderson, shout at her to leave.

She sailed past him and was out the door before he could say goodbye to Ethan and Mrs. Anderson. Kimberly gave him a big smile, and as they left, he could tell from the way Rebecca stomped across the parking lot, she wasn't happy with him.

Here it comes. And it did. Not one second after she climbed into his truck.

"Dammit, Hudson. You did that on purpose."

"What?" He played dumb, but she wasn't having it.

"Now everyone and their mother is going to know you're the person I'm going away with for the weekend. Jesus. We should just have taken out a billboard. A whole weekend of sex with Hudson Blackwell." She was trying to get her seat belt buckled, and he hid a smile when he reached over to help her.

"Who said anything about sex?"

She glared at him. "I'm serious. I don't want anyone to know what we're…what this…" She cursed. A lot. And then sank back into the seat with a long sigh. "I don't even know what this is anymore."

"Well, it's a good thing, then."

"What's a good thing?"

He headed out and turned onto the road, but instead of heading back to town, he pointed the truck in the opposite direction.

"It's a good thing we've got the whole weekend to figure it out."

She picked at an invisible piece of lint and then sat up a bit straighter, glancing out the window. "Where are we going?"

"It's a surprise."

"Well, I didn't bring anything fancy to wear, so…"

"Won't be a problem."

"Why not?"

"Because you won't be wearing much of anything for at least forty-eight hours."

He saw the first hint of a smile. "You're damn sure of yourself."

"I am." He flashed a grin and cranked the tunes as they sped down the highway that rounded Crystal Lake. It was the first week of November, and the snow they'd been promised had fallen a few days earlier, though most of it had already melted. With the temperatures hovering just above freezing, and precipitation on the calendar, the roads would be dicey later. Didn't matter to Hudson. He planned on spending most of the weekend inside, indulging in a lot of indoor activity and having a conversation or two with the woman beside him.

They drove in silence for nearly twenty minutes, and when he turned onto Ingalls Side Road, she perked up. Rebecca looked his way, but Hudson kept his eyes on the road. He'd already been up here and knew the potholes weren't exactly vehicle friendly.

The road twisted and turned, taking them deeper into the bush, and another twenty minutes passed before the conifers and evergreens began to thin. He saw the sparkling water in the distance. They'd nearly reached their destination.

When he rolled into the clearing and cut the engine, the two of them sat for a while, their silence more like a companion as they gazed up at the large rustic cabin in the woods. The sun was setting just behind it, the last rays of orange and gold slowly disappearing as dusk fell. In the distance, several more cabins dotted the shoreline, each with their own dock, though they were smaller.

"This place looks the same," she murmured, reaching for her seat belt.

"Yeah."

She turned to him and his chest tightened. He was hot and cold, and his heart beat so damn fast, it hurt. Him. Hudson Blackwell. He was scared. She shook her head, a catch in her voice. "I forgot about this place." Her gaze wandered back to the cabin before claiming him again. "Or maybe I just wanted to forget."

Hudson waited a beat and then reached for the door handle.

"I didn't."

He opened the door and got out, and as he followed Rebecca up the steps to the veranda that ran the length of the cabin, he hoped like hell he knew what he was doing. He knew they'd reached the end of whatever it was they'd had in Crystal Lake. He'd seen that in her eyes the weekend before.

This right here was new territory for him and Rebecca. He couldn't screw it up.

CHAPTER TWENTY-EIGHT

The door was unlocked, and with one last glance at Hudson, Rebecca turned the handle and pushed it open. It was like walking back in time. She stood at the threshold for several moments as a wash of memories hit her.

Hudson carrying her over his shoulder to the rug in front of the fireplace.

Hudson smiling down at her as she told a funny story.

Her hands on his strong, young body.

His mouth on hers.

Rebecca exhaled and took a step inside. She breathed in the past and turned in a full circle. The large cabin was part of an old resort that at one time had been popular in the area with city folk looking to experience the wilds of Michigan. Fishing. Camping. Canoeing. Hiking. Sledding in the winter. The smaller cabins were always full. But when the car industry collapsed and folks didn't have as much money to spend, this place had died a slow death.

It became the go-to for local teens to hang out and party. And do other things.

"Do the Edwards still own this?" she asked.

"They do."

"It looks clean," Rebecca said as she walked farther into the great room. The fresh scent of pine was in the air. Heck, even the windows looked crystal clear, as if they'd just been washed.

"I got the key off Jake a few days ago and came up to make sure there were no critters running around. I was surprised to find everything in working order. The fireplace has been checked out, the bedrooms are made up. Even the kitchen is up to snuff."

"Are they planning on reopening?"

Hudson shrugged and dropped their bags. "He didn't say, but obviously they've pumped some money into the place over the last while."

He walked past her, and Rebecca watched as he got busy with the fire. The fireplace was the focal point of this great room and was built into stone and granite. Above it hung the requisite stuffed head. In this instance, a large moose. The furniture was still the same. Massive pieces, leather and suede, with a few dark rust-colored chairs as accent. They were more than a little threadbare, but considering the age, they were in good condition. She noticed a large bag beside the sofa, one full of pillows and blankets.

Seemed as if looking for critters wasn't the only thing on Hudson's mind.

She wandered over to what had at one time been the reception desk and spied several framed photos on the wall. Her father, Ben, had never brought his children out here, but Hudson's family had spent time at the lodge.

Her heart took a tumble, and she walked around the desk, eyes on the last frame to her right. She stood staring at it for so long, her neck ached. And then on tiptoes, she reached up, but her fingers couldn't quite grasp the edge of the frame.

"Here." Warm breath touched the back of her neck. "Let me."

She froze as Hudson's hands reached overtop and grabbed the photo from the wall. He held it in front of Rebecca so both of them could see it. It was black and white. The image simple. Powerful.

A woman sat at the edge of the water surrounded by three young boys. Her laughter was frozen in time as she gazed up at the photographer. Long hair hung in wet ropes down her chest, and the oldest child leaned against her, his head on her shoulder, his arms tucked into hers. The look on her face was one of pure, unrestrained joy. She was happy. Her boys were happy. She was loved.

"I forgot this was here." Hudson spoke quietly, and Rebecca moved so that she could see him.

"She was beautiful. Your mom."

He nodded. "She was."

When he glanced up and looked at her, a knot formed in her throat. He made no effort to hide his pain, and the sadness reflected in his eyes touched something deep inside Rebecca. She knew what it was like to lost a parent. Sure, Ben was still alive, but he'd surrendered to the bottle a long time ago. What had it been like for the Blackwell boys? She took the photo from Hudson's hand and ran her fingers over the images. All three of the boys touched their mother in some way, and their love was evident. She was their life.

Rebecca set the photo down onto the counter and slid her hands around Hudson. He pulled her into his arms, and they embraced for what seemed like forever. She laid her head against his chest, listened to the strong, steady beat of his heart, and in that moment, she let everything go. As if a weight lifted.

She didn't want to think about what they were doing. Or what the future held. Right now, all she wanted to do was *feel*. She wanted a connection. She wanted the love she saw in that photo.

"We should talk," Hudson said quietly.

"No." She shook her head. "Tomorrow is for talking."

Gently, she wriggled out of his grasp, and Rebecca slid her smaller hand into his large one. She slowly led him back toward the now-robust fire, and for a few seconds, the only sound she heard was the whistling wind outside the windows, the cackling sound of the wood as it burned, and their breathing.

She looked up at Hudson. At his dark, dangerous eyes. The sensual curve of his mouth. The fast-beating pulse at his neck. His hands slid down her body until they came to rest at her hips. He lifted her, and she automatically encircled his hips with her legs and sank her hands into his hair. He hesitated, just for a second, as if considering his actions, but then, with a groan, his mouth claimed hers. It was a kiss to end all kisses. It was hungry and tender. Demanding and coy. His mouth ravaged hers as if he were starving, and when he finally broke contact, they both had to take some time.

She was trembling in his arms, her body on fire, and the throb between her legs was hard to ignore. She began to gyrate her hips, her head thrown back as his mouth slowly made its way down her throat.

Hudson gently lowered her and took a step back. His erection strained beneath his jeans, and she licked her lips, eyes on the prize, as her heart rate skyrocketed.

"Don't," he said hoarsely.

When she met his gaze, the look in his eyes made her mouth go dry.

"I mean it. Don't make that sound again unless you want this over before it starts."

A slow smile curved her lips. "What sound is that?" she asked breathlessly, reaching for the top of her deep-blue sweater.

"You know the one." His voice was rough, eyes dark as onyx, and his hands hung loosely at his sides.

"I don't." She pulled her sweater over her head and let it drop to the floor. "You'll have to be more…specific." Her tongue touched the top of her lip, and she loved how his eyes followed the movement. She felt powerful. Sexual. In total control.

Rebecca slowly tugged on her zipper and then bent over provocatively as she stepped out of her boots and then tossed the jeans beside her top. When she straightened, his hands were no longer loose but fisted, and she knew he was close to the edge.

Hudson moved toward her. "It's like a half sigh but with a hint of whiskey."

"Whiskey?" she asked, tilting her head so she could see him better.

"Yeah," he murmured as he reached for her bra strap. She inhaled sharply as his knuckles grazed her bare skin. "This is a good look on you."

"Demi bra?"

"That what this is?" His mouth drifted over where his knuckles had just been, and she stifled a groan.

"Yes," she managed to say as he nipped her collarbone. "There was a sale and…"

"Thank God for commerce." His hands were at the back clasp.

"I remembered you liked blue."

"Best damn color in the world." Her bra joined the clothes on the floor, and then his hands moved down her hips, his touch urgent as he ripped at her panties. There was a fever between them. A need to connect that fed a deep-rooted urgency.

Rebecca's fingers worked to get him as naked as she was, and when he tossed aside his jeans, she kissed him again. A long, soul-searching kiss that made her head spin and her body shake with need. She was wet and swollen and so damn worked up, she felt like crying.

"I need you inside me," she gasped when his mouth closed over one of her nipples. Each time he pulled and suckled, desire and need converged, shooting through her body and settling between her legs.

"Hold on," he said, voice gruff. With one last nip at her breast and then a kiss that made her knees shake, Hudson moved toward the fireplace and rifled through a bag. He unfurled a large blanket onto the floor in front of the fireplace, but she was there pushing him back onto it before he could do or say a thing.

She grabbed the condom wrapper from his hands and smiled. "You really did think of everything."

"I tried."

She tore it open with her teeth. "I like that you're so organized." She stood over him, eyes smoldering at the look in his as he gazed at the junction between her legs.

"It's one of my strong suits."

She straddled him, smiled when he groaned and then swore, and she unrolled the condom over his cock. The muscles in his shoulders strained, and the look on his face was fierce. She leaned forward, her sensitive nipples grazing his chest as she kissed him again. God, he was like a fever she couldn't shake. She needed to taste and touch, and she didn't break contact as she slowly slid down on him.

He groaned against her mouth, and she nearly wept at how good he felt inside her. He'd been her first. Their connection was both organic and chemical. No one would ever satisfy her the way this man did.

They made love with a passion so raw and full of need, it left Rebecca speechless. Their bodies strained. Their hands clutched at each other. And when she came, it was his name on her lips. His body and mind that held hers. His soul that touched the very core of her being.

And yet as the aftershocks of their lovemaking rolled over her, Rebecca should have felt content. And wanted. And satisfied. But she didn't. She slammed her eyes shut and held him, hating that fear was blossoming inside her.

CHAPTER TWENTY-NINE

Hudson woke up with an uneasy feeling in his gut, and that was worrisome, because he'd learned a long time ago to listen to his intuition. He didn't know when or what, but something was headed his way, and he was pretty damn sure, whatever that something was, it spelled trouble.

He rolled over but made no effort to get to his feet, because no way in hell was he giving up the warmth of the woman beside him. Instead, he watched the gentle rise and fall of her chest as she slept. She looked so damn relaxed and—a ghost of a smile touched his face as he reached for a long strand of hair that fell across her nose— so thoroughly loved. Her lips were swollen from his kisses, her skin flushed from the touch of his hand. He wouldn't be surprised if she ached in new places, because he'd been tenacious in his quest to love every single inch of her. And then some.

The fire had long since burned out, and while it was cool in the lodge, he wasn't worried. Rebecca would be plenty warm beneath the pile of blankets they'd hauled out of the cupboard from one of the upstairs bedrooms. Restless, he slid from beneath the comforter, careful not to wake her and pulled on his jeans. He didn't bother with a shirt and, barefoot, trudged over to the window. Dawn was breaking, and the horizon was lit up with streaks of gold that illuminated the frost-covered tips of the trees in a shimmery haze. Fog slithered across the still-unfrozen lake, long plumes of white shadow that moved in the breeze.

It was going to be a gorgeous day up here, and Hudson had Rebecca all to himself until Sunday night. He was going to make the most of it. With one more look at the still-slumbering form, he headed to the kitchen and got busy preparing a feast of eggs, bacon, hash browns, and cornbread. In no time, he whipped together something to be proud of, and he'd just poured himself a coffee when Rebecca slipped into the kitchen, wearing nothing but his plaid shirt and a smile. It hung to mid-thigh, and even though the sleeves fell past her hands and covered more than it showed, she looked sexy as hell. With her tumbled hair and sleep-heavy eyes, she was something to behold.

He took a mental picture, because it was one he'd be pulling out in the future.

"What's all this?" she asked, voice sleep heavy and sexy as hell.

"I brought it up yesterday."

"You were sure of yourself." There was a teasing lilt to her words, and he smiled.

"Of what?"

"Sure that I'd still be here."

"Can't help it. I've always been an optimist. And besides…" He shot her a wicked grin. "I'm pretty good in the sack, so I assumed you'd be up for more."

She picked up a tea towel and threw it at him. He loved this. This ease they'd managed to find.

They ate a hearty breakfast and talked about anything that struck their fancy, but nothing that really mattered. It was as if they were both ignoring the elephant in the room—which he supposed they were—but Hudson was content to just *be* with Rebecca and ignore anything that might spoil the moment.

He'd told her to bring boots and warm clothing, and after a quick shower, they both got dressed. Rebecca was just pulling on her boots when she stopped and looked at him quizzically.

"You don't find it funny that this place has been renovated and updated? The bathroom we used is nicer than the one I just installed in my house."

Hudson buttoned his shirt and dropped a kiss on her nose. "Maybe Jake's thinking of reopening."

"He never said anything?"

He shook his head. "Nope."

"Weird."

Hudson grabbed their backpack and slipped it over his shoulders and pointed to the door.

"Where are we going?" Rebecca gave him a quizzical look.

"Follow me, and you'll find out."

The two of them headed into the early morning sunshine. The snow clouds had given way to a clear blue sky, and the wind from the north was minimal. It was crisp and cold, but altogether a perfect November day. Hudson pointed to the path that led to the cabins, and the two of them moved in that direction.

Here, the trees were mostly evergreen, pine, spruce, and fir. The smell of pine needles was heavy in the air and brought to mind hot chocolate, snow, and Christmas. They trudged along the path and stopped near the first cabin. Made of logs, like the rest of them, it boasted new windows, a new roof, and the bronze nameplate above the front door had been freshened up. Dry Run.

Hudson stared at the name for a long time, unaware his easy manner had changed until Rebecca moved to his side.

"Everything okay?" Rebecca asked, her voice light.

"This was ours."

"What do you mean?" She followed his gaze.

"This cabin. We'd have family reunions up here, and this cabin, Dry Run, was always ours. I liked it because it was the closest to the main lodge, and I'd beat all the other kids over there for breakfast. It was the highlight of my day."

She chuckled. "You weren't hard to please."

"None of us were. We had it easy. So damn easy, and we didn't know it. As long as Mrs. Thompson had her homemade strawberry freezer jam and biscuits, I was good to go. We spent our days on the water." He pointed to a clearing just to the left of Dry Run. "And our nights around the fire. Wyatt was the singer. Jesus, nothing could get that kid to shut up. Dad would bring out his guitar, and the two of them would sing Hank Williams songs all night. They'd always end with a sing-along. 'American Pie' or something." He stopped. "Huh. I forgot my dad played. How crazy is that?"

Rebecca grabbed his hand and squeezed it.

"It's not crazy. It just is."

He shook off the memories and cleared his throat. "We should get going."

They hiked for nearly two hours, following a well-worn path that told Hudson the area was still used even though the resort hadn't been in use in years. It wasn't overgrown, and easy to follow. The higher they climbed, the less dense the trees were and the rockier the landscape became. When they finally reached the clearing, the sun was high in the sky, and Hudson doffed his jacket and slid off his backpack.

"Oh my God." Rebecca walked to the edge of the stone clearing. They were at the top of the hill they'd just hiked, one with deep ravines that led straight down into a neighboring body of water, Silver Lake. And in the distance, several smaller lakes stretched out, liquid blue among patches of evergreen and the many bare trees that had lost their leaves to the oncoming winter.

"I forgot how beautiful this place was."

She turned in a full circle, and though her eyes were on the scenery below, Rebecca had his undivided attention.

"Yes," he murmured, walking toward her. He followed her gaze. "It's incredible." He wasn't talking about the view, and when she glanced up at him, a gentle smile lit her face.

"Do you remember the last time we came here?" she asked.

Hudson nodded. "Best prom party ever."

She giggled. "I can't believe us girls hiked up here in running shoes and gowns in the dark."

"Hell, Nash carried the whole damn sound system on his back."

"That's right."

"And a small generator to run the thing."

She giggled. "And his date quit halfway up." "Thank God. She whined the entire way." Hudson opened up the knapsack and retrieved a blanket, two hot thermoses of soup, and biscuits.

"You really thought of everything."

"You seem surprised." He handed Rebecca one of the thermoses.

"No. I just…" She shrugged. "I wasn't expecting all this."

"You like?" he asked lightly.

"I do."

They settled down on the blanket and ate their lunch, both enjoying the fresh air and amazing view.

"So, FBI." Rebecca looked at him quizzically.

"Yeah."

"How'd that happen?"

He shrugged and swiped at a bunch of crumbs on his lap. "I ended up at college on the West Coast and was recruited."

"Do you like it?"

He was quiet as he considered his answer. "I do." It seemed like the right answer, so why didn't it feel right? He did like his job. It was rewarding, and he made a difference.

"How'd you end up in Ohio?" Hudson changed the subject, leaning back onto his elbows as he gazed up at the sky.

Rebecca chewed off the edge of her biscuit. "David had a job waiting for him. His uncle owned a car dealership, and he was a mechanic so…"

"You don't talk about him." Hudson glanced up at her. He was curious as hell about her husband. Hell, he'd even gone after Nash for information, but that hadn't gotten him anywhere. The guy was loyal to a fault and had no problem telling Hudson to back off. If Hudson wanted to know about Rebecca's marriage, then he'd have to find out on his own.

"No. He was…" She seemed to struggle for words.

"Hey, we don't have to talk about this."

"No. It's fine." Rebecca picked at the edge of her cuff. "David was…well, he was the answer to my prayers. At least, at first. I mean, I needed a distraction. A way to forget."

You.

Rebecca didn't have to say the word, but he heard it ring out inside his head. And he felt like an absolute shit.

"He was a way out of this town, and I wanted to leave." She turned her head slightly, but he saw the tremble in her lips and heard the quiver in her voice when she continued. "I'd known him all of two months when he asked me to move to Ohio with him. I figured you weren't coming back, and by that time, I was so angry and hurt that even if you did, I'm not sure what I would have done. Ben was home again, and I just needed to get away."

Hudson sat up. "What about college? I know you'd taken off a few years, but you were all set to go."

She didn't say anything for the longest time, and when she turned to him, her eyes were heavy, shadowed with a pain he was just starting to understand.

"You left, Hudson, and I was broken. I can't explain it any other way. I was empty, and I didn't work anymore. I didn't talk to anyone. I didn't want to see anyone. I stopped eating." Her voice broke, and he reached for her, but she moved quickly and got to her feet.

"Violet tried to help. She knew how screwed up I was, but I wouldn't let anyone inside. I locked myself in my room and kept the phone in there because I was sure you were coming back for me. I stared at that stupid thing for hours at a time, but it never rang, and you never came."

She shivered violently and wrapped her arms around her body. "One night, I found some pills, and I swallowed every single one."

"Jesus, Becs." Pain lashed at him. Pain and self-loathing and anger at his weakness.

"My mom found me, and Ben actually got me to the hospital." She laughed bitterly. "He had a sober night. I guess it was a sign. The doctor said they saved my life, because I would have died within the hour. I spent a few weeks in the psychiatric ward, saw a counselor, and then they said I was good to go home. By then, I'd missed the first week of college, not that it mattered. I didn't have it in me to go." She turned back to him, not bothering to hide the tears that shimmered in her eyes. "Then I met David."

"I came back."

He saw the shock on her face, and it only made him feel worse. "You came… When?"

"About a month after you'd left for Ohio."

"No one told me. No one… I…"

"I was back in Crystal Lake for all of five minutes before I ran into Nash and he filled me in. I came back for you, but you were gone. I didn't bother with my father and didn't make an effort to see my brothers. I left and didn't come back for years."

Rebecca exhaled a long, shaky breath. "Look at us," she said, attempting a smile through her tears. "We sound like a goddamn Nicholas Sparks movie."

"They usually have happy endings, don't they?" He was going for something light, but it didn't have the desired effect.

"Sometimes," Rebecca said softly.

A big gust of wind tumbled across the clearing, and Hudson reached for his jacket. "We should head back," he said quietly. They gathered up their things and began the trek through the bush to the lodge. By the time they reached the first of the small cabins, clouds were moving in, and Hudson could smell snow on the air.

They were discussing dinner, which wine to open for dinner, the pinot noir or the merlot, when they spied a dark gray sedan parked beside Hudson's truck. It was nondescript. Four door. Domestic. It screamed government.

"Are you expecting anyone?" Rebecca asked, tugging on his arm because he'd come to a complete stop.

That feeling was back, another punch to the gut, and this time it packed some power. He frowned darkly as he approached the front steps to the main lodge. Woodard leaned against the railing, a cigar hanging from the corner of his mouth, a bright red knit hat covering most of his balding head. He wore a gray suit, white shirt, navy tie, and light brown leather shoes. Totally inappropriate for the area, but so Woodard.

Even out here, he was on the job.

"How the hell did you find me?" Hudson stopped at the bottom of the stairs and glared up at the man who was about to ruin his day. Or week. Hell, maybe even his month.

"GPS on your phone. I've been calling you for over twelve hours." Woodard nodded to Rebecca, and Hudson made the introductions. Of course, Woodard barely gave his hello before he got to the point of his visit.

"He's surfaced."

Adrenaline kicked in at the man's words. Dartmouth. "When?"

"Twelve hours ago."

"Where?" he asked harshly. Dumb question, because he wasn't going to discuss something like this in front of a civilian.

Woodard arched an eyebrow, his eyes moving in a subtle shift toward Rebecca. "We need to leave now."

"Hudson?" Rebecca's expression was shuttered.

"Give me five minutes," he said to Woodard.

"You've got two."

Hudson took Rebecca's elbow, and the two of them walked past Woodard and entered the lodge. Fucking Dartmouth. Anger rolled through him, and he didn't speak because he couldn't. It took a bit, but he got his emotions in check enough to try to explain.

"Woodard works out of the DC office."

"So he's an FBI agent?" Rebecca asked, watching him carefully.

Hudson nodded. "There's this target we've been after for years. He's one of the worst I've ever come across. The things he's done…" He had to take a moment and breathe because he was shaking with anger. "I can't go into specifics, but I know this guy inside and out. If we're going to nail this son of a bitch, I'm the best shot we have.

"I've got to do this, Becca." He took a step toward her. "I don't want to go. I don't want to leave you. But—"

"You don't need to explain, Hudson. We knew this was going to happen sooner or later. And maybe it's good it happened now, before things got too complicated." She shook her head and turned from him. Hudson watched her in silence as she moved toward the folded blankets near the sofa.

"Maybe this is a good thing," she said softly.

"What's that supposed to mean?" His voice held an edge, and he wanted to punch the hell out of something. He clenched his hands and moved toward her.

"You leaving is a good thing," she repeated, turning her head slightly so he could see her profile. "We're getting too comfortable, and as much as the sex has been great—"

"This is not just about sex," he interrupted, voice dark and angry.

"No," she answered after a few seconds and turned back to him. "It's not. It's about what's going to happen today. Or tomorrow. Or next week or next month. You'll leave here again. You've built a life for yourself, a career in DC, so I get it." Her voice broke, and he took a step toward her, but she shook her head and held up her hand. "But, Hudson, I can't go back to the girl I was. I refuse to be broken again. I have Liam. I just can't do it. I deserve someone who will stay. Someone who *can* stay."

Hudson watched Rebecca begin to gather up their things from the floor in front of the fireplace. And though he wanted to grab her and hold her close, inhale that scent that was all hers, listen to her heart beat against his as her warmth bled into his body... He did none of that, because she was right. She deserved more. He was a bastard.

And he would leave.

"I don't know how long I'll be gone, and I'll probably be off the radar. I won't be able to call you." He hated the pain in her eyes. Pain he was responsible for. Again. "But I'm coming back."

She offered a small smile and shrugged. "Okay." Woodard banged on the door. "You should go. I'll lock up and drop your truck at your dad's."

"Becca."

"Please, Hudson. Let's not make this a big deal. Go get the bad guy."

Less than a minute later, he was gone.

CHAPTER THIRTY

Funny how time made some things sharper, like pain and regret, while others, like joy and pleasure, became less memorable. It wasn't exactly fair, but then, as Rebecca had learned early on, life was not about being fair. Life was about getting knocked down and picking your sorry ass back up.

In the three weeks since Hudson had left town, a lot had happened. Some of it good, but most of it unfair. John Blackwell was doing wonderfully, and Darlene had moved in with him. Liam had won an academic achievement award for the month, and she couldn't be more proud of her son.

But Sal wasn't doing so good, and with only a few days until Thanksgiving, Rebecca feared he wouldn't make the holiday with his family. This man had come to mean so much to her, and even as he stared down the face of death, his humor and compassion were there. He cracked jokes through the pain and asked for only the minimal dosage of medication.

He'd told Rebecca he wanted to be aware. To cherish these last moments with his loved ones. Salvatore believed that death was beautiful. A beginning. And that the journey to the next world wasn't one he wanted to miss. He would see his beloved Rosa again.

He was a hero in Rebecca's eyes and the grandfather Liam never had. The man saw everything, and as she stole a bit of quiet time with him, she wasn't surprised that his focus was on her and not himself.

His voice was low, his strength not so good, but there was still a twinkle in his eye as she bent forward to listen better.

"How's Liam? He seemed quiet the other day."

"He's good. I mean, he's upset." Her throat tightened. "He loves you, and this is hard."

"He's a good boy, Rebecca. You should be proud." Salvatore winced, and she stroked his forehead.

"Can I get you anything? Do you need more pain medication?"

Sal smiled weakly. "No. I'm not ready for that yet." He focused on her. "What's going on with the Blackwell kid?"

She smiled at that. Salvatore referred to anyone under the age of forty as a kid.

"Nothing," she answered quietly.

"He come back yet?"

That surprised Rebecca. "How did you know he'd left?"

"Nash." She shouldn't be surprised. It wasn't as if Sal didn't know all about her history with Hudson.

"I don't know if he's coming back, and even if he does, he won't stay. His life is in DC, and now that his father is on the mend, there's no reason for him to hang around Crystal Lake."

Sal's voice was harsh. "You're all the reason a man should need."

"You're too sweet."

"I'm old and dying is what I am. That gives a person a certain amount of freedom to say what's on their mind. Your light belongs to someone, Rebecca. Remember that. It's strong, and if he's deserving, he'll find his way back to you."

It was the last thing Salvatore said to Rebecca. He died early Sunday morning, just as the first major winter storm of the season hit Crystal Lake. It was as if the sky was angry, filled with bulbous gray clouds that produced enough snowfall to close the roads and make travel dicey. Schools were closed, and by the time things settled down, it was Wednesday.

Salvatore's funeral was much like the man. Simple. Direct. With a wake held at the Coach House. Rebecca found herself behind the bar, pouring drinks for family and friends. Tiny tried to get her to relax, but she couldn't. Besides, Violet was there to keep her company. Rebecca's son was somewhere, running around the place with Sal's grandsons. Which was nice to see, considering he'd just lost a man he considered a grandfather. Not to mention he'd asked after Hudson more than once.

But kids were resilient. Adults? Not so much.

"You don't look so hot." Violet leaned closer and cocked her head to the side.

Rebecca offered a wan smile. "I hope I'm not coming down with something. My stomach has been all over the place."

"Oh no." Violet frowned. "The flu's going around. My God, Becs. I can't afford to get sick. Maybe I should slide down to the other end of the bar?"

Rebecca's retort was cut short because a wave of nausea rolled over her. She quickly turned away and closed her eyes, hating how the room seemed to move. It took some time but it passed, and when she turned around, Violet was frowning.

"What?" Rebecca wiped her damp forehead and nodded as Nash asked her to take two drinks over to John Blackwell's table.

"Nothing," Violet replied slowly. And she had that look on her face. The one that said she was thinking way too hard. Rebecca had no time to dwell on it. She grabbed the drinks and moved through the thick crowd until she reached the far corner where John sat. It was amazing, really, how the man had bounced back. He still had health problems, but he was mobile and he was here.

"There you are," he said, smiling up at her. He patted the seat beside him, and maybe it was the crowd or the flu. Whatever it was, Rebecca took him up on his offer and sat down.

"Just for a minute. It's crazy in here, and Tiny needs my help." She looked around. "Where's Darlene?"

"She's having a word with Mrs. Lancaster. Something about the flowers from the ceremony."

"Good." Rebecca rubbed her temple and tried to think of something to say, but the only thing that came to mind was Hudson.

Have you heard from him?
Do you know where he is?
Is he safe?

"I want to tell you something." John turned to her, and her stomach tumbled again. There was something in his tone. Something quiet. Serious.

"I should go," she said, mouth dry.

"It won't take long, and while I can appreciate this isn't exactly the place to have this conversation, I need you to know something."

His hands were shaking, and he clasped hers tightly. His lined face looked peaked, and the air rasped through his lungs. The man was on the back end of sixty, but life had aged him. Everything was there to see, mapped out on his face like a story.

"Are you okay?" she asked gently.

"I will be." He glanced away, his fingers loosening a bit, and the noise of the bar seemed to melt away. It was dark in this corner, but she could see clear as day. John Blackwell was about to change the game. She felt it deeply.

"John?"

"I'm the reason Hudson left town all those years ago. He won't talk about it, but it's the least I can do. Share my shame so that maybe…" He lifted his head and made no effort to hide the tears in his eyes. "Maybe the two of you could fix what you had."

"What are you talking about?"

"He never told you why he left, did he?"

She shook her head but remained silent.

"He took a phone call meant for me. It was from a woman in Louisiana. A woman who claimed I'd fathered her child." A tear slid down his face, and Rebecca gently wiped it away.

"Did you?" she asked, watching him carefully.

"I don't know. It's possible."

Rebecca didn't quite know what to say, so she kept silent. Though she grabbed his hand and held it, trying to give him some warmth, because the man looked ashen.

"I knew her as a business acquaintance. Angel and I…" His voice trembled, and he swore. "We had a rough patch. She was just so damn busy with the boys, and I was working a lot. I was weak and self-centered, and I have no excuse other than that, in the moment, being with this other woman felt good." He sighed, and his shoulders sank. "It didn't last. These things never do. I loved my wife. Our sons. Our family. I ended it because I had to. Because I knew I had to be better. But life, such as it is, doles out the good and the bad indiscriminately. For me, it was too late."

John was silent for a few moments, a faraway look in his eyes. "You see Hudson had met Susan before. Years earlier. The day his mother was killed. Susan had been to the house when Angel was out with Wyatt. She left a message with Hudson asking Angel to meet her. And Hudson, not knowing any better, passed it along when his mother called home to check on eggs. *Eggs.*"

Lost in thought, John remained silent and then with a start, continued. "If not for that phone call things might have turned out differently. But as it was, Angel left from the grocery store with Wyatt in the car, not knowing what she was heading into. I don't know if it was by God's grace that she never made it to the diner, because she died not knowing of my infidelity."

Rebecca's eyes widened, and her mouth dropped open. Horrified, she could only watch as the painful events of that long-ago night flickered across John Blackwell's face.

She knew the details. Everyone did. A drunk driver crossed the center line and hit Angel's car head on. It was tragic, and the only good thing to come of it was the fact that Wyatt, sitting in the backseat, escaped with only a few cuts and bruises and a broken arm.

"After the accident, I never heard from Susan again. I'm not sure why. She just up and vanished. It was easy to place the blame for my loss on others. Most notably Wyatt. Somehow, I put it in my head that she was on the road because of him. I buried all of it and didn't think of that woman again until Hudson..." His lips trembled. "Until that day she called again, and he realized exactly who she was. The woman who his mother was supposed to meet the day of the accident. He raged at me. As young as he was, his anger and disgust was a thing unlike any I'd seen before."

John sighed and shook his head. "I denied it, of course. All of it. And then Hudson threatened to go find this woman. To go find this supposed love child. I told him then that if he left, he was dead to me. Told him there would not be a reason for him to return. I played a bluff, and he called it."

His sad eyes broke her heart. "Unfortunately, you got caught in the crosshairs of his rage and anger and need to do something. I know he didn't want to hurt you. He just didn't know how not to. He couldn't come back here because I would be a constant reminder of all that he'd lost."

John closed his eyes. "He made a life for himself. Something to be proud of. All of my boys have, and that's saying something, because I was a miserable excuse for a father."

"No." Rebecca grabbed his cold hands. "It says everything about you and Angel and what both of you instilled in those boys. Love can be buried. It can suffocate and go away. Or it can linger as if waiting for the right moment to spark again. Your boys know you love them. They know you're human."

She thought of Salvatore's words and smiled, a sad, wistful sort of thing. "I have to believe they'll find their way back to us."

John's eyes flew open. "Us?"

She simply shrugged. "One can hope." Rebecca cleared her throat and jumped to her feet. "I need to get back and help out. Thanks for telling me this." She paused. "Did he ever find this Susan?"

"He did." John's gaze slipped away.

"And the child?"

"He never said, and I'm ashamed to say I never asked."

Darlene joined them just then, her smile faltering when she sat down across from John. "You don't look well. Should we go?"

"No. Rebecca just brought us a cocktail. We'll have a drink in Sal's name and then head home."

Rebecca dropped a kiss to each of their cheeks, and then left them alone. She spent the rest of the evening thinking about family and love. About hatred and blame. And Rebecca realized a few things.

It didn't matter what social ladder you clung to or which tax bracket was checked off on your income tax return. No one was immune from pain or betrayal. From loss and heartache.

Hudson had left and told her he'd be back. She wanted to believe him. But it had been three weeks, and she'd heard nothing. Three weeks of sleepless nights and an ache inside her that was so sharp and strong, it left her nauseated. Empty.

It was her past all over again.

She thought again, of Sal's words, but they brought her no comfort. Because she knew that love was not always enough. Sometimes love just made things worse.

CHAPTER THIRTY-ONE

When Hudson flew into Detroit Metropolitan, he was sporting a headache from lack of sleep, and lack of caffeine. The latter he'd stayed away from, as he was so wound up, the muscles across the back of his shoulders were like steel ropes.

He needed a massage, a shower, possibly a haircut, but more importantly, he needed to be back in Crystal Lake by six o'clock. He picked up his rental, checked the time, and then made his way over to the MGM Grand Detroit. Leave it to Wyatt to put himself up in a casino.

He called his brother on the way over and spied him signing autographs near the entrance. Funny as hell that Wyatt Blackwell, a celebrated NASCAR driver, didn't own a goddamn vehicle. Hudson wasn't exactly sure what to make of that, but he didn't feel much like dwelling on it.

He put the window down and shouted, "Get in."

Wyatt posed for one last selfie with a cute redhead and then hopped in.

"Travis gonna make it?" Hudson asked as he eased into traffic.

"Think so." Wyatt yawned and leaned back in his seat. "He doesn't play till Saturday, and I understood he would be home by noon. So I'm guessing he's already there."

"You pull an all-nighter?" Hudson shook his head. His brother reeked of cigars, booze, and women. It was the trifecta of all trifectas, and it currently had Wyatt by the balls.

"Damn right I did, so keep it down. If I want to enjoy my Thanksgiving turkey, I need to catch some shut-eye."

Hudson didn't say a word. Twenty-four hours earlier, he'd been holed up in a dive in San Francisco, running on zero sleep and a rush of adrenaline so high, it gave him the shakes. After weeks of knocking down doors and calling in favors, his team, combined with local law enforcement, had been able to nail down Dartmouth's location. It had been under the radar, and he'd been off the grid for weeks. Hudson was the lucky bastard who'd been given the green light to bring him in, which should have made him feel like a fucking king.

Professionally speaking, it was a big win, and yet, in the minutes just after he'd cuffed Dartmouth, the only thing he could think about was Rebecca. The instant gratification was gone. He'd been congratulated, and then his mind moved elsewhere. And here he was, about to change the game. He just hoped she was up for it.

After debriefing, she'd been the first person he'd called. But just like the past few hours her phone went straight to voice mail. Pissed him off. He needed to hear her voice like he needed air to breathe.

Needed to know she was still waiting.

Hudson drove like a son of a bitch—Wyatt would have been proud—and they reached the familiar sights of Crystal Lake at just after six o'clock. His brother must have sensed he was home, because he pushed back his Dodgers ball cap and gazed out the window as they crossed the bridge and sped along River Road.

"This place doesn't change."

It did. And it would. But Hudson didn't bother pointing that out. Wyatt would figure it out eventually.

They pulled up in the drive, and Hudson hopped out before Wyatt even had time to put his hand on the door. He spied his father's car, a rental he was going to assume belonged to Travis, and—his heart jumped—Rebecca's modest vehicle.

He strode up the steps, uncaring that his jeans were wrinkled or that the boots he wore were still caked with dirt and European mud. He knew he looked like shit, but he didn't give a crap. It was the least of his worries.

He pushed into the house, was immediately assaulted by the familiar scents of turkey and stuffing and all the fixings that went along with that. Voices spilled out of the great room. Liam's, then his father's, laughter.

Then Rebecca's soft rejoinder.

He didn't take his boots off, even though there would be hell to pay from Darlene, and strode into the back room as if the hounds of hell were nipping at his heels. Maybe they were, because if things didn't work out the way he'd envisioned, Hudson would probably spend the rest of his days putting out fires and taming the beasts.

He saw her right away. She was bent near his father, a smile on her face as John recounted a story or joke. When Darlene gasped, she glanced up, and that was when everything went wonky.

The room sort of faded away, and he blinked rapidly until his vision cleared. He was aware that Wyatt was beside him and that Travis got up from the chair by the fireplace. This should have been a monumental occasion, considering it was the first time all the Blackwell men had gotten together in years. But Hudson didn't give a crap about that. In this moment, all he cared about was the pale woman standing beside his father.

"You look like shit." That was Travis.

Hudson ignored his brother. There was time for all that later. He crossed the room and nodded to his father before pausing in front of the one person on the planet he needed to see more than anyone.

"I'm back."

Her face was blank, though she was breathing fast and hard, as if she'd just run a mile.

"Becca."

Liam had gotten to his feet and taken two steps toward him, but stopped in his tracks when he sensed the tension in the room.

"Bec?" he asked again, swallowing a hard lump as he tried to gauge just where her head was at.

"Not here." Her words were whispered.

"Becca, we need to talk."

She shook her head, chin trembling slightly. "Not here. I can't…"

Wyatt walked by him just then and slapped him on the shoulder. "I'm not real up on the way relationships work. But I'm going to guess you need to do some groveling before this situation improves."

His brother continued by him and gave Rebecca a big hug. Wyatt kissed her on the cheek and then crossed over to the bar to help himself.

Wyatt was right.

"You mind if I steal your mother for a bit?" Hudson aimed the question at Liam, though his eyes never left Rebecca.

Liam looked surprised, but shrugged and glanced at his mother. "I don't care if she doesn't."

"Becca?" He held out his hand. She raised her chin. Pursed her lips. And at first, he was afraid she was going to tell him to go to hell. Instead, she whispered something to John, kissed Darlene on the cheek, and grabbed her purse.

"I won't be long," she said to Liam, ruffling the top of his head. "Are you going to be okay?"

"If you are." Her son looked at Hudson, and his expression said it all. *Don't mess with my mom.*

She turned to Hudson, her voice clipped. "Where are we going?"

God, she looked beautiful. Jeans and a simple blue sweater never looked so damn good. Her hair was loose, piled around the cream, red, and blue scarf she'd wrapped around her neck. Her lips were soft and pink, and her eyes... A guy could lose himself inside them.

"You'll see." He waited for her to pass and followed her outside to his rental.

They rode along in silence, which was strange considering they hadn't spoken in weeks. Maybe Rebecca was feeling exactly the way he was. Nervous. Afraid to open his mouth and somehow shatter the image he'd kept in his head. The image of where this was going.

Of where he wanted it to go.

He knew exactly when she realized where it was they were going. She sat up straighter. Her breathing began to quicken. Her hands were balled in her lap.

When he pulled up in front of the lodge, Hudson didn't cut the engine because he needed her to see. So he got out of the truck and opened the door for her. She blinked up at him and hesitated, but when he offered his hand, she accepted.

They walked up the steps and stood on the porch, and when he pointed to the window, to the bright red-and-blue sign that was there, she began to shake.

"It says Sold."

"It does." He cleared his throat, tried to dislodge the big old lump that was there, and then gave up. So what if he sounded like a wuss. Nothing was going to stop him now. "I bought it."

She jerked her head back. "I don't... Why?"

Hudson turned to her and grabbed her hands in his. He stared down into the only face that had ever owned him body and soul. No more just getting by. He was finally ready to live his life, and he needed this woman in it.

"It was our dream, once. Remember? Everything about this place is us. What we wanted. What we envisioned for our future."

"But, Hudson. We were so young. God, we knew nothing. Sometimes the things we think matter, like our dreams, don't make sense in the real world."

"Sometimes we need to cling to those dreams. Sometimes we need to work to make them happen. I'm ready now."

"Ready for what?" Her voice was barely above a whisper.

"Ready to work. Ready for a family." He paused, because this was the biggie. "I'm finally ready to be the man you deserve. I'm here to stay. I want a life with you and Liam. I want this place to be part of our life. I know it's a big change—"

"Damn right it's a big change. And you seem to forget that it's not just me I have to think about. You left, Hudson. Again." She thumped him in the chest. "You left for over three weeks with no word. Not one phone call."

"Babe, I couldn't call. Our operation was dark. I was undercover. Trust me, if I could have made contact, I would have."

"I..." She shook her head. "I know you said that but...Sal died." Her voice broke, and he inched toward her. "And I'm used to dealing with that kind of stuff on my own, but I just thought..." She shook her head and closed her eyes. "I just thought maybe this time, I'd have a shoulder, you know? I thought that maybe the past wouldn't bite me in the ass again." A sob escaped. "I let myself hope, Hudson. And I—" "Becca. I'm not leaving again. Ever."

Her eyes flew open. "What are you saying?"

"I'm saying the hounds of hell couldn't drag me from you. I'm saying a goddamn tornado could cut through here, and no way would I let go." He stepped closer yet. "I'm saying that I love you, and I want us to have a life together. I want—"

He didn't have time to finish his sentence on account of the warm body pressed so tightly into his. Rebecca's mouth found his, and they clung to each other in a kiss that spoke volumes. It was sweet and tentative, bold and daring. It was all-consuming, and when she finally dragged her mouth from his, Hudson literally felt weak.

"I'll take that as a yes," he murmured against her cheek. "I love you, Becca. I don't think I ever stopped." He moved again and cupped her chin, because he needed her to understand. "I'll never leave you again."

He kissed her nose. "I."

And then dropped one on her forehead. "Love."

Then he made his way to the corner of her mouth. "You."

She shivered against him and rested her head against his chest. "There was never anyone else for me, Hudson. Never. I loved you with all my heart. From the time I was fifteen and first met you. I love you even more now."

She sighed and looked up at him. "You do look like shit, though. Why don't we head back, and you can have a nice, long hot shower, and we'll fill your family in on our plans."

He dropped another kiss to her nose, because, damn, it was a cute nose. And just, well, because he could.

"You must be hungry."

Her eyes widened. "Um. No. I had turkey dinner at my brother's, but John insisted Liam and I come by this evening. Now I know why." She bit her bottom lip, her forehead furrowed. "He told me. About your mom and the other woman."

Hudson stilled.

"About why you left." She paused. "Do your brothers know?"

"No." He shook his head slowly, as the familiar wave of pain hit him. "It's not my secret to tell."

"Sometimes it's best to let things be."

Hudson wasn't so sure about that, but right now, his focus was Rebecca and her son, Liam. He didn't want to think about the sins of his father or the way they'd changed the dynamics of his family. There was still a lot of pain there, and he had a feeling the day of reckoning would come. There was a sibling out there. Somewhere. Would the lure of Crystal Lake be too much for him or her?

He shook the thoughts from his head and pulled Rebecca back toward the still-running truck. "You mind driving? I haven't slept in forty-eight hours."

She gave him one last slow and sinful kiss, and then they hopped in the truck. Seconds later, they were headed back down the road that would bring them to town.

"You're not going to miss your job?"

He shook his head. "No. I've got a lot of good I can do here. Things I'm passionate about. Namely you."

Hudson turned up the heat and got comfortable.

"We'll have to take it slow with Liam. I'm sure he's figured out we're more than friends, but he's used to being the only man in the house."

"Sounds like a plan." God, the heat felt amazing.

"Like we'll date for a few months."

"Okay."

"No sex at all."

"Sounds good."

"Like maybe never."

God, he was drowsy. "Yep."

"Never again. The no-sex thing."

That got his attention, and he smiled to himself. "Nice try."

"Thought I'd slip that in there. Just to see if you were paying attention."

Her voice was like a song, and she chattered away, filling his head with love and hope and contentment. Hudson had taken the long way, but he was finally home.

EPILOGUE

Christmas Eve Day
Rebecca

For the first time in years, Rebecca was caught up and ready for the holidays. She'd done her shopping early, wrapped the presents the week before, and with the vet clinic closing at twelve, had the afternoon to relax for a busy evening ahead. She and Hudson were having an open house at their completely renovated lodge, and they were expecting a host of friends and family to come out.

Kimberly had just locked the clinic door and turned the sign to CLOSED when Ethan Burke, who'd just officially taken over from his father, walked in from the back office with the older Burke, carrying a decanter and four glasses.

"Merry Christmas," Ethan said, indicating the girls should each have a drink. "Thought we'd toast to the holidays with a rum eggnog."

"Sounds lovely," Kimberly said with a grin. "I've got some Christmas cookies in the back."

Rebecca's smile faltered. Eggnog? The thought turned her stomach. Whoever'd come up with the idea of combining eggs and cream for a drink was nuts. She shuddered and reached under the reception desk for her purse.

"Sorry, guys. I can't stay. I've got a ton of stuff to do before the open house tonight and need to run." She slipped into a slate gray wool coat and wrapped a cream-and-navy scarf around her neck. Hiking her purse over her shoulder, she wished everyone a Merry Christmas and made sure they knew to pop in any time after seven.

"Wouldn't miss it for the world," Kimberly said with a smile and a hug. "I'm so happy for you, sweetie. You deserve the best Christmas ever."

Feeling more blessed than she could ever remember, Rebecca headed to her mother's for a cup of tea before going home to soak in the tub. Snow was falling yet again, large flakes that filled the sky and covered the roads. The tops of the evergreens were heavy with the white stuff, and just the day before, several inches fell, so that Crystal Lake and the town that shared its name looked like a winter wonderland. Everything glistened and looked new and fresh.

She hummed along to her favorite Christmas carol, and a feeling of melancholy stole over her as she picked her way along the snow-covered path up to her mother's front door.

She made a note to get Liam to shovel it and pushed open the door, stomping snow from her boots as she called for her mother. She took a moment to breathe in the smells she loved—ones that made her think of Christmas. Gingerbread, fresh from the oven. Cinnamon. The fresh scent from the evergreens on the Christmas bough across the fireplace. *Cinnamon!*

"Mom?"

Rebecca slipped off her boots and hung up her jacket before walking to the kitchen. The gentle strains of Bing Crosby echoed down the hall, and she followed his voice. "White Christmas" indeed.

The table was filled with Tupperware containers as well as Christmas tins, all filled with Lila Draper's homemade goods. Her mother was a whiz in the kitchen—always had been—and as much as Rebecca's childhood had been dark and sometimes filled with despair, Christmas, with its sense of hope, coupled with her mother's amazing cookies and cakes, was a memory she would always cherish.

Her mother was at the sink, staring out the window, and with a deft movement, Rebecca lifted the lid on the closest tin and snagged a cookie. She glanced down at it and smiled. Win! It was shortbread.

"I'll grab the kettle," Rebecca said, taking a bite from her cookie. She reached into the cupboard for a couple of teabags.

"Oh. Becca. I didn't hear you."

Rebecca glanced sharply at her mom. Saw the side profile, the puffy eyes and red nose. The lightness she'd felt all morning suddenly vanished, and Rebecca quietly set about making them tea. She forgot sometimes. Forgot that her happiness, her absolute contentment with her life, didn't belong to anyone else other than Rebecca and Hudson. The holidays were tough for a lot of folks, and with her father still in jail, she knew her mother was grappling with sadness and heartache.

Rebecca was glad her father wasn't around to ruin things, and she knew Mackenzie felt the same. But that didn't negate or lessen the fact that in spite of her father's many shortcomings and fondness of the bottle—their mother still loved him.

Lila was quiet as Rebecca made the tea, and when it was ready, the two of them took their cups into the dining room. They sat in silence for a good long while, and then, with a sniffle, her mother offered a wan smile.

"I'm sorry, Rebecca. I'm not great company today."

"You don't have to be sorry about anything." Rebecca grabbed her mother's hand, wanting to provide some kind of comfort.

"I was hoping your father would call this morning but…" Her mother grabbed a tissue from her pocket and dabbed the corners of her eyes. "He didn't. He hasn't called in over a month." Her mother attempted a smile through her tears. "I guess he's busy, or…something."

"He probably is," Rebecca eventually said, taking a sip from her tea. What else could she say to that?

Lila held her cup, hands shaking. "Did I ever tell you how I met your father?"

Rebecca shook her head and spoke softly. "No."

Her mother smiled, though it didn't quite make it to her eyes. "It was a Christmas dance at the community center. I wore this beautiful red velvet dress. The crushed kind, you know? It shimmered when I moved and fit me like a glove." Lila winked at her daughter. "I was quite the looker back in the day."

Rebecca smiled. "I don't doubt that you were a hottie. Still are."

Lila squeezed Rebecca's hand as a smile stole over her face. "I was there with another man. One of the Bradley boys. Can't remember which one." She chuckled. "I dated both of them."

"Mom." Rebecca was shocked and giggled. "You tart."

"I had my moments." She seemed lost in thought for a few seconds. "I knew who your father was, of course. He was the most handsome man in Crystal Lake. All the girls were crazy about him. But he only dated older women, and I'd never been alone with him." Her voice trailed off, and she got a faraway look in her eye. "Until that night. I got in a fight with whichever Bradley boy I was there with. Hank, maybe? He wanted to leave and go somewhere to do something I had no interest in doing."

By the look in her mother's eyes, Rebecca had a pretty good idea what that something was.

"I left and went outside for a smoke." Her mother shrugged at the look on her daughter's face. "I know, honey. But back then, everyone smoked. Anyway, your father followed me outside. He walked right up to me and, without saying a word, held up the tiniest piece of mistletoe you've ever seen. I remember he pointed to the cigarette in my hand, and I tossed it in the snow. He took another step closer, and good Lord, but he was so handsome. He held the mistletoe above my head and said I had to kiss him. I was shocked. I told him I was there with another man, and he just looked at me and said..." She lowered her voice and mimicked a man's baritone, "'Not anymore. Now kiss me.'"

Her mother blew out a long, shaky breath. "And I did."

The grandfather clock chimed just then, and both women jumped in their seats. It was loud and startling, and her mother started to giggle. Which made Rebecca start to giggle. And before too long, both of them were doubled over. When their laughter finally subsided, Lila sat back in her chair, and almost immediately, a fresh batch of tears filled her pale green eyes. She swiped at them.

"I'm a silly woman. Look at me. Blubbering like an idiot."

"Mom. It's okay. The holidays are emotional for a lot of reasons."

"I need to say something." Lila's fingers worried the edge of her tissue. "I know your father isn't a good person. He's selfish and mean. He's a lousy husband, and he wasn't good to you kids." She glanced up, and the look in her mother's eyes broke Rebecca's heart.

"But I need you to know he wasn't always like that." She shook her head. "He wasn't. I don't know when he changed or why, but he did. I tried to leave him once. You were a baby."

Shocked, Rebecca was silent.

"I made it a week without him, and then I came back. I just...can't give him up. I made mistakes. A lot of them. And I'm sorry. I wish I'd been stronger for you kids. But that saying, love is blind, is so true. In spite of Ben's faults, and there are many, I love him. And I know people think I'm crazy sticking by a man who..." Lila's chin trembled, and a knot formed in Rebecca's throat.

"A man who did the awful things that he did. But I won't abandon him. I can't."

"It's okay, Mom." Rebecca didn't understand that kind of love, one that was so lopsided, but after all the things she'd been through, who was she to judge?

"I need you to know something, Becca. I never wanted that for you."

That damn knot was bigger now, and Rebecca clutched at her mother's hands.

"I was never as proud of you as I was the day you left David. As a young mother to strike out on your own like that, well, that's some kind of strength. That takes guts. More guts than I ever had." She cupped Rebecca's face and pressed a kiss to her cheek, her breath warm against Rebecca's suddenly cold skin.

"You are my princess, and I want you to have it all. I want you to have what I never did because you are strong and deserve it."

Rebecca opened her mouth, but her mother shushed her with a finger.

"I believe that one day, your father will get better, and the man I met so long ago that night at the Christmas dance, well, I believe he'll come back to me." A tear slipped down her face. "I have to believe that."

Rebecca hugged her mother tightly. "I love you," she said.

"I know, honey." A pause. "Hudson is deserving of your love. I've seen that over these past weeks." She smiled softly. "That's one gift I'll treasure this Christmas."

Rebecca gave her mother another hug and a kiss. "Mackenzie will pick you up around six thirty." She glanced back toward the kitchen. "Don't forget the shortbread."

Rebecca headed home. She cranked the tunes in her car and sang "Jingle Bell Rock" as loud as she could. What a feeling she had inside. It was big and strong and filled her right up. It was love, anticipation, and joy. There'd been darkness in her past, but the future sure as heck looked bright. And while David had nothing whatsoever to do with his son, other than making sure his support payments were deposited each month, she hoped one day, things would change.

She thought of her mother. That was the thing about life. There was always hope.

She was still humming Christmas songs when she got home and

checked her watch. Liam was with Hudson out at the lodge, doing whatever it was that men did when getting ready for an open house. Rebecca planned on making the most of her time alone. She filled the tub with hot water and slid inside. She had two hours all to herself before swinging by Violet's to pick up her special present for the man she loved. She smiled at the thought and closed her eyes.

Christmas Eve Night
Hudson

A year ago on Christmas Eve, Hudson had been nursing a whiskey in some dive bar in DC, trying like hell to forget about the holidays. It said something, this turn of events, that found him in a place he loved, surrounded by people he loved even more.

And sure, some of those relationships needed work. Like anything, relationships weren't simple things. They were messy and complicated. Sometimes painful and hard. He'd made amends with his father, as best he could, and hoped one day his brothers would find a way as well. At least before the old man passed. Neither one of them had been able to make it back for Christmas, and though John accepted their lame excuses, Hudson knew it hurt.

He also knew his father expected it. He'd said about as much when he and Darlene had left an hour earlier. "Thanksgiving wasn't exactly a success, son."

That was an understatement. It had been awkward and uncomfortable. Travis had left town within twenty-four hours of arriving. Hell, Wyatt had only managed to stay a few days longer. He'd stuck around to accept an award given out by a local car enthusiast organization. Given the fact he'd somehow managed to get into a fender bender leaving the ceremony, Hudson was guessing Wyatt wished he'd left when Travis did.

Nash slapped him on the shoulder. "This place looks great. You and Becca did an amazing job."

The two men had just finished gathering up glasses and trays. Rebecca had taken Liam up to bed, and once Nash was gone, that was exactly where Hudson was headed. The thought brought a smile to his face as he tossed a dish towel onto the counter.

"Seriously, Hudsy. You keep that goofy look on your face, and

Rebecca is going to know."

"Know what?"

"That she's got you fully and completely by the balls."

He followed his friend from the kitchen. "She's the only one who's got permission to go near them. Totally fine with it."

"Yeah," Nash murmured as he slipped into his leather jacket. "I see that." He glanced outside. "Taxi's here."

The two men stared at each other for a few moments and then slapped shoulders and hugged the way men do.

"Look at us," Nash said, hand on the door. "All respectable and shit. Never thought we'd both be back here, me with a bar and you with this place. When you opening?"

"We'll start slow. Advertise for some bookings in the summer and go from there."

Nash nodded. "Merry Christmas, Hudsy."

Hudson closed the door and locked it. He turned off the lights and made sure everything was off in the kitchen before heading up to the second floor. The main lodge featured four bedrooms, with the large master at the back, overlooking the lake. The door was open slightly, and soft light spilled onto the hallway.

He walked inside and found Rebecca sitting in front of the fireplace. She'd wrapped herself in a large blanket, and he paused, drinking in her profile as the light cast shadows over her face.

It hit him then—hard in the chest. Could a guy get everything he wanted? Was it possible to have this much love and keep it?

"Everyone gone?" she asked, turning slightly and gazing up at him.

Hudson nodded. He didn't answer, because there was no way in hell he could speak. His throat was closed up as tight as a damn drum. Being here with Rebecca had him humbled. The woman didn't know it, but she could bring him to his knees if she wanted. That kind of power was scary.

But then, being totally and unequivocally in love with someone was scary and thrilling and wonderful and a whole bunch of things he didn't have words for.

"Everyone's gone," he replied. He sat beside her and gazed into the fire. "It was a great party."

She nodded slowly and turned to him. "It was."

Her eyes were luminous, their depths like glass. Hudson couldn't help himself. He leaned over and pressed a soft kiss to her mouth.

Already his body was hot and tight, filled with the need for a woman he would never let go of. She opened beneath him immediately, letting him inside, and he kissed her with all the passion and want and need he possessed. When he finally dragged his mouth away, he was breathless.

He rested his forehead on hers. "Hold on, babe. I need to do something before we get carried away."

With his heart nearly beating out of his chest, Hudson got to his knees and reached into the front pocket of his jeans. There, nestled for the entire evening, was a small box. He fingered it for a few seconds and then withdrew it. It was black velvet and delicate.

Her eyes widened, and her kiss-swollen lips parted.

"I had this big speech prepared for you. A bunch of words that were supposed to ease my way into this. But, Becs, there are only three that make sense. Only three that I need you to know. I love you. I've been in love with you since that Fourth of July party, and I, well…"

Hudson held out his hand and offered her the small box. Her fingers trembled slightly when she plucked it from his palm.

"I want us to be a family. I want to marry you. I want to grow old with you. Fight with you. Make love with you. Hold you. There's never been anyone else."

She slowly opened the box. Nestled inside the black silk pillow was a ring. White gold with a single square-cut diamond. It was elegant and classy, and his chest welled up tight when she picked it up. Gently, Hudson took the ring from her and slid it onto her finger.

"I'm hoping that's a yes," he said, voice husky.

For several long moments, she said nothing and kept her head bowed. When she finally looked up at Hudson, everything inside him stilled. He wondered if she could hear how heavy his heart was beating, or how hard it was for him to draw air into his lungs.

"Yes." She smiled through tears, and his heart melted. "It's always been yes."

He reached for her and drew her into his arms. For the longest time, they held each other, and then she wiggled out of his arms and got to her feet.

"I have something for you."

Hudson watched her cross the room and pick up something from the night table beside the bed. She still clutched the blanket around her, but it had fallen, showing off a lot of skin. He liked that.

She came back and knelt in front of him, the fire once more casting shadows that only served to enhance features he could trace in his sleep. Those big eyes of hers settled on him, and there was something there…something that got his attention.

Rebecca blew out a breath and smiled. "I had Violet pick this up for me in the city. I'd ordered it special, but there was a mix-up, and I couldn't make it in, and then she said she could do it and…" Rebecca stopped, obviously nervous, and Hudson looked down.

In her palm was an ornament. It was silver and round and engraved.

Daddy-to-be. 2017

Hudson's eyes flew to her face. "Becca?"

She nodded and shrugged, fighting tears. "I know we never talked about it or anything, and that this is probably the biggest surprise of your life. But that first time we were together, the night of the fair dance, we didn't…we never used any protection and well.…"

He couldn't speak. Literally couldn't speak.

A small frown appeared on her face, and her voice shook with uncertainty. "Hudson? Are you okay with this?"

He nodded, and then, as if a rubber band pulled tight had broken, he slumped forward and grabbed her into his arms.

"Becca, I can't wait for what's coming. I can't wait." He held her and breathed her in, loving the way her body curled into his. And when she let the blanket drop and pulled him down to the fluffy rug in front of the fireplace, Hudson Blackwell knew he was a goner. His hands and his eyes hungrily swept over her body, and within seconds, he was as naked as she.

"Merry Christmas," Rebecca whispered into his ear as she straddled him.

Hudson gazed up into the eyes of the woman he loved more than life itself and sank his hands into the hair on either side of her face.

"Thank you," he said simply.

"For what?" Her breath hitched as his hands slid down her body to cradle her still-flat stomach.

His hands splayed across her abdomen. "For this." He kissed her shoulder and made his way back to her mouth. "For letting me back into your life."

"It was a no-brainer, Hudson." She cupped his chin. "Without you, I had no life."

Hudson reached for Rebecca. He kissed her. He loved her. He worshipped her. And much later, when they were spent and limp as noodles, he carried her to the bed and buried both of them beneath blankets and comforters. He kissed the top of her head and drew her close. And as her breathing evened out and he knew she was asleep, Hudson thought that maybe, just maybe, it was the best sound in the world.

Because it was Rebecca. And she was his. They would be a family.

They had found their way back to each other, and Hudson Blackwell would never let her go again.

-THE END-

Printed in Poland
by Amazon Fulfillment
Poland Sp. z o.o., Wrocław